# CAN JOB

### a comedy

## Kirsten Mortensen

This book is a work of fiction. Names, characters, places,
and events are either products of the author's imagination or are
used fictitiously. Any resemblance to actual events, locales, or persons,
living or dead, is entirely coincidental.

*Manufactured in the United States of America*

*For Ken, without whom my life would be a train wreck of math mistakes and erroneous sports references*

# DRAWING CONCLUSIONS

*"No comment. Absolutely no comment. I signed the piece of paper, my friend. The little piece of paper. Didn't want to, had to. Because believe me, I'd love for the real story to get out—I mean, people want to blame a child for this? For destroying an entire company?"*

—Brad Tankard

You never know what impact a piece of Art might have on this world.

Take Ethan Tankard's work, for example.

His artistic genius—at least, as far as his father was concerned—was obvious from a very early age, from the day Brad Tankard was babysitting (sort of) and Ethan crawled over to the dining room wall and raised his Violet Blue Crayola above his head and . . .

And a few minutes later Brad remembered he was babysitting and walked into the dining room and saw the boy.

Brad froze.

He stared.

He was astonished.

"It's the way he holds his crayon," he gushed later to his wife. "Look at that line!"

And so Ethan was pronounced a prodigy.

A few years later he started school.

He abandoned Crayolas in favor of Bic and colored pencil.

And his style evolved. He still dipped occasionally into Cartoon Derivative and Primitive Figure Drawing but his true oeuvre was Diagram.

They were enigmatic, Ethan Tankard's Diagram drawings. Some appeared to be structures of some kind. Some were apparently vehicles.

The majority were devices of uncertain operation.

But if Brad was perplexed by the direction his son's art had taken he hid it well. On the contrary: Brad cheerfully disassembled various household gadgets—an old 35 mm camera, his PC chassis, as many pieces as he dared unbolt from under the hood of his car—and laid their innards bare, to give Ethan fresh sources of inspiration.

Each time Ethan finished a new drawing, he offered it to his father for praise.

Over and over, Brad gasped and praised.

Ethan's imagination was, after all, relentless. And the connection between it and the tip of his pen gloriously unbroken.

Then his father took a job.

Brad's new position wasn't a "full time salaried." It was a contract job, destined to be tossed one day into the dustbin of corporate budget cuts. But that would come later. For the time being, the work kept Brad occupied and, even better, alleviated some of the fiscal tension that continually threatened the wary calm of the Tankard household.

The job also allowed Brad to style himself as A Writer, which was one of his ambitions. Granted, the writing Brad was paid to do—technical documentation, drafts of spec sheets, compliance docs—left little room for his Creative Genius. And the committee members whose views on each piece were solicited, politely and rigorously, by Brad's new boss, Andrew Spittleton, were all too ready to pounce on any whiff of Style, highlight it, select Insert Comment, and issue a terse reprimand. "Can't say it this way." "Please see the 1/28 version of the Technical Messaging Map." "Sentences too long? Rec we bulletize."

Not that the reviewers were mistaken. On the contrary. They knew their stuff. They had to. They worked for DipTych Corporation, a company that is more than a company; it's a household name, the company that has manufactured 9.83 of every 10 can openers purchased in North America— 8.17 of every ten worldwide—since its founding in the 1890s. The name you see every time you pop open a bottle of beer or slice off the lid of your canned cat food.

A venerable institution.

So venerable it easily weathered the early 20th century transition from manual can openers to electric. So venerable that when, last year, it announced the formation of a brand new subsidiary—DipTych Digital Can— the event was recognized instantly as a show of brilliant strategic leadership.

DipTych's stockholders went giddy. The household consumer goods analysts swooned in joy.

It was DipTych Digital Can that gave a writing contract to Brad Tankard. And therefore gave him a front row seat to what would no doubt prove to be An Historic Event, at least within the galaxy of blue chip American corporate icons.

The effect on Brad's son, however, was more ambiguous.

Until recently, Ethan had always boarded the same bus after school—bus #6—and dismounted at the end of his ride a few yards from his driveway.

There, he'd be greeted by his father.

Now he took bus #12 instead, which discharged him in front of the Middle School.

His mother was a teacher there.

She met him and led him to her homeroom.

She held his hand and looked around as they threaded the maze of sweaty-smelling, high-ceilinged hallways lined with banks of pale orange lockers that he was forbidden to touch.

He spent the next hour drawing on the chalkboard or flipping through picture-books while Mama sat at her desk and graded papers or stood at the classroom door to chat with other teachers who happened by.

Then he rode home, belted into the car seat in the back of Mama's Prius, and once home made his way to the corner of the spare bedroom that served as his father's office.

His father wasn't home yet.

The swivel chair was empty.

Ethan climbed into it, pulled a sheet of paper from the stack sitting in the laser printer feed tray, and began to draw.

He knew exactly what he wanted to draw today, too, because shortly after lunch his class filed behind the teacher, out the back door, and to the field at the rear of the school.

There, a man with a closely cropped beard had set up his collection of telescopes.

Ethan and his classmates were allowed to peer through one of the scopes.

It was pointed at a house that bordered the far end of the school yard.

When Ethan's turn came and he looked into the tube, at first he saw . . . nothing.

A trick!

But no! Just as he was about to give up, he shifted the angle of his face just so and it happened. A small, circular image wobbled into view within the darkness—he calmed himself—the circle grew larger and then a gigantic slice of a fantastically flattened world suddenly presented itself in all its distorted glory.

Ethan gasped, entranced.

"Ethan."

The main feature of the scene was a window in a house. He could see the pattern of the curtains on either side of the window frame. There! He could see inside the house. A ceiling fixture. A cupboard, door ajar. Plates . . .

"Ethan!"

. . . A coffee mug. A small orange plastic container like where Mama keeps her headache pills . . .

"ETHAN!"

Three times, his teacher had to call his name before he even heard her.

His turn was over.

And now he was back home, but still enmeshed in the spell cast by that magical machine.

He began to draw.

The machine's legs were short, shrunken to reflect Ethan's assessment of their importance. The exterior controls were depicted as a system of dials and levers. A cutaway revealed the machine's interior: some wiring, a circuit board, a delicate cable carefully entwined around a pulley.

It was a masterpiece.

From some papers strewn across his father's desk, Ethan found the perfect label with which to crown his work, and laboriously copied it across the top of his page—the words RESTRICTED USE, rendered laboriously in a thick serif typeface.

He believed he would show his new masterpiece, RESTRICTED USE, to his father as soon as he got home.

But then his mother called up to him and he darted downstairs to SpongeBob. And he forgot about the drawing.

Left it on his father's desk.

Brad found the drawing later, after the boy had long gone to sleep.

He picked it up, rotated it in his hand, marveling.

Then he set it down and opened his appointment book.

Reviewed the next day's schedule.

The R&D department's weekly status meeting was noon tomorrow.

# THE NUMBER

*"Look, corporations have to take risks. If you don't take risks, you don't grow. We're proud to be proven risk-takers."*

—Van Prentice, Executive Vice President of Operations,
DipTych Corporation

DipTych's roots, like those of most contemporary corporations, are rooted deep in the proverbial clay. But climb up into its branches and you'll encounter a different world altogether.

Now three gentlemen who made their home in this divine bower sat around a computer. They were DipTych CEO Paul W.G. Scally's immediate reports, and they'd been there since 9:40 that morning.

They were all three entranced by a slick little corporate analytics program called Quantme.

The software's ingenious claim: it renders any executive into an astute fiscal modeler. Just input a handful of readily available figures—last quarter's gross receipts and the like—and sit back. A few voluptuous purrs of the hard drive and voila, your fiscal projections are output in a variety of selectable formats suitable for importing into other documents, emailing, or printing.

Van Prentice, Executive Vice President of Operations, had requisitioned it.

The other two Executive VPs were now watching him run it.

"It combines Gaming and Chaos Theory," Van repeated as he left-clicked his mouse button to highlight another input field.

"Genius," said the Executive VP to his left.

Secretly, the third Executive VP agreed, but he reflexively tempered his colleagues' enthusiasm with a show of skepticism. "What did Flagner and Wright say?" Flagner and Wright being a Best Practices Consulting Firm with elegant tendrils entwined throughout DipTych's upper branches.

"Very favorable. Flagner himself suggested we evaluate it." Prentice tapped his keyboard enter key. "There. Now we just wait."

"They used to do this with calculators."

"These programmers today. Young kids. You know the guys who developed this, what they did before? That online game—Druid something."

"Druidscape? My son plays that."

"Yeah, that's it. Kids sold it, made a fortune. Now they develop business software. And consult." Prentice leaned forward. "Okay, here we have it."

The other two Executive VPs leaned forward as well, their chests puffed, and pointed excitedly at the screen. Oh! The bonuses they would bring home next December!

"Mr. Prentice?" Van's admin leaned into the open office door. "Rocco Pinnoccho here for the ten o'clock."

"Send him in, Grace." Van leaned back. "And Grace, I've just sent a document to the printer, bring it in when it's done." Van's printer was out by his admin's desk. Somewhere. He wasn't quite sure where.

Rocco entered. He shook hands with all three Executive VPs.

They towered over him.

He pointed his chin upward during the greetings to compensate.

Then pulled up another of the room's cushioned meeting chairs and sat.

Grace returned with the printout.

"Rocco, my man, we have good news. It's going to be a fantastic year for DipTych Digital."

Rocco nodded emphatically. Good news.

Van handed him the printout. "We've just run the numbers," he said. "Here they are."

Rocco looked at the report.

His face stilled.

"Very doable," Van told him.

The two other Executive VPs nodded in agreement.

"Aggressive. But doable." Van nodded back. "We dare to target."

*Dare to Target* was the Quantme tagline. The Executive Vice President who had feigned skepticism mouthed the words silently to himself as Rocco studied the printout, running his right index finger over the numbers as if he were checking them.

"This is just what we needed," Rocco said when he was done. He nodded. "Right in line with what my team worked up internally."

"Excellent," Van said.

And the meeting was over.

Back in the polished privacy of the elevator, Rocco stood for a moment after the doors had closed before he pressed the button for his floor.

At one time, a meeting like that would have perturbed him.

Not today.

The elevator floor sank smoothly between his feet. Down down down.

They thought they controlled him. And once, they probably had. As much as he liked to believe he'd achieved his corporate success through his own machinations, he knew better. He knew none of his past promotions had been squeaky clean, he'd won them because they'd met someone else's political needs. And now, just as surely, he knew the executives who made their home within Scally's inner circle were determined to keep Rocco in check. They didn't like the way Rocco was winning the DipTych Digital numbers game. They didn't like how Scally admired Rocco for driving his team so hard with so few resources.

They were determined to make sure he stayed here in his little pond.

But they had misunderestimated him. And soon they'd see it for themselves. That he'd changed. Evolved. That he was made, now, of different stuff. That he acted, now, under his own power.

Because don't let the whiff of Metrosexual fool you: beneath that perfectly exfoliated skin stretched an endoderm of far sterner stuff. A classic strength-born-of-adversity situation, because Rocco labored under a severe liability. In a world that prefers the beautiful, Rocco was born with a noticeably asymmetrical face. Nose not quite centered, one eye slightly higher than the other. He had learned, as an adult, to disguise this native disfigurement somewhat. Notice the carefully sculpted strip of moustache above his full upper lip. The hair combed straight backward—no part, nothing to trick the eye into comparing one side of Rocco's face to the other. Grooming tricks to lend a kind of balance that his face otherwise lacked.

Rocco was that sort of a person, always resourceful. Even as a boy he'd been so. When he was nine or so and the older boys had taken to bullying him, for instance, he'd used his father's hammer and a nail from the jar on the work bench, poked holes through the sides of two tin soup cans, labels removed, run a length of twine through the holes, and using the twine as reins had stood himself up on the cans, adding dizzying inches to his height.

*Voila.* Short no more. Short no more!

And take his most recent career accomplishment. He'd been languishing as the operations manager at Traditional for 18 months. But he'd also guessed, correctly, that Scally and the Board were ready to double down on their digital bet. And through a combination of ruthless maneuvering, a little bit of luck, and the careful seeding of a few rumors about his rivals—rumors carefully chosen to be just believable enough to stick and just salacious enough to circulate—Rocco Pinnoccho, in his 53rd year on the planet and his 12th year with the company, had secured not only a Vice Presidency, but the Vice Presidency of a shiny new corporate division.

The cans of his youth were once again solid beneath his feet.

Veeee peeeeee!

Veeee peeeeee!

Veeee peeeeee!

How he relished his title.

But. Again the but.

Corporate advancement, to Rocco's perpetual grief, is not an absolute. On the contrary. It's relative. So while he might be astride the shoulders of the youthful Digital Canning Division, a lofty perch relative to the Rest of the World, within the DipTych hierarchy there remained reaches well above his head.

So Rocco Pinnoccho was looking ahead. He was considering his future.

His original plan: the burgeoning fortunes of DipTych Digital would burst like an aneurysm through the tissue thin layer stretched above Rocco's head, carrying him up to a seat at the C-level round table.

But Rocco was beginning to appreciate the fact that this plan had been unrealistic. At least without some major tweaking.

He'd done everything he could. He'd run DipTych Digital Can masterfully since day one.

But there was nothing he could do about the economy.

The damn economy. Which, even after the EasyCan launch, threatened to exert an uncontrollable drag on what should have been a graceful piloted yacht flying fast as the wind.

Not that DipTych Digital wouldn't do well. How could it not, with the money DipTych was dumping into it? But the pond that had looked so large eight months ago now looked puny and insignificant. Hell, Rocco couldn't even count on approval to create a couple more directorships before fall. How was he supposed to become a Senior VP if there weren't future regular VPs waiting in the wings to fill out his division's executive roster?

In better times, he'd have abandoned the original plan entirely and engineered a lateral move. But the timing wasn't right for that—it would feed him back into the waiting teeth of any number of still-too-freshly angered enemies.

Rocco needed something fresh, a Grand Strategy that would supersize the cans beneath his feet from puny #2 1/2s to massive #10s.

And so he paced.

His office door was shut.

The blinds were drawn.

He checked his watch and lifted today's edition of the Borschtchester *Deign and Pontificate* from his desk. He didn't bother to re-read the front page article above the fold. Even the first time he'd glanced at it, some three hours earlier, it was no surprise—the company had broadcast the gist to all of its employees the afternoon before, a deft little mid-week email pep talk. "DipTych is virtually recession-proof." Quote from Scally. "During times of trouble, people open more cans than ever. We've got the data. They stand over the sink and eat right out of them."

Rocco folded the paper in his left hand and rapped the article with the back knuckles of his right. Right across Scally's pixilated photo. Then he paced back across his office, opened the door, dropped the paper in the cobalt blue recycle box next to it, sat at his computer, and opened a new spreadsheet.

He typed for a few minutes, referring occasionally to Van's Quantme report. Then he picked up the phone and summoned his first lieutenant, Darryl Fiegit, Sales and Marketing Director, DipTych Digital Can.

"Okay. As promised," Rocco said as Darryl settled into the chair on the other side of his desk. "Here are your numbers."

Darryl took the sheet.

He looked as if he might vomit.

"I know this is higher than we'd discussed, but given the market growth potential it's very doable."

"Doable? Rocco—"

But Rocco was having none of it. "We're about to launch EasyCan."

Darryl looked at the sheet again. It was vibrating slightly in his hand.

"According to the marketing plan you submitted."

"Come on, Rocco." Darryl was still looking at the print-out. "You know we were blue skying."

"We're paid to be aggressive."

"Aggressive, sure. But—"

"Darryl. You know the facts. There are 2 million people in the United States with a net worth of a million or more. All you need to do is sell an EasyCan to 20 percent of our millionaires and we're there."

"You can't make assumptions like that, Rocco. You know you can't. The focus groups . . ."

They'd commissioned the focus groups weeks ago, and had argued about how to interpret the results ever since. Rocco insisted that the lackluster reception of the EasyCan concept could be fixed by tweaking the feature set. Darryl, by nature more morose, suspected the issues might be more fundamental.

"We've agreed to disagree about the focus groups," Rocco reminded him.

But Darryl wasn't done. "And we've made no headway in the Dimpling licensing deals. None."

This was another sore point between them. Because EasyCan was intended to be more than a mere can opener.

It was intended be a Digital Can Opening System.

Imagine a device that looks not like any can opener you've ever seen before, but more like a high-end home coffee maker. To use it, you'd open a little door in the front and set a can on the platform inside. No need to position the opener's blade yourself—after you closed the little door, sensors inside the unit would identify the size and shape of the can.

You'd hear a little whir, as the device mounted the can onto its blade armature.

This functionality was the heart and soul of EasyCan, because the mechanical innards wouldn't work properly on a standard can. No, they would not. To be compatible with EasyCan, the sides of the can had to be configured with specialized and highly proprietary indentations: EasyCan Dimpling Technology®.

If a can didn't feature EasyCan Dimpling Technology, the EasyCan system wouldn't be able to mount it on its cutting arm.

So take that, world. Bwa ha ha ha ha. A successful realization of the EasyCan dream would create a de facto market for cans that could only be opened by DipTych's own device.

And DipTych would control a portfolio of licensing deals and partnerships the lucrativity of which not even founder Musgrave Diptychowski (1851 – 1933) could have dreamed.

The Colossus of Can Openers would become the Colossus of Cans.

It was for this that Rocco and Darryl had many weeks crisscrossing the country, calling on executives at the big consumer goods corporations.

The response, unfortunately, had been uniformly unkind.

The executives at big consumer goods corporations insisted, the fools, that old-fashioned cans were perfectly good enough, thank you very much. They'd suggested that DipTych might better stick to the old fashioned can opener business.

Nonetheless, Rocco's faith in the plan was unshaken.

"We've beaten this to death too, Darryl," he said. "They're all bluffing."

Darryl restrained himself from shaking his head. What good would it do?

"All it takes is one," Rocco repeated for the hundredth time. "Then the others have to follow. If they don't, they'll lose their customers to the competition."

Darryl wasn't so sure. You see, there was a downside for any company that licensed EasyCan Dimpling Technology. It would add more cost to their canning operations. Which would be passed on to consumers. Who might balk a bit, on the heels of a particularly nasty recession, at seeing prices go up on their baked beans and tuna fish and canned corn.

"I'd feel better," Darryl muttered, "if we did some market research on consumer price sensitivity to EasyCan compatible cans."

"The market research we have is rock solid."

Those damn focus groups again. Sure, the participants had warmed to some of EasyCan's rich feature set—on paper. Who wouldn't? Come on! A built-in scale? A little keyboard and a mini-printer—you can use the EasyCan System to create and store shopping lists, imagine! And built-in intelligence! Say you buy a can of cannellini beans. You place the can inside the EasyCan chassis, close the door, step back and wait for EasyCan to complete its one-touch hands-free open operation. Then the system's LED display lights up. It says you've opened a 16 ounce can of cannellini beans. It's read the bar code on the can! A little icon flashes. You last opened a 16 ounce can of cannellini beans on March 18! Wow, two cans of cannellini beans in just under a month! This must be one of your household staples! And so the EasyCan Opener System prompts you to add Cannellini Beans, 16-oz to your weekly shopping list . . .

"I'm not talking about the EasyCan feature research," Darryl said. "I'm talking about the cans. And without the income stream from Dimpling deals I don't know—"

"Darryl!" Rocco leaned forward slightly, his voice turning gentle, concern creasing his forehead. "Look. You know the hundred million isn't my doing. If it were my choice . . ."

"You have to push back on them."

"I tried."

Darryl looked unconvinced.

"I did. I told them this was way out of line with our internal projections. They wouldn't budge. I tried."

Darryl still looked unconvinced.

"I go to bat for you every single day, Darryl, you know that."

Long pause.

What could Darryl do?

Nothing.

He rubbed the back of his neck. "I'll need . . . I'll need to accelerate my staff-up."

Rocco's voice got even silkier. "Of course. We've discussed this. You have my okay to get that admin you need."

"No." Darryl was not a particularly robust-looking man, but even a squirrel can muster a semblance of ferocity if cornered. Now he jutted his jaw slightly. "You want me to make those numbers . . . I need my staff—a full department."

Rocco opened the marketing plan. He flipped to the section titled Budget and looked sadly at the column of figures.

But Darryl cut him off. "Rocco, I cut my budget projections by 75 percent, just like you asked. We've got Kich-N-World coming up. We have less than three months. You know as well as I do. I need an army."

Rocco sat back, smoothing his moustache to give himself some time.

"A full department, or I fall flat, Rocco. There's no way."

Numbers flashed through Rocco's head. The plan—Rocco's plan, not Darryl's—had been to shoestring the operation for a bit longer. Keep labor costs down, sit on the cash . . . it had worked well, it was the way he'd murdered the other divisions for more than two quarters straight, Scally now regularly grilled the others on why they couldn't run lean the way Digital did. Of course it couldn't last forever. He knew that. But it had been so . . . nice. It had played so well into his long-term plans . . . or what used to be his long-term plans.

He stroked his moustache again.

This Darryl. A weakling. But a weakling with absolutely no life other than his job at DipTych. Which meant he had all the time and energy he needed to execute a reasonable approximation of a marketing organization single-handedly if he were forced to. Throw together the launch plan, leverage the U-Ful Utensil sales channel, pump some orders through the books. Then you add the fat. After you get the money coming in. That was how you goose the engine of your executive fast-track. Those guys upstairs, Prentice and those other idiots, they'd be the ones with prickling scalps when Digital turned a profit its second quarter after EasyCan launch.

But a hundred mill.

A hundred mill.

That changed the scale of things.

Rocco frowned.

Damn that Van Prentice anyway. Him and his Corporate henchmen, they'd found a way to get back at Rocco for his paper numbers.

They'd changed the paper.

Rocco looked again at Darryl's list of staffing requests.

It was a long list.

"Scally's okayed it. You know that, and I know that," Darryl said.

"Fine." Rocco dropped the folder onto his desk with an angry flick of his hand.

He shut his office door after Darryl left and then sat down again, petting his tie, thinking, thinking.

He'd known this day would come.

He'd hoped it wouldn't come so soon.

He needed something different. Something that would carve a mark so monstrous that Scally would have no choice but to reward Rocco handsomely.

He needed a backup plan. In place. By the end of Q1.

# A THING OF BEAUTY

*"What keeps me up at night? That's easy. My staff. These are my people. They're good guys, every one of them, solid engineers. They put their hearts and souls into their work. I hired them, it's my job to look after them, make sure they're taken care of, and I take that very seriously."*

—Andrew Spittleton, Research Director,
DipTych Digital Can

As a contractor, Brad wasn't allowed to roam the hallways of DipTych by himself. He had to be escorted, something that Andrew Spittleton, Research Director, DipTych Digital Can, generally did himself.

So Brad waited inside the foyer, chitchatting with the guard who sat next to the badge swipe machines.

It didn't bother Brad Tankard one bit that he needed to be babysat, because the indignity was more than cancelled out by the knowledge that he was part of the soon-to-be-magnificent DipTych Digital Can.

Brad recognized greatness when he saw it.

He was thrilled to be associated with—in fact technically a Member of—the Team.

And he displayed his enthusiasm enthusiastically. He was never merely punctual for work. He arrived today 20 minutes early, dressed impeccably as usual, impeccable as a mid-Century ad man in his altered-to-a-perfect-fit Italian suits, smartly-styled black leather messenger bag tucked under his arm, brimming with ideas and an outsider's enthusiasm for following the byzantine rituals of DipTych's technical communications programs.

11:51.

Andrew descended the half flight of stairs leading to the foyer, greeted Brad, greeted the guard. Brad swiped his contractor's badge and stepped over the line separating the mundane from the DipTych. Actually he kind of bounded over.

The building is one of dozens DipTych owns globally, and the second largest of the properties it owns in its headquarters of Borschtchester, New York.

The company, you might have guessed, is a behemoth.

It hadn't always been so. In Musgrave's day, DipTych was content to be nothing more than a successful and lucrative can opener company.

But then Musgrave died, and a generation that had never known him ascended to DipTych's executive offices, and then another, and then along came the 1980s, and DipTych—eager to burnish its reputation for forward-thinkingness—joined the rest of corporate America on the then-fashionable binge diet of Strategic Acquisitions.

To an outsider, some of these purchases may have seemed a tad incongruous, if not manic.

"Why a confectionary company?" you might ask.

Perhaps you haven't seen DipTych-branded fruit-flavored candies. They're sold in 3-inch circular tins with the whimsical tagline "no can opener required!" printed on the side. Brilliant cross-branding, you have to admit. After you taste those candies, you never look at your can opener the same way again.

Acquiring U-Ful Utensils gave DipTych unprecedented access to the European kitchenware market. Again, brilliant. If the U-Ful sales reps sabotaged Corporate's efforts to integrate its other division sales reps within their own network, that was hardly the fault of the Board of Directors.

The most far-reaching acquisition, now re-styled as DipTych Window & Door, at least made sense from a cash flow standpoint. The more cynical members of DipTych's professional class often joked that if it weren't for Window & Door, there'd be no roof over Candy & Nut.

In any case, no matter how far afield DipTych's eye might wander, the company also maintained a prideful and possessive sense of its ancient heritage, illustriously rooted in the 19th century industrial blossoming of its home city. And if, today, its corporate frame sagged fearfully under its own weight—one could sometimes even hear it creak ominously—DipTych paid well—very well, by Western New York rust belt standards—and its cheery benefits packages periodically garnered mentions in the national press.

All was well.

As a contractor, Brad wasn't given full access to the trough, of course. But it was more than he'd earned as House Husband. And the work gave him the opportunity to brush the dust from one of his fine Italian suits and Attend Meetings.

Like the one about to start.

"I'm going to get a cup of coffee. Want one?"

Andrew was habituated to approximately 18 Styrofoam cups of free DipTych coffee per day.

"No, thanks."

The coffee habit may explain Andrew's stunning career, in fact. A true DipTychian to his bones, Andrew had been hired right out of college as a young engineer and for the next 26 years toiled away, head down and head first, on analog can opener technology. Earning, en route, the undying respect of legions of other DipTych engineers. And the right to spend three quarters of his time flying to overseas manufacturing plants to troubleshoot manufacturing issues. His eyes, always solemn, had long since taken on a cast of virtuousness that shone through even when he was feeling particularly stubborn, which was often, as he was a precise and opinionated man.

Also, his wife's cousin is married to the DipTych CEO's niece.

So it was Andrew Spittleton, a middle-aged Andrew Spittleton with pale streaks like spilt milk coursing through his neatly trimmed beard, who'd been tapped to head up R&D for the newly created DipTych Digital Can, an honor as heavy as it was exhilarating. And not only because the buckets of cash allocated to the new division had flowed, so far, mainly through his budget. Far more important to Andrew: it was his job, and he knew it, to ensure that the products that would one day issue from the division's loins would be without peer, unmatched and unmatchable. In fact, the only thing more important to him than this was his wife, and she was pretty much self-managing at this point in their marriage.

He returned to the conference room with his coffee and sat down. Over half of the chairs around the conference table were now occupied. A couple of hardware guys were there, a couple of materials engineering guys, a couple systems engineering guys, the Mechanical Design Engineer, and the woman Andrew had just hired to head up Quality Assurance.

"Who are we waiting for?" He took a sip of his bitter and Styrofoam-infused brew.

People murmured a few names.

Were these people all at work today, did anyone know?

Yes, so-and-so had seen so-and-so, and so-and-so had said he was going to be there but a few minutes late.

Andrew glanced at the clock.

The QA woman—the only female in the room—passed around the agenda.

A couple more engineers came in and sat down.

Andrew glanced at the agenda. One other person still missing. The marketing guy. But he was coming from corporate, across town. "Let's give folks another minute."

Brad drew a small stack of manila folders from his messenger bag.

Andrew picked up his own briefcase from the floor and placed it on the table in front of him. He didn't always place the briefcase so—this was to prepare for the marketing guy. The briefcase was now a metaphorical castle wall over which no marketing asshat could possibly clamber.

Another engineer entered and sat, joining the chit chat.

Brad pulled his son's latest drawing from one of his folders.

"What are you working on now?" Andrew asked him.

"Neon Tetra."

DipTych, in an admirable display of humanizing humor, uses aquarium fish names as code words for its R&D projects.

Andrew nodded.

"Take a look at this," Brad leaned down the table. "My 8 year old's work. He's quite the draftsman, isn't he?"

He handed the drawing to Andrew, who took it in one hand while he sipped coffee with the other. "Cute."

"The composition is exquisite, isn't it?"

Andrew nodded.

"The way he captures dimensionality. And that line . . ."

Andrew nodded again. He glanced at the clock. "Okay, folks, while we're waiting for Darryl, let's get started." He dropped Ethan Tankard's drawing onto the table on top of his copy of the agenda, then noticed he couldn't read the agenda and pulled it out from under the drawing. "George?"

George Bonmont was Head Systems Engineer. This made him second only in power to Andrew himself, and not only because his tenure had cracked the 35-year mark—rendering him ten DipTych Years older than Andrew—but also by virtue of the enormous responsibility he bore. For to George fell the task of governing all of DipTych EasyCan Technology's integration points. And there were a lot of them. In fact, it's perhaps a vast oversimplification to call the EasyCan Opener System a "system." It's far more. It's multiple systems, systems-within-the-system. The scale, the printer, the cutter, the screen. Not to mention potential add-on modules. One that allows can lids to be ejected into a recyclable paper wrapper, for instance. Making them safer to handle during transport to your recycle bin. And a steam cleaner to keep the EasyCan Opener System's innards pristine and hygienic.

Fortunately, George had an uncanny and DipTychian grasp of the high level implications of all this interconnectedness.

He'd even coined a new phrase to capture the magnificent-ness of all that interconnectedness. "Tangential Integration."

"First up," George started. "We think we've got a possible solution to our bus architecture issue."

Oh, the data port thing.

Ugly.

All of the EasyCan systems-within-a-system need to pass data to one another, you see. Not to mention pass data to DipTych's future canning technology concubines—oh, sorry, "partners." Passing data was the blood flow that would keep Tangential Integration alive. The trick was enabling data to be passed without growing EasyCan to the size of a 6000-BTU window air conditioner unit—which EasyCan had, at one point two months back, begun to closely resemble.

"It will require some customization," George continued, "but Paulie here says it's doable, right, Paulie?"

Paulie nodded.

Everyone in the room already knew about the whole bus architecture issue and proposed fix, of course. In fact, George had used it as an example in a paper he'd submitted, "The Challenges and Rewards of Tangential Integration," for an upcoming engineering conference. And he'd blogged about it some, too—George, being one of DipTych's senior R&Ders, was permitted to post on the company's technical blog portal. George, you see, was smart, possibly one of the smartest guys on the DipTych payroll, not that anybody besides George and a handful of his closest colleagues would know it. And Tangential Integration was the kind of concept that could make a guy's career. That could pass into the engineering lexicon with a fellow's name forever in close association, *Tangential Engineering . . . as first described by George Bonmont*.

"So that takes us to the next open integration issue, the LNN bus."

The engineers paused in a collective moment of thoughtful silence as they shifted their attention to the issue of the LNN bus.

The door opened.

Darryl had arrived.

Greetings, head nods, handshakes.

Darryl took a seat at the conference table.

The conversation recovered from its respectful pause.

"Question." Tim, User Interface Design Engineer. "If we move to a customized LNN bus, will it enable us to boost the MPS to the LED at all? Or are we still constrained by the overall RDQL?"

Darryl avoided looking at Andrew. He looked at Tim, and nodded as if he knew exactly what Tim was talking about.

"That depends," answered Placido, Mechanical Design Engineer. He pulled out a pad and sketched a quick schematic. Then, with short hard strokes, an arrow. "With a VRN bus, you've got inherently more capacity here—" he drew another arrow, "and here. The LNN should approximate the VRN, assuming we don't run into any quadrant issues in our LSR."

"Quadrant issues," Andrew said. "I thought we'd settled quadrant when Alex moved the scale from the side to the top."

"He did, to an extent," said Placido.

"To what extent."

"About 22 percent." Placido smiled, because answering 22 percent was an inside joke. The team always answered 22 percent when it didn't know what the right answer was.

Andrew didn't smile.

"We could look at quadrant again," one of the other hardware engineers suggested.

Andrew flicked his hand. "Okay. We have Darryl here, let's table this for the time being." He reached out and popped his briefcase open so that the back of the lid faced Darryl, Battleship Game style.

Darryl's only defense, on the other hand, was a pad of lined paper. He drew a retractable pen from his pocket and clicked it into note-taking mode.

"Okay, Darryl. I'm guessing you'd like an update on where we are with the prototype."

Darryl nodded.

"Right," Andrew said. He pulled a sheaf of documents from his case, extracted one single-page report from the sheaf, and pushed it across the table toward Darryl.

Then he separated the rest of the stack into two piles which he arranged on either side of his briefcase. This spread his defenses laterally in a kind of paper moat.

Darryl was reading the sheet of paper.

"This looks like the same report from two weeks ago."

Andrew took a virtuously contemplative pull from his coffee. "Yes. You may have noticed, Darryl, based on our conversation when you walked in. We've got some issues we're working through. This isn't a 1945 folding hand opener unit. This is high tech. We have to get it right."

Darryl flinched.

The edge of the paper Andrew had handed him was damp and rumpled now from the moisture of his hand.

Andrew, on the other hand, looked contented enough to just about purr.

"When we have something we can prototype," he said, "you'll be the first to know."

"Andrew. There's a lot riding on this. Corporate has given us some pretty aggressive numbers. And we have Kich-N-World. It's only, what, eleven weeks away now? We gotta do our launch. And to do our launch, we gotta have something to show at the show."

"So you tell me. But like I said, as soon as we have something we can prototype—"

"Andrew. You're making me nervous."

Like Andrew needed to be told. Darryl wore nervousness like some men wear designer clothes. Only he never took it off. He looked nervous even when he was drooling on his throw pillows during late night reruns of *One Hit Wonders from the 80s.*

Now he stared at the status report for another moment, considering his options. He could show a little sympathy for Andrew, and thereby align himself as an ally against the perennially bone-headed DipTych management. But that was risky. There was no natural basis for an alliance between the two. Andrew didn't really have any use for Darryl.

And Darryl was a cautious man.

That left an option that was nearly as weak. Darryl evoked a higher power. "Look, Andy. You know this isn't me. Making these decisions. Management—straight down from Scally—we need a product." Darryl pushed the report back across the table and up against Andrew's open brief case. "We have to get past concept. Concept's going to get us all marched to the guillotine."

Fail. Andrew still looked contented. Even vaguely triumphant. He picked up the report, placed it on one of the stacks of paper spread around the briefcase, then merged that stack with the rest of the papers and, with long graceful fingers tapped them together against the table like an oversized deck of cards.

He took a very long time to do this, while Darryl's shirt became yet more damp with the fruits of his growing anxiety.

"I understand the stakes perfectly well, Darryl," Andrew said. "But my chief responsibility is to the product, not the marketing department." He returned the papers finally to his briefcase. "As soon as we have something new, you'll be the first to know." He took another swig from his Styrofoam cup.

Darryl stood up. His chair wobbled drunkenly from the force of his movement. He managed to catch it. "I'll phone you up next Monday to check, Andy."

"I'm out of the country all week. Friday," Andrew answered. "Or the Monday after would be better, actually, I don't know if I'll really have anything new for you by Friday."

He picked up his agenda and scanned the room. "Okay, who's up next. Kevin?"

"I don't think George is done," Kevin said.

"Oh, right. George, then."

Darryl capped his pen and crept away.

# STAFFNATION

*"Everyone was treated with the utmost dignity. We offered both counseling services and generous severance packages structured in accordance with standard DipTych HR policies and procedures."*

—Ambrose Dial, HR Director,
DipTych Corporate Division,
in a written statement

Darryl's position didn't warrant an office with a door.

Granted, his cubicle was spacious—a good 4 square feet larger than anyone else's in the immediate vicinity. He had extra file cabinets. He had a larger desk.

His spoils.

Trinkets, compared to what he really needed, which was soldiers. FTEs. Warm bodies lined up and ready to do his bidding. All the fresh young talent that a venture like the Digital Canning Division so richly deserved.

Now more than ever. Because there were two ways Darryl could respond to the news that he was on the hook to generate a hundred million in top-line revenue within the next 12 months from an LOB only eight months old and which happened to lack an actual product to sell. One was to dash his lance at the windmill for real, revise his strategic sales and marketing plan and insist to the death that he could move a million—give or take a few thou—DipTych EasyCan units through an infant sales channel.

Darryl had already considered this and dismissed it. It was crap. The only reason Rocco believed it was possible was that he'd long ago burned out his bullshit detector. Or—more sinister interpretation here—maybe he didn't think Darryl had a bullshit detector of his own.

No, Darryl needed to do something different. Peg his fate on that time-honored American tradition. Become too big to fail. A strategy which, as a welcome side benefit, would also serve up plenty of candidates for spreading out the blame, should blame be necessary. A perfect foil for when Rocco laid the blame on Darryl.

Darryl pulled up his copy of the ops plan on his computer. Three divisions. Sales. Marketing. Public relations. He pulled out a pad and began drawing an org chart, lines and boxes. Not quite big enough . . . he needed a fourth. Call it Strategic Development. Then, within each of those divisions, subdivisions. Each with a managerial layer of its own, then a secondary layer of foot soldiers, and sprinkled throughout a few dozen administrative staffers. Darryl poked at the sheet with his pen and counted. Yeah. He could get to 45, 50 people easily.

He picked up the phone and dialed the Human Resources extension.

He didn't catch the name of the woman who answered. It was either Sooley or Surley. But she had a cutesy voice and seemed happy to hear from him.

He gave her the list of titles. "Sales Manager. Channel Relations Manager, will report into sales. Marketing Manager, direct report. Marketing Assistant. Public Relations Manager, direct report. Website Development Manager, report to Marketing Manager. Strategic Development Manager, direct report."

"That's wonderful!" Sooley/Surley said, tapping the titles into her computer.

"So what's the next step, then?"

"I'll email you job descriptions and salary ranges. It's pretty much boilerplate. You just review them, and let me know if you see any issues."

"Right. Then you run ads, right? How soon would—"

"Well, not necessarily," Sooley/Surley interrupted. "We start with an internal search."

"Oh."

"We give priority, as you may know, to DipTych employees who have been displaced."

DipTych had recently announced a reorg. Five thousand layoffs by December 25.

"I see," Darryl said. This was not good news. "Look, uh, it might be a good idea to go outside for, uh, some of the more critical—"

"Certainly, if we aren't able to find qualified employees among the displaced."

"I don't want people who, uh—"

"All of your candidates will be highly qualified."

Darryl knew the highly qualified employees she meant. He'd seen them. You could always tell. Wandering in the cafeteria, huddled in the parking lot. Alive, but robbed by pink slip of their animating resolve—it was this shuffling army, then, from which Sooley/Surley wanted to draw his mighty soldiers.

A hundred million.

Darryl thought things over for a minute. Then he remembered the rumors around the time Andrew Spittleton had started beefing up DipTych Digital R&D. That he'd drained Tradition of its best engineers.

"The internal search—we'll be targeting current employees who haven't been pink-slipped too, right?"

"Not initially, no. In accordance with DipTych HR policy, we start with the li—the employees who—"

"Oh. So it does exist," said Darryl.

"What does exist."

"The list."

"I'm sorry?"

"The Can't Be Fired list."

"I don't know what you're talking about." Sooley/Surley's girly voice had suddenly cooled and deepened. "There's no such thing as a Can't Be Fired list."

"Look, Sullerrrly" said Darryl, slurring her name so that it would likely at least resemble whatever it really was. "This new division. It's not like . . . the talent I need. We need fresh thinking."

Silence.

He tried again. "And let's be honest with one another. We both know that if someone is . . . identified as a candidate for downsizing, chances are that person is . . ."

"Is what?"

"You know."

"I'm not sure I do." Sooley/Surley's voice sounded downright chilly. That might even have been the sound of ice cubes clinking between the words.

"Chances are most of these people are . . . not at the top of their games."

"Mr. Fiegit. May I remind you that DipTych is firmly committed to the wellbeing of each and every one of our employees?"

"Well, of course it—"

"—and may I also remind you that each and every employee of this company was hired only after passing through a rigorous screening practice, designed to ensure that we employ only the top talent—"

"Right, but digital—"

"You know, I'm thinking, there is a training we offer."

Darryl heard keyboard clicking again.

"Training?" For a momentary lapse into stupidity, Darryl assumed she was suggesting that DipTych offer training to the dull and underqualified candidates she was planning to squeeze chute into his organization.

"There's a module in our Sensitivity program." More keyboard clicks. "It will help you understand the importance of valuing your staff. Ah, here it is! What is your availability, let's see, next week."

Darryl shot up out of his chair, knocking his computer keyboard off its little pull-out tray as he did. "I'm, ah, I'm, ah—I'm tied up in meetings all week, I'm afraid."

"Perhaps the week after, then, let me check . . ."

Darryl's keyboard had been saved by its cable from falling all the way to the floor. It dangled now, swaying slightly.

"Oh dear," Sooley/Surley said. "It seems we're not offering it again until . . . hmmm. Next month, it looks like."

One last chance . . . he knew it . . . gasping, must get the words out . . . "My calendar . . . update . . . I'll need to . . . call you back with . . . availability."

"Yes, that would be fine. Middle of next month. Now. Let's see. You need admins, right? We have a lot of admins."

An understatement. One of the first thing a DipTych manager did, as soon as there was budget, was to hire at last one admin. Borschtchester born and raised, most of them, the vast majority now 50-something women, smokers, cynically wise—and they made great human shields any time a round of layoffs was announced. Need to cut your staff? Fine. Lay off a few admins, presto, a 10-20 percent reduction and hey! None of your golf buddies got hurt! Genius.

So no surprise that admins were well-represented in the latest 1000 layoffs.

Darryl slumped back into his chair and reached for his dangling keyboard.

"Hold on," Sooley/Surley said. "Looks like we've already got a hire for you. Digital Canning Division PR Manager." Again with the keyboard keys clicking. An evil sound. "Taylor Song."

"I'm sorry?"

"It's a somewhat unusual situation." More evil clicking.

"I'd prefer to interview candidates before you—"

"I understand. In this case, we've already offered the position."

Darryl opened his mouth to protest, then considered that an objection might remind Sooley/Surley of his sensitivity deficiency.

"The candidate is highly qualified."

No doubt.

"Here comes a job description for Marketing manager. What else. You said Strategic Development Director, right?"

Darryl slumped under the weight of sudden exhaustion. "Manager. Manager. Not Director."

"Thank you, Darryl. Job description on its way. Next?"

# IN WHICH TAYLOR'S CAREER
# SUDDENLY DEFLOWERS

*"Flowers you can hold in your vase. Beauty you can hold in your hand.
An aesthetic sensibility you can hold in your soul."*

—Orwin's print ad

Taylor's entry to DipTych Canning Division was, in fact, a more unusual situation than Sooley/Surley even knew, considering that Taylor herself, at the time of Sooley/Surley and Darryl's conversation, didn't know that she had the job.

She thought she worked at a flower shop.

It was her dream job. First, because the shop was an oasis of greenery and life all the more luscious this time of year, when everyone outside was gray and dead. Second because everyone she worked with and for was generally pleasant and good-humored, and the pace of her work—even during the busiest times, like right before Christmas or some weekend in June when every high school in the greater Borschtchester area scheduled their senior proms—the pace of work always seemed natural and manageable, always yielded little pleasures and satisfactions as if time itself were the handmaiden of the shop's unending cascades of blooms.

And third, because it was the florist shop in town that sold the most gloriously artistic and fantabulously expensive arrangements featuring the most exotically creative twists, like a single rose bound in a cluster of carved antique chopsticks, or bouquets of brown dried daffodils interspersed with sprigs of brilliantly colored autumn leaves (long-dead spring, just-dead summer, get it?) or holiday wreaths woven of poison ivy. Sold with complimentary latex gloves of course.

The shop was never boring, never prosaic. You felt like you were part of something larger.

That said, something had troubled her that day. She'd noticed it again during the last half hour or so her of her shift. She was cleaning up the flower arrangement room, always a bit of a wistful time anyway, inhaling the fading scent of the discarded blooms strewn over the work table, or a step away the more poignant odors of the not-yet-used blooms languishing in their display vases—the dusky mintiness of the mums, the lilies' rosiny perfumes, the undertones of pollen with its minerals and pepper—if only it would all just linger in her hair and clothes for just a bit longer . . . until she got home maybe, that wasn't too much to ask, was it . . .

She pulled onto the expressway, peering into her mirror to check traffic, frowning.

And then the thought rose, the one she'd been trying to refuse, transparent at first, then taking on a translucency until, ghoulish, it gave itself over to its words.

*If there was a way to treat flowers with fixatives—like they use in perfumery— to enhance their scents, make them last longer, carry better . . . would people pay more for that, I wonder?*

The car swerved slightly as she shuddered in horror.

Imagine.

Perverting flowers.

*Damn it.*

Where had *that* come from?

She slapped herself on the side of the head. She shouldn't have let it form. She shouldn't have listened to it . . .

Somebody somewhere near her tapped his horn—she'd drifted slightly in her lane—she yanked the steering wheel back to the right.

*Stay on track, Taylor.*

But it was too late. She could still feel the pulse of that demonic thought. And her day had seemed so fine . . .

"That wasn't me," she said aloud. "That isn't me."

And it wasn't.

But the eerie traces of it wouldn't go away. She still felt uneasy when she exited the expressway and threaded a short progression of downtown city streets.

She wished now that she was headed straight home. But she was not.

She was on her way to a protest.

25

Not a particularly robust protest, as it turned out.

Taylor saw them as she drove by hunting for a parking spot: a little clutch of activists standing in front of State Assemblyman Stewart "Bo" Valgus' office

She joined them a few moments later, and her friend Aimee hugged her and handed her a sign and asked her if she knew the three other protesters.

She did. She'd met them at their last rally. It had been better attended, because the organizers had worked local activists into a frenzy by vigorously re-tweeting a remark Bo had made during an interview with a local radio morning show. The DJ had asked his opinion about same-sex marriage and he'd answered "I haven't had a chance to think about it, to tell the truth." The idiot. Everyone knew that a same sex marriage would have come to the floor if ex-Governor Eminent Flipzer's ungovernable hetero sex drives hadn't led him to disgrace and ruin. Well, if not ruin, then a brief time-out to think about what a bad boy he'd been.

Overnight, the legislature had become suddenly paranoid about any issue associated with the letters s-e-x.

And so here they were, to express their chagrin with Bo Valgus. Only this time, the protest lacked much support, because unfortunately there had been no precipitating event to fire up the masses.

Taylor glanced at Bo Valgus' office.

It appeared to be somewhat deserted, although there was a light on in the back of the room.

The property was a storefront facing one of Borschtchester's storied old city streets, and had once housed "Ray's Deli." Nobody could really remember Ray's Deli, but the lettering of the deli's sign had protected the plastic facing behind it, and since Bo hadn't installed a new sign over top, you could still make out the words on the facing.

Bo's sign was a big cardboard placard leaned up against the inside of the plate glass windows, facing the street. The lettering of the placards was red and blue. No hint, not even the slightest, of his party affiliation was anywhere in evidence.

Taylor glanced again at the storefront as she picked up a sign. It read: "The only Civil answer is Marriage." Aimee's read: "I DO support gay marriage."

They stood in front of Bo's windows.

Cars trickled by a few at a time, typical for Borschtchester's alarmingly anemic evening rush hour. Nobody honked.

"You know, I don't think anyone's here," Aimee said.

She had cupped her hand over the grimy window and was peering inside.

Taylor stood next to her and looked in, too. "How's Jenna doing?" she asked after a minute.

"Not great. I think it's over."

"If you need a place to stay . . ."

"With my ferrets."

Some people have baggage. Aimee had ferrets.

They turned around and faced the street again.

The protestor named Zeke lit a cigarette and as he threw his match onto the sidewalk said, "Oh Christ, here come the anarchists."

Three young men, about a block away.

Taylor glanced at her friend. "Aren't they supposed to wear masks?"

"They aren't radical anarchists," said Aimee. "They're more mainstream anarchists."

The one in the middle was kind of cute. He looked at them and then said "Hey" like he was saying it to Taylor.

"Not much of a protest," said the tall anarchist.

"Thanks for coming by," Aimee said. "We had more people the last time."

"We're not here to support gay marriage." The tall anarchist again. "We're here to protest all marriage, gay or straight."

"Oh," said Aimee.

Zeke blew out a cloud of smoke. It drifted over Taylor and Aimee and the three anarchists.

"Down with marriage," the cute one said.

Zeke crushed out the butt with his boot. "You can't drink beer here. Open container. You'll get us all busted."

The third anarchist's doughy look suggested he should probably lay off the beer for other reasons as well. He shrugged and took another sip.

"You're not really helping, you know," said Aimee.

"What, not helping. We just about doubled the size of your movement."

"You know that Bo's not around," said the cute one. "He's in Albany until tomorrow morning."

"Maybe we should chant something," Taylor suggested. But nobody answered.

Traffic had picked up a bit. Still no honks.

Taylor and Aimee paraded up the sidewalk and back again.

"Well. My beer's gone." The doughy anarchist. "We've done our bit, comrades."

"See ya," said the cute one, and the anarchists left.


"I always feel so let down after these things," Aimee said as she and Taylor walked to their cars.

"At least it wasn't snowing. Have you met those anarchists before?"

"Not really. I've seen them around. That one was checking you out."

"No, he wasn't."

"He didn't look that bad, for a dude." Aimee was on her way to work. She was a tattooist and preferred to work with post-Happy Hour customers. And she wore her hair in a Cupie doll cut that made her look younger than she really was, which made drinking in bars problematic, since it was beneath her dignity to carry ID.

"Have fun," Taylor said. "Call me if you get bored."

It was getting dark by the time Taylor exited the expressway again.

She negotiated the ever-diminishing trickle of suburban streets that led to her neighborhood.

And was about to pull into her driveway when she saw the lights.

A lot of lights. Every window on the broad blank face of her house, in fact, was alight.

She pulled up to the curb a half block away. Heart thudding. Dialed 9-1-1.

"I think someone's broken into my house."

The dispatcher took some information and a few moments later two police cars slid up, and then a third, quiet as sharks.

And in that moment, Taylor thought of something.

It wasn't a burglar. It was—

She jumped. She hadn't seen the officer walk up alongside her car, he'd startled her when he'd tapped on her window.

"You Taylor Song?" Muffled through the glass.

She nodded and reached for her door handle but he shook his head. He wanted her to stay in the car.

He muttered into his pager as he walked away and a moment later had caught up to the other officers.

And all three were walking up the driveway, approaching the front door.

Their guns were drawn.

*If it's her,* Taylor thought, *let's hope they don't freaking shoot her.*

She turned her key in the ignition to get some juice to her electric windows and lowered hers.

The expressway was only about a quarter of a mile away. Its traffic, shushing by, was the loudest noise of the neighborhood this time of year, when there was no foliage to deaden it.

The front door opened.

And over the traffic sound, Taylor could hear a woman's voice, speaking.

Her officer walked back up the street.

He got out. The officer was tall and big-gutted and redolent of drugstore aftershave. Taylor choked back a gasp when the smell of it hit her.

"A Brenda Song," he said to Taylor. "She says she lives there. She says she's your—"

"My mom. Yeah. I'm sorry officer. I didn't realize—she's been away . . . a number of years—"

"Yeah, she said. On a business trip. I guess you weren't expecting her back tonight."

"No. No, not really. No, I wasn't."

Taylor waited until the police cars were gone.

The front door was shut again. But unlocked.

Taylor pushed it open.

Brenda rounded the corner from the kitchen.

She looked the same. Dark gray pantsuit. Two-inch heels. Hair clipped short, stiff with spray, parted on the left, square gold earrings clasping her lobes, fingertips perfect pearls of polish. Face perfect as a diamond.

"Mom."

"Hi, dear. Sorry I didn't phone ahead. What are all those plants in the dining room?" She gave Taylor a quick hug, then picked up a wheeled cloth suit case, burgundy with a paisley pattern and faux gold hardware. "Coffee?"

Taylor followed her back into the kitchen. "I called the cops."

"Yes, I gathered that. I was on the phone. Conference call. Chantilly board meeting. They're planning a re-org and the stockholders are getting restless. Did you say you wanted coffee?"

"No, thanks." Taylor unbuttoned her coat. Slowly.

Brenda began opening and closing cupboard doors. "Speaking of boards, I put in a word for you at DipTych. Marketing should suit you, I think? They'll start you out at 36 a year."

"What are you looking for, Mom?"

"Taylor, where are the coffee mugs?"

"Over the sink. I'm sorry—I—moved them. What did you just say, something about DipTych?" The same ominous feeling Taylor had felt at Orwin's that afternoon had come back, only this time it was worse. Like the creature from the doom lagoon had finally started slithering forth. There was the nose . . . a muck-covered claw . . .

"Ambition is worth fighting for, Taylor. Your generation doesn't appreciate that. I see it a lot. It's easier for you, you don't remember what it was like before women were encouraged to have careers."

"Mom, I don't—"

"It's time you had a real job, Taylor." Brenda filled her mug and returned the coffee pot to its burner.

"I have a job."

Brenda had opened a laptop that was only slightly larger than a deck of cards. Now she plugged one end of a power cord into the back of the laptop, and the other end into the outlet on the side of the kitchen island. She pulled up one of the four retro bar stool-style chairs and perched herself on it. "I know you have a job. Just because I travel a lot doesn't mean I don't pay attention."

"I don't want to quit Orwin's. And you don't travel a lot. You travel all the time."

"Is that where all those plants in the dining room came from?"

"I don't know anything about marketing."

"The humidity has taken the finish off the windowsill. You should call in a contractor to give an estimate. But you'll need to get the plants out of there before he comes."

"Mom."

"I heard you. You have a job at Orwin's." Brenda tapped her notebook's mouse pad. "You can always go back some day. That's the nice thing about . . . those kind of jobs. There are always plenty of them."

"They say I could take it over eventually."

Brenda looked up at her daughter, fixing her eyes on her for the first time. "Take it over?"

"Yes." Taylor had straightened up and faced her mother, waiting. Businesswoman to businesswoman.

"So you're saying you'll just stay there. Forever."

"Well—" It wasn't exactly the fulsome praise Taylor had expected. "It's where I want to be."

"That's not possible."

"They said—"

But Brenda was finished. "I pulled strings to do this for you, Taylor. It's a personal favor. I promise, it's in your best interest."

"I don't know anything about—what will I even be doing?"

"You have a communications degree."

"But I—"

"Fake it, dear." Brenda touched her hair, smoothing a non-existent ruffle. "A useful skill in its own right." She pulled a cell phone from her briefcase.

Taylor began backing slowly from the room.

Brenda flipped open her cell phone. "Do well for yourself and you can buy Orwin's someday," she called out. "If you still want it. You start at DipTych on Thursday. Ask for Darryl Fiegit. He's your new boss. Do you have some business suits? You can borrow some of mine until you get a chance to shop for some. Archie? Brenda here. Yes. I reviewed your numbers on the plane . . ."

Brenda had moved one of the plants from its spot on windowsill and put it on a trivet in the center of the dining room table. A bromeliad. It had produced its spike of bright red bracts, which made it a suitable centerpiece. Although for a bromeliad, the bracts signaled the beginning of the end, because next it would flower, and after it flowered it would die.

Taylor had adopted it when it was tiny, a pup fallen from a full-grown bromeliad at the shop.

Marketing. Marketing. How hard could it be.

"Aimee."

In her bedroom, on her cell.

"'sup?"

"Busy?"

"Nope."

"Guess who's here."

Aimee guessed immediately. "No kidding. How long has it been this time?"

"I can't keep track any more. At least four years, I guess. Maybe five."

"I'm telling you, these aren't business trips. Nobody leaves for a business trip and then doesn't show back up for five years. She's got another family somewhere."

"She sits on a lot of boards. I've looked it up."

"She's like these men who have two families. Two identities."

"She got me a job. At DipTych."

"Oh geez."

"It pays a ton."

"Spend it all on tats," Aimee advised. "But you love Orwin's."

"Orwin's is paradise."

"Don't cry."

"I've been kicked out of paradise."

"Like Eve. But you know, I'm sure getting kicked out of DipTych will be even easier. Play the game for a bit, show Brenda that it's not a fit, then you can go back to your old job."

Taylor hadn't thought of that.

"Right?" Aimee said.

"I hadn't thought of that."

"See? It will work out. And in the meantime, think of all the extra pocket change you'll have. We'll finally be able to take that trip we've always dreamed of. You can pay."

Taylor sighed.

"There, better?"

"Yes. Thank you Aimee, you're the best."

"Hey, I can try to find out that guy's name if you want."

"Nah. Don't bother."

"He didn't look too bad."

"Don't bother."

"You said you were over . . . *him*." The name that shall not be spoken.

"I am."

"Okay." Aimee sounded skeptical. "Let me know if you change your mind. Cute anarchist awaits."

# A PARADE OF LITTLE
# WORKPLACE JOYS

*"Marketing is war. Marketing is war. PR is the air command. You send it in, it drops its ordinance, softens the enemy's resistance. Direct mail, that's your ground troops, back it up with advertising which is your big guns, your cannon. And social media, that's the counter-intelligence. You use social media to win the minds and hearts of the natives."*

—Basil Bane, Marketing Manager,
DipTych Digital Division

It was Taylor's first day on the job.

There were two open seats left when she walked into the conference room.

One at the head of the table. Nope, not sitting there.

She took the other seat. Sat down. Looked across the table.

And found herself looking into the eyes of . . . that cute anarchist.

The cute anarchist?

She dropped her gaze, startled.

He must have recognized Taylor, too, right? But he'd rewarded her with little more than a mild glance, deflating immediately the little flutter she felt when she realized it was him.

She fussed with the supplies she'd brought. Notepad. Pen.

The big clock on the wall whirled and clicked.

8:58.

They were waiting for their boss, Darryl.

They chitchatted. Taylor listened. Eavesdropped, rather. Little of it made sense to her. Although she gathered after a bit that everyone else in the room had come from elsewhere in DipTych, had been reeled into Darryl's org chart from the divisions she knew only as tabs on the company's home page, DipTych Traditional or U-Ful Utensils. And now, here they were, assembled into a brand new company-within-a-company, bewildered a little, still, at their fantastic luck. They had jobs? They'd been given cubicles? Budget even, some of them? And didn't even have to cast off any of their old work habits?

Heaven.

So they chitchatted, taking each other's size. For despite having worked for the same company for years, few in the room really knew anyone else. DipTych might have passed its crest, a few years back, as Borschtchester's largest employer, but it was still a huge place—you have to think of it as a little city to understand how huge. You could work there for decades and never meet more than a few hundred people out of the hordes and hordes that wander its buildings and halls. So now the room buzzed with the ritual of placing one another, a soft jockeying for status. Did you know so-and-so from Labeling. Never met him but the name's familiar. Oh, if you were in Specialty sales, you must have met so-and-so. Yes, she was my boss until she moved to Classic. Great boss.

All this made Taylor more than a mere outsider. Fortunately, she had no way of knowing how out of place she was. She was an innocent. She was aware of nothing more than the normal awkwardness you feel when you walk into a party where the only person you know is the hostess and she's nowhere in sight, she must be in the kitchen or something.

Then the door shut and the chitchat died away.

Darryl took the last remaining seat.

"Well. Here we are," he said. He glanced around the table, the path of his glance jittery. He avoided Taylor's eye. Perhaps avoided everyone's eye. "Suppose we start by introducing ourselves. Since we're all new here."

They did so, one by one, a ring of introductions around the table.

The cute anarchist's turn. He said "Miles Chacuderie." And instead of following his name with a title, like the others did, he just added "graphics."

"Okay, guys," Darryl said when they were done. "As you know, we have a lot to do. A ton. We're setting up a whole marketing organization from scratch, and frankly the future of DipTych depends on whether we can pull it off. So we have to pull it off. Failure is not an option, as the saying goes. And our number, the number we've been given, I'll be honest with you, it's an aggressive number. It's going to take all we have to—"

"What's the number, Darryl?" That from the man sitting two seats down from Taylor, Basil Bane, Marketing Manager.

"It's an extremely aggressive number."

"So I gather. What is it?"

"I'd rather not—"

Taylor glanced around the room herself, now. It was as if the ring of people had suddenly tightened. They were leaning forward—all except one. She avoided looking at him. So this must be something momentous? She picked up her pen.

"We're going to find out sooner or later." Basil's voice was rising slightly.

"A hundred mill," Darryl muttered.

"Oh for Christ's sake," Basil said. "I knew there'd be a catch."

Everybody was suddenly talking all at once.

"Look," Darryl said.

Nobody stopped talking.

"Hey!"

They stopped now and looked at him.

"It's just a number, okay? This is . . . uncharted ground for this company. I'm working on it. You really can't worry about—"

He seemed to have forgotten what they shouldn't worry about, because he stopped speaking and looked around the table at peoples' faces, then realized he was looking at them and closed his mouth and looked instead at his watch. It crossed Taylor's mind that perhaps the poor man had some trouble at home or something. He didn't look particularly well.

"You need to talk reason to them," Basil said. "There is just no way this division is going to make a hundred million in the first year. That's insane."

"Let's just not worry about the number now, okay?" Darryl muttered at his watch. "Forget about the number."

The momentous thing must have passed, because people settled back into their chairs. Except, out of the corner of Taylor's eye, the cute anarchist. Because he hadn't leaned forward in the first place.

"Look, I'll worry about the number, okay?"

The people around the table nodded thoughtfully.

"You worry about Kich-N-World. As I'm sure you all are aware, it's our biggest trade show."

"Maybe," said Basil. Taylor turned to look at him again. He was not a particularly attractive specimen. Flabby. The particularly soft sort of flab, it slumped down his body like a sock slumps around your ankle when its elastic is spent. "Lucky Big World Kitchen and Bath in Beijing had 15,000 booths last winter."

"Lucky is kitchen *and* bath," said Sherry Snells, E-Commerce and Web

Portal Developer. "Kich-N-World is just kitchen. Pure kitchen."

Taylor had placed a pad and pen on the table in front of her. Now she shifted her weight and pulled at her skirt. It was a black pencil skirt and had twisted slightly, which was causing it to pull at the waist. Perhaps not the best choice in skirts. Taylor's hips were somewhat pear shaped.

"You weren't in Beijing, were you?" Basil asked Darryl.

Darryl ignored the question, because he hadn't been in Beijing. Instead he picked up his notepad, tapped it on the table, and pressed on, like any good boss. "So guys, here's the lowdown."

Basil rolled his eyes.

"Digital is the new kid on the block. In the booth. The new kid on the booth."

Darryl's eyes flicked nervously around the table.

"All of DipTych is watching us. Thanks to EasyCan. Biggest thing since Musgrave put rubber grips on our can opener handles in 1922."

Taylor wrote a note on her pad. Grips on handles, 1922. Then she realized Miles was watching and could probably guess what she was writing. She blushed and flipped quickly to a fresh page.

"And Rocco kept control of the launch here with us. Corporate wanted it, Corporate fought for it, but Rocco kept it here in the Division. That means hard work, we get first dibs on press, the whole tamale."

"In other words," Basil said, "we're stuck doing everything."

"Not everything. You'll need to coordinate with the other divisions. Taylor, you'll need to work with your counterparts in Traditions and U-Ful to give them press time for any of their announcements.

Taylor forced herself to project calm. Press interviews, press interviews . . . she'd spent the last five days cramming. Dredging up bits of things from the PR courses she'd taken in college. And there was Google, of course. But her feet weren't touching bottom in this room and she knew it. And so she fumbled. Grasped in a vague way that her prestige depended on her appearing to be at least competent. So. How hard could this be. She cleared her throat silently, then forced out the words. "What are the dates? Of Kitchen—" Was it World? Or Universe?

"World," Basil enunciated carefully. "We have less than ten weeks."

Taylor took that to mean they should all be worried. She glanced accidentally at Miles. He shot her a quick grimace of exaggerated terror. She snapped her attention back to Darryl, but also touched the scarf below where it was knotted over one shoulder. The scarf, like the skirt, had also been a poor choice, apparently. She was way too warm in this room.

Darryl had passed a little stack of papers around the table. The stack got to Taylor and she took her copy. The top was a glossy brochure from a company that apparently had something to do with trade shows. That, anyway, is what she gathered from the tagline, "Exhibit Our Way: All Your

Trade Show Booth Needs." The stack also included a stapled sheaf of photocopies. Taylor looked at them. Ah. They must be drawings and schematics depicting the DipTych Kich-N-World trade show booth . . .

Basil shuffled through his copy of the documents, then dropped them on the conference table. And then he began to speak. The gist of his speech was to explain to everyone in the room all the reasons they couldn't accomplish anything they needed to accomplish in time for the show. The booth configuration was all wrong. They didn't have any collateral. They needed a video demo but it wasn't shot yet. The Kich-N-World content on the DipTych website wasn't developed. And a press kit—here, with the corporate killer instinct honed by years of practice, he looked at Taylor and waited for her to respond.

She was still too innocent to panic. Or anyway, to panic more than she already was, considering that she had only the vaguest and conceptual acquaintance with Press Kits. "That should be no problem. It's my first priority."

"It's all your first priority," Basil corrected her. "Trade shows are PR." He looked at Darryl. "Corporate should handle the EasyCan launch. You know that, right?"

"That's not possible. We're keeping it here in Digital," Darryl said. "Strategic decision."

"We're going to have some tough nuts in the press over this whole thing," Basil said.

"Not sure I follow you, Basil."

Taylor looked back at Basil. What were they talking about?

"Kyle Shillelagh."

Darryl didn't answer.

"Excuse me, but—who is Kyle Shillelagh?"

"He's the editor of *Kitchen Industry Insider*," Sherry said.

Taylor must have had a blank look on her face, because Basil made a huffy noise and stared at her. "*Kitchen Industry Insider* is nothing. Nothing at all. Except it's the trade pub that the entire kitchen industry reads. And the trade pub that hate hate hated DipTych's last digital offering."

DipTych had had another digital offering?

Taylor could feel her brain starting to hit overload. Already. In the first hour of her first day.

Basil turned back to Darryl. "You see? We have a PR person who is—" Taylor waited, but whatever Basil never finished the sentence out loud, which made it worse. A PR person who is what? Profoundly inexperienced? Out of her depth? An obvious dimwit? "And we're supposed to handle Kyle Shillelagh."

"I'm sure Taylor—" Darryl's voice cracked slightly and he didn't finish.

"We can't handle this at the division level," Basil said firmly. "We should turn it over to Corporate. Or Hedy."

"No! Not Hedy." Darryl flushed. "We'll be fine. Handle it, Basil. Taylor will come up to speed just fine."

Basil scowled. "Okay. But I'm going on record. *Kitchen Industry Insider* is going to have their fun, just like last time, and next thing you know we're going to have *The New York Times* calling. The *Washington Post*. Like I'm going to talk to some hot shot journalist who wants to crack my nuts in print just for a few laughs." He looked back at Taylor. "You're going to be busy." Basil held up a hand so he could tick off Taylor's fate, one finger at a time. "You need to schedule who's going to be in the booth, schedule press interviews, write the press kit and background materials, and develop the web content."

Darryl nodded. Taylor took notes.

"Does Pinnoccho need help with the panel?"

Taylor recognized the name, although she hadn't met him yet. Darryl's boss.

"He says no—he says he'll prepare himself." Darryl must have noticed Taylor's blank look. "Rocco has been invited to sit on the Kich-N-World Chips and Clicks panel discussion."

"Okay."

"The press will want time with him," Basil told Taylor. "You'll have to coordinate with his schedule. He'll be there the second day. And—" he directed this at Darryl— "we need a Twitter presence."

"I believe web content is marketing, not PR."

Miles had said that.

Taylor stiffened.

But Basil was having none of it. "It's PR." His voice was nasal and he drew out his vowels for emphasis. Peeaar. "It's always been under PR. Since DipTych first launched the site."

Taylor watched Darryl hopefully but he didn't appear to be paying very close attention. And she felt, as much as saw, Miles give a little shrug. It wasn't his battle. He was done.

"Darryl, we discussed this yesterday." Basil knew when to keep the pressure on. "Now that we have a PR person on board, we need a Twitter presence."

"It wouldn't hurt," Darryl agreed.

Taylor added "Twitter" to the list on her notepad.

"Taylor." Basil wet his lips. "We should probably get together right after this. Are you free?"

Taylor nodded.

"Good. Meet me in my office. We have a lot to do. If you need lunch, we'll order up from the cafeteria. I don't usually eat lunch."

She nodded again.

The meeting dragged on.

Taylor's notepad filled with scribbles. Hire photographer for press kit photos, check with corporate communications on list of press contacts, check with corporate communications on list of analysts, tradeshow back wall/customer quotes? She smiled at everyone and nodded her head until her neck ached. Fake it fake it fake it.

Finally it was over.

Everybody stood up.

"See you in a few minutes," Basil reminded her as they were leaving.

"Sure thing."

She turned toward her cubicle.

"Hey, protest girl." It was Miles. He'd caught up with her and was speaking now just above a whisper, his lips close to her ear. "Blow him off."

"I can't blow him off. You heard Darryl."

"Yeah. Darryl's an idiot, too. But I'm telling you. Baz is going to dump his entire job onto you. He's a lazy fuck and he's spotted a sucker. That would be you."

"Thanks, you're a gem yourself. What are you even doing here? I didn't think anarchists stooped to working for multi-national corporations."

"This isn't a job, it's an infiltration." He grinned at her. Ouch. He was very cute. His eyes were hazel in the middle and brown around the edges, and his hair curled out at the tops of his ears.

She looked away.

They were at her cubicle. She stepped inside and hesitated. She should be doing something, getting something, but what was there to get? Maybe . . . another pen.

Miles stood at the cubicle entrance, watching, seeing too much.

Taylor rounded her desk and opened the top drawer.

Miles stood aside to let her back out into the aisle. Aisle. Really a passageway, a beige fabric alley formed by the walls of her neighbor's cubes.

She hesitated again.

"That way," Miles pointed. "Turn left at the copier."

"Thanks."

"Yeah. And don't say I didn't warn you."

She went on to meet her fate.

# MEALTIME FOR BO

*"When you think about it, politics is about listening. Politics is 99.99 percent listening and only one percent the other stuff—doing. So I listen to my constituents. It's what I do. And I'm proud of it. Nobody is going to vote for Bo Valgus if they think Bo Valgus isn't listening."*

—Bo Valgus, State Assembly Representative

The alarming thing about the city of Borschtchester—everyone agreed—anyway, everyone who wasn't perfectly happy to live in the 'burbs—the alarming thing was how weak it was before the sheer force of demographic entropy. Turning and turning in a widening gyre and the downtown cannot hold.

It was awful. A downtown punkie as an ancient stump, once-majestic commercial properties carved up and patchworked into shiftless little shops, some boarded up, the rest catering furtively to a poverty-line clientele and frightening off everyone else with merchandise that was, inexplicably, both underpriced and overvalued. Oh, here and there you'd find more respectable blocks, grand old buildings that still housed lawyers' offices or the delis and little restaurants that catered to the lawyers at lunchtime. But that was only by day. At night, when the last professional armed the last office alarm system, and the little shop owners stepped outside and pulled their black cages down over their storefronts, then the ever-encroaching decay was truly undeniable.

An intolerable situation.

The good citizens of the city were obsessed with it, teething at it constantly, even in their sleep.

The local pols shared the citizens' concern.

They came up with an idea bound to lure people back to the center.

Their thinking was rock-solid in its simplicity.

Want to trap a mouse? Use a piece of cheese.

Want to lure a toddler into a dentist chair? Try a lollipop.

Want to rebuild downtown?

Build bars.

Of course, our public officials, despite being as clever as they are visionary, can't actually build the bars themselves. That would be unseemly. Not to mention put them at unnecessary political risk. Should the bars fail.

What they could do was stimulate others to build some bars. Easy peasy.

And so we come to Middlins Brewery, the latest resounding Downtown Stimulus Success Story. Bo Valgus himself, in fact, had presided over the grand opening only a few short months ago.

It was now one of his regular lunch spots, which ensured its glory would continue to rub off on him on a regular basis. Not the only of his regular lunch spots by any means—Bo spent a lot of time in restaurants, which was one reason he was more a Bo-and-a-half if consider total weight and/or girth. But restaurants are to politics what freshly plowed fields are to Monsanto sales reps. A place furrowed with opportunity, where swords have been put away and the natural rhythms of things always work in an enterprising fellow's favor.

Today, however, Bo was uneasy in his mind.

His angst had nothing to do with the brewery. On the contrary, Middlins was still awash with the fizzy afterglow of the opening. Middlins, by virtue of its novelty alone, drew teeming lunch crowds from DipTych headquarters two blocks away. Employees who had sustained themselves for over a year now on DipTych cafeteria fare—ever since LowJoe's Brewery, Middlins' immediate predecessor in that space, had filed for bankruptcy. Following that unfortunate gunfire incident that pretty much killed off, no pun intended, its after-sundown patronage. Without which no restaurant in this location could survive—teeming lunch crowds or not.

But the gunfire incident had been wiped away completely by the tax payer-funded renovations that preceded Middlins' opening.

So Bo wasn't worried about Middlins.

His problems were closer to home.

Closer than close to home.

In his bathroom.

You see, Bo was having his master bath redone. And it was taking longer than planned. The job had been launched, complete with dramatic gutting of the old bathroom's tile, fixtures, and lighting, exactly twenty-one weeks and four days ago.

The room was still a gutless mess.

And Bo's wife was getting cranky. This morning. Dahlia in those pink silk pajamas with the black and white poodles printed on them, her hair wound up in a towel, sobbing at him in the kitchen. "You can't even get him to stop by with a lighting catalog," she'd said. "What kind of a man can't get a contractor to stop by with a lighting catalog?"

Ouch.

Dahlia was tired of using the bathroom down the hall. Dahlia was tired of the dust and the drop cloths and sawhorse on the balcony. Dahlia was too embarrassed to have house guests.

Bo, truth to tell, had grown so used to the dust and the drop cloths and sawhorse that he didn't really notice them anymore. Dahlia, perhaps sensing this, had pointed out that because the master bath, like the home's bedrooms, opened onto the balcony overlooking the living room, you could see the drop cloths and sawhorse not only from the living room, but from the dining room and even the kitchen, if you happened to be standing by the stove. Horsie was inescapable, in other words. And driving Dahlia Valgus to near madness, apparently. Perhaps she was not a true animal lover.

Bo sympathized, but he was in an impossible situation. Not only that, but if you looked at the situation honestly, it was really Dahlia's fault, not Bo's. It was Dahlia who'd picked the contractor, that Trevor Mancely, because she'd wanted the best of the best. An Artist. Bo had never even met the guy, Bo wasn't generally home during the day.

This whole thing was Dahlia's project, not Bo's.

Bo learned it was in trouble like he learned about most details of his home life: Dahlia going on about it from her side of the bed while he was drifting off to asleep.

"So guess what?"

"Mmmmm." Bo lifted his head enough to re-adjust his pillow.

"You know how Trevor's been acting so down in the dumps lately, not himself?"

"Mmmmm."

"I found out why. It's his marriage."

"Mmmmm."

"He told me all about it today. His wife has walked out on him. He said he knew they were having issues but he had no idea things were that bad. He came home a week ago and all her stuff was gone. He's been trying to call her but her sister keeps picking up and telling him . . ."

But Bo could no longer keep track of it because he was asleep.

Maybe if he'd known how Trevor's personal heartbreak would wreak havoc in his own life, he'd have been more attentive.

But at first, the repercussions were mild. Night after night Bo, from his pillow, would let Dahlia's updates hop by him as benign as fluffy little cartoon sheep. How broken-hearted Trevor was. How today he'd managed to drag himself to the Valgus bathroom for a few minutes but could only sit and stare at the walls, the poor thing. He seemed to be losing weight? He should eat more. He'd started framing the shower stall today but fifteen minutes later he was nowhere to be found.

Then, as the weeks dragged by, the tone of the nightly tales started to change. Now it was "Trevor didn't show again today." And then, "He's not answering his cell." And then his voice mailbox was always too full to accept any more messages. And then it was "I emailed a new treatment to my agent. The show title will be 'Master Disaster.' Our bathroom will be the first episode, of course."

Huh what?

Bo's eyes opened.

"What was that, Dee? About our bathroom?"

"Weren't you listening?"

"Of course I was."

"No, you weren't."

"I had a hard day, Dee."

"So you weren't listening. You were sleeping."

"I'm sorry, okay?"

She rolled from her back to her side, so that her back was to him.

"Dee, please tell me again what you said? About our bathroom?"

"If you care at all, what I said was I had a new idea for a show, and this one is about people whose bathroom renovation projects go horribly wrong."

Bo was wide awake now, and alarmed.

Dahlia was a big Reality Show fan, and entertained solemn fantasies about breaking into the biz herself. Bo generally ignored them. But this was different.

"Dee, you can't have our house—us—on a television show about disasters."

No answer.

"Dee, you want me to lose my job next year?"

He listened. Was she snoring slightly?

"Dee. I'll get Trevor in here to get the thing fixed up for you, okay?"

"I told you before. He doesn't return calls."

So she was still awake.

"I'll handle it, I promise."

And so the whole mess was dumped into Bo's lap.

He was the man of the house after all.

That was nearly eight months ago.

Thankfully, Dahlia's agent hadn't been too crazy about "Master Disaster." He felt it wasn't ready to pitch to the networks. And Dahlia had since moved on to a new idea, which Bo secretly also doubted would stand a chance—it might be technically difficult from a production standpoint to shoot a series with the entire cast suspended 24x7 in a Plexiglas box several hundred feet above a major city, as Dahlia so adroitly envisioned. Not that Bo didn't encourage her. He did. He had a vague idea she might be happier if she were working. She'd quit her job as a medical transcriptionist when Thomas was born and, to Bo's eye, seemed to be kind of drifting a bit since the boy had left home.

Nonetheless, the bathroom had been festering for far too long.

Bo pushed open the plate glass door and stepped into Middlins.

He greeted the hostess by name, scanned the room, and then strode in and started strutting his stuff. There was an election coming up that fall. Table to table. These DipTych folks, they knew him well. He pressed his well-stuffed hands into theirs just to make sure. Whatcha havin. Thinkin about the chicken wrap. Might try the special. Not sure yet. Wait staff squeezing past him. Lots of eye contact. Working the room.

In another 10 weeks it'll be two years, that bathroom job undone. Damn it.

"Bo."

He turned. "Mr. Pinnoccho," he said, extending his hand.

"I'd like a word with you."

Bo glanced back toward the door. He hadn't made plans to eat with anyone else, but if someone suitable were walking in, he could pretend . . .

The holding area between the foyer and the hostess station was empty.

"Anything for you, Rocco, my man." He gestured toward a window booth.

"Not here," Rocco said.

"What do you have in mind?"

"Where's your car?"

Bo was by habit compliant when someone was about to ask a favor. So he relented and they headed toward the door. Waylaid briefly en route by a slender man with a goatee who asked a question about funding for the troubled Borschtchester Performing Arts project. Actually less a question than a complaint. The state should step up with funding. Bo fixed his smile and agreed wholeheartedly and explained how staunchly he supported programs like tax incentives for Middlins Brewery that bring jobs back to downtown.

Rocco pretended to listen but didn't quite suppress the annoyed look on his face.

At last the bearded man was finished. Bo shook his hand and reminded him to vote for Bo that fall.

"Would you mind driving while we talk?" Rocco craned his neck, looking up and down the street. No sign of any DipTych execs. Good.

They pulled out onto the main street.

"So. Rocco. What's on your mind."

"The arts center. It's going to crash and burn."

Bo didn't answer.

"The feds are going to pull funding."

"I disagree. The feds aren't going to pull funding," Bo responded evenly to hide his suspicion that the feds were going to pull funding. Stupid economy.

"*We* keep our promises, remember." Also a disingenuous statement, but one with a critical subtext. At one point, there was an understanding that DipTych would be a major corporate supporter of the Performing Arts Centre project. But six months ago, following another disappointing quarter, the company had abruptly and unceremoniously changed its mind. Since the agreement had never been formalized or even publicized in a formal way, Bo couldn't claim he'd been publicly embarrassed. But privately he was pretty miffed. He hid his annoyance when he was in front of the real DipTych bigwigs, of course. But around a Rocco, he let it peek, like a bit of frayed bra strap that won't stay put beneath a middle aged woman's tank top.

Rocco, not having been involved in the arts center backing machinations, pushed forcefully ahead. "We're all good guys, Bo, when we have interests in common. We can flip this around."

"Scally's dead set against it," Bo said. For this, he was missing his lunch.

"Not the arts thing." Rocco smiled without his eyes, and with one corner of his mouth raised a touch higher than the other corner. "We're going to do a switcheroo."

"A switcheroo."

"DipTych has a new vision for the space. Something Scally and the board are prepared to back one thousand percent."

Bo pulled onto a side street and parked the car. "Okay, Roc. What does DipTych have in mind."

"A cannery."

Rocco watched Bo carefully.

"A cannery." Bo looked highly skeptical. "DipTych is can openers. Not canning."

"That was the old DipTych. The new DipTych has bigger plans."

"DipTych wants to build a cannery in downtown Borschtchester."

"Well, let's call it a manufacturing facility. How about . . . the Valgus Enterprise Zone for Light Manufacturing."

Bo nodded. But he didn't look entirely convinced.

"Bo, we're talking DipTych Digital here." Rocco leaned toward the politician, lowering his voice as if someone might overhear. "Expanding into canning is a huge strategic move for us. And we were going to site our cannery operations in Mexico. But with the arts center in trouble it occurred to us, why not create jobs right here at home."

"How come this is the first I heard about this. About you guys getting into the canning end of things."

Rocco nodded and lowered his voice even further. "We've kept it very close to the vest, Bo. We don't want our friends in consumer packaged goods to get wind of it before we're ready, know what I mean?"

Bo frowned. "Mexico's cheaper."

"Work with me here, okay? The fact is, we need to be very careful, it's about managing risk. Canning is a new business for us. There's a solid argument to be made for keeping it close by, for now at least. And there are security issues. We have some extremely valuable intellectual property with our new digital product. We want it where we can keep an eye on things."

Bo fiddled with his keys.

"It's job creation, Bo."

"I've fought long and hard to re-establish manufacturing in our Upstate communities. Nobody has fought harder or longer."

"Why send jobs to Mexico when we could have them right here," Rocco answered.

"Sending jobs overseas hurts us here at home. I've fought long and hard to keep jobs here in the U.S. where they belong."

"We'd need to deal with the Zoning Board."

"And the greenies." Bo made a face. "They aren't going to like this one bit."

"They can't be any worse than the art center haters."

Bo nodded, then frowned. "You're not bullshitting me, Roc. Scally's behind this?"

Rocco hadn't talked to Scally yet. He took care, therefore, to avoid committing himself to the sort of lie that he couldn't deny later. "Scally's never 'behind' anything, Bo. He's at the top. At the top."

Bo's eyes narrowed further. "But you're saying he knows what's going on."

"He knows everything he needs to know."

"Rocco, if I find out you're bullshitting me—"

"Bo, you have my personal word that we will have no trouble whatsoever with Scally."

"Mmmmm. So what about Fusee."

Rocco twisted perceptibly in his seat. Because Bo was referring to Fusee & Madelaine, the local marketing and PR agency that counted as its clients both Bo Valgus and DipTych Inc. Unfortunately Rocco did not have—shall we say—the sort of "close personal relationship" with Fusee that he would have liked, given the agency's importance to his scheme. "Let's just say we're proceeding with extreme caution, and there are no red lights from that direction." Truth was, Fusee & Madelaine would be Rocco's toughest customers. And he knew damn well that if he'd gone to them first he wouldn't have gotten past the outer ring of admins on their offices' ground floor.

But once he had Bo and Scally, Fusee & Madelaine would have to at least listen—and Rocco had a nice little deal sweetener in his back pocket. A nice fat chocolate-covered sweetener with a gooey caramel center. It was a gamble worth taking.

"I see Switch later today. I'll see if I can get five minutes with him."

"No! No, not a good idea, not quite yet, Bo."

Bo scowled over at Rocco's face. "And why is that?"

"Let me handle it, for now."

"Don't bullshit me, Rocco. Is Fusee on board or not?"

It was time to give Bo a peek at his hand. "Bo. You can trust me. And I can trust you, right?"

"I'm listening."

"The Digital Division originally planned to keep all of its marketing in-house. Strategic decision on my part. But this—adding the cannery, I'm rethinking things. I'm thinking that we're going to use some outside help."

All Bo knew about business was what he picked up here and there—from conversations with constituents, and once in a while he'd skim the first few paragraphs of an article in the *Deign & Pontificate* business section. But of course he knew a horse trade when he saw one. "How much we talking?"

"We're talking a campaign that will last three to five years," Rocco said. "We'll need to spend eight figures, easily."

Bo started up the car. "Let me make some phone calls."

"It would be nice to keep some of the federal backing, of course."

"Should be doable."

Rocco opened the passenger door and re-buttoned his coat. "I'll walk back to the office . . . and Bo, this is still very hush hush. You, me, Scally, not many more than that. So keep it quiet for now."

"Right."

"If you need to reach me use my cell, for now."

"Right."

Bo pulled away, leaving Rocco standing on the sidewalk.

The pol's mind began running through its gears.

Because of course, the arts center was dead.

It's not that the city of Borschtchester didn't appreciate the arts.

On the contrary, it was a very art-friendly city.

In fact, the vast majority of its citizens were part-time artists. This depressed the hell out of the Real Artists, of course, because they couldn't gain a toehold in the local market. Peoples' homes were already stuffed with their own paintings and prints and sculptures and mixed media creations, not to mention those of their nieces and aunts and grandchildren. The Sunday NOW BREATHE section of the *Deign & Pontificate* was devoted almost entirely to the celebration of local artists, complete with full page interviews. One week, a retiree who carves totems out of recycled Christmas trees, another week a college undergrad whose work represents the ageless interplay of Hope and Angst. At times, the city seemed like it was one big unending celebration of the arts.

And FairARTS! had its staunch supporters. Borschtchester's mayor had signed on enthusiastically from the start. And in the private meetings in the mayor's office, Fusee & Madelaine had emitted a wondrous and unending stream of ideas for FairARTS! tie-ins and promotions and cross-marketing that were practically guaranteed to ensure that people would appreciate the project once it got off the ground. And one of Bo's most prized voter niches—the local construction industry—was very much lined up behind FairARTS! They knew it would create jobs, and jobs were always good to come by in this part of the country.

Borschtchester's voters, on the other hand, tended to be a bit peevish when it came to funding. Perhaps they weren't making enough side income from the sales of their art. Some of them periodically phoned Bo's office about their combined property, state, and county taxes being the highest in the country. Bo could sympathize. He was a seasoned empathizer, after all, what politician isn't? And he acted on his empathy. He promised federal funding. And he meant it.

Frank Drulian, U.S. Senator, being, of course, his natural ally when it came to making good on that promise.

They'd made a fine team, in fact.

Not that it had been an easy stunt to pull. You see, it would never do to just rely on federal money earmarked for the Arts. The trick was to tap into different pieces of the federal budget.

But Frank was the master. He got some Homeland Security budget money, for instance, by agreeing to modify the FairARTS! roof so that the Department of Defense could use it to test its civilian surveillance and crowd control technology. Farm Bill money was also pretty easy. The Borschtchester Historical Farming Society. The Society happily committed to creating a permanent Tribute to Beets exhibit for the FairARTS! building main entrance, which would in turn raise public awareness about Borschtchester's illustrious farming heritage.

Transportation Bill money was a bit tougher. Bo and Frank floated a proposal to combine the FairARTS! Center with a new bus terminal, but squashing a bus terminal into the Center's footprint had proved a mite challenging.

J.D. Holmes, the architect originally selected to develop the Center's conceptual design, had a minor nervous breakdown and had to be replaced.

Meanwhile, the fragile coalition of artists who did support the Center began showing signs of strain. They argued that replacing the originally-conceived performance hall with a smallish puppet theatre, in order to make space for a bus terminal, violated "the sacred spirit" of FairARTS!

Spontaneous protests began springing up whenever Fusee & Madelaine scheduled a FairARTS! public comment forum.

The pols in the state capitol started to sound spooked.

There was a brief reprieve when the fine strategic minds at Fusee & Madelaine came up with a new plan, this one inoculated with a gloriously ingenious twist: it invoked those magical words, "light rail." Nothing like the words Light Rail to make the Borschtchester Philistines flip, oh yeah, slick as a crowd card stunt during the halftime show at a college football game.

But the reprieve was short-lived. Bo was tricked by a clever local radio host into using the word "silly" when discussing the light rail idea. Mind you, the quote was fine when taken in context. "IF we had to build a Center with no space for any art, it would be silly," he'd said. IF. If if if if if if if if.

Obviously, nobody had EVER said there would be NO space for arts.

Puppetry is Art.

And a Tribute to Beets exhibit. That's Art.

For a city with so many artists, Borschtchester swarmed with Philistines.

The FairARTS! project started to run straight down the ol' drainpipes. From a PR perspective. Between the gang that claimed Bo had called the bus terminal idea "silly" and the other gang who claimed he was anti-art.

And then came the DipTych setback. Which didn't matter so much in terms of funding—DipTych's non-commitment had never mentioned any specific figure—but it definitely hurt from a momentum standpoint. DipTych, stumbling fiscally? It brought the reality of the Great Recession home as nothing else had. Public support for FairARTS! reached its all-time low. And whenever Bo brought up the federal money to Frank, the Senator changed the subject.

(Bo did get his revenge on DipTych by the way. For years, the state budget had funded the Borschtchester Pigeon Waste Control program. But that year, Bo accidentally on purpose failed to keep the funding in place. Times are hard! Urban beautification is nice, but times are hard! Of course, the Borschtchester Pigeon Waste Control program happened to double as a way to underwrite DipTych's exterior building cleaning costs. It's expensive to wash pigeon scat off a sky scraper a couple of times a year.

See, supporting a project like FairARTS!, it looks like an expenditure. But when you consider the whole picture, the offsets you gain here and there when you've made the right friends, it's not as expensive as you think. Now is it. Take that, DipTych.)

Bo's face softened.

Because until today, he'd been feeling a trifle stymied. All those Borschtchestarians, sputtering about why taxpayer money was going on FairARTS! when the state was digging around in its sofa cushions looking for loose change and the federal deficit resembled more than anything else an Orc army surging across the face of the U.S. economy.

But things have a way of working out. And now—assuming Rocco wasn't full of horseshit . . . manufacturing . . . a wonderful new twist. New. Different. It had Potential. And with Bo at the helm, it would be Bo re-divvying all the goodies. Favor time.

Favor time.

Bo's eyes suddenly widened as a new thought occurred to him.

A car honked. Bo may have nearly sideswiped a nearby Chevy.

He paid no heed.

He was thinking about bathrooms.

Because as funding for the Performing Arts Centre had looked tighter and tighter, one of the first cuts made was to reduce the number of bathrooms.

But with a factory, everything was different, and not only because they'd be starting over from scratch, and with DipTych money to boot.

Bo sat on the State Assembly labor committee. So he knew. In private commercial buildings OSHA regs would kick in, and OSHA regs mandate 6 toilets for the first 150 employees, plus another toilet per each additional 40. That was 14.75 toilets for 500 cannery workers. Maybe more, since DipTych wouldn't dream of installing more men's rooms than ladies, even if the labor force skewed male. Plus probably a nice private bathroom somewhere in case Scally ever toured the place and needed to take a wee.

Bo tapped his steering wheel and broke out into song. To the tune of the My Sharona chorus. *Mah mah mah mah b-bathroom!*

He pulled his car into the alley next to his office building.

*Nothing like the promise of a juicy public contract to shake that Trevor out of his divorce proceedings doldrums.*

It was time that boy made the jump from residential bathrooms to big time public jobs.

Bo pressed the lock button on his keychain fob. His Buick horn beeped sonorously.

It was enough to make the man practically giddy.

He finally had a way to get his bathroom reno done.

# DAHLIA, O DAHLIA

*"I predicted Graham would show his true colors. So what, we all know you are his biggest fan. Your entitled to your opinion. But you seem to think you can jump on this board and hijack the thread and nobody will remember the bs you spouted back when G was all over Tracy and setting Rob up to make it look like he was stealing from the community security zone when everybody with any brains new he wasn't. This forum isn't nazi germany and you can't treat it like you're a reality show hitler coming in here and telling us all how we should think."*

—RealMe21,
posted on xtremerealityshowfandom.com

Bo strode through the front door of his office.

It was hardly what you'd call posh. It had been painted after Ray's Deli had closed, but that was long ago, and the walls had since surrendered their virtue to the ensuing onslaught of chips and scuffs. The carpet was frayed badly where it met the front entrance threshold. Long dingy tendrils of Olefin yarn lay limply, pushed first one way, then the other like tendrils of seaweed on the seabed, depending on whether the last foot to shuffle over them had been entering the office or leaving it.

Kelly, Bo's part-time admin, looked up from her Windows Solitaire game when Bo approached her desk.

"I need to talk to Frank."

"Okay." She paused. "I think the Senate might be in session this

51

morning."

"Try his cell. Keep dialing him until you get him."

"Right."

Which she did, after about 15 minutes.

Frank was as receptive as Bo figured he'd be. "So you're saying we just pull a little switcheroo," he said.

"We go from the arts to the can."

Yes. It was eminently doable. The public might be momentarily confused, but Bo and Frank knew what to do about that. Pass it into the capable hands of Fusee & Madelaine.

That left the federal earmarks.

"We'll poll it," Frank said. "Manufacturing jobs . . . we haven't polled manufacturing jobs in a few years. But given the country's mood today, people are going to like it."

Frank's action items. Have his aides quietly draft some slight wording changes to slip into the Farm and Transportation bills.

Bo's action items. Work a little Valgus magic on the mayor and the county exec. Pull a few strings with Zoning Board members.

He looked up from his day planner. "Kelly, what time's my shoot?"

Bo was appearing in a spot for the Borschtchester Tourist Board's "We're In The Soup" promotional campaign."

"You've got an hour and a half."

Bo twiddled his fat class ring (Borschtchester City School District, class of '82) for a moment. It was kind of premature to mention any of this cannery business to Dahlia. On the other hand, if it solved the Valgus' little bathroom issue as neatly as he suspected it might, peace would be restored to their happy home, and the sooner the better on that.

His stomach rumbled. Reminding him how long it had been since his last meal.

It was an omen.

"Call my cell if anything comes up," he said to Kelly. "I'm having lunch with Dee."


From a distance, Dahlia Valgus looked like a mid-20th Century throwback. It was her hair. Cut short on the sides, longer on top, and her natural curl drove it high as the grandest bouffant.

She'd grown up on a dairy farm.

When she and Bo first met, her datedness had been even more pronounced and was one reason he'd fallen for her.

This afternoon she was sitting in the living room scooping fruit-on-the-bottom strawberry yogurt from a single-serve cup and watching the latest episode of the hot new reality show Kill or Be Killed. She had TiVo'd it and was watching it now for the third time—in other words more studying than watching.

As Bo tossed his keys on the table in the foyer Dahlia picked up the remote and hit pause. Jotted a note in a spiral notebook that she kept next to her on the couch, exchanged the notebook for the remote again and pressed "resume."

Bo walked past her to the kitchen to get a diet cola.

Then he stood behind the couch and popped the can open and pretended for a minute to watch the show with her.

"Hear from Thomas?"

She didn't answer, just watched the screen.

Thomas was living with his girlfriend in Holland. Bo had encouraged the move. The kid had developed an insatiable appetite for marijuana. It seemed prudent that he should take up residence in a country where smoking it didn't get one's name in the papers.

"So. Dee. I've got some news."

Dahlia jotted something else in her notebook. "I never wanted you to go into politics," she said without turning her head.

"I know."

"You made a good living selling insurance."

"You keep saying that."

"I need to keep saying it because if I don't keep saying it you'll never hear me saying it."

Bo knew better than to pay too much attention to statements of that nature. He attempted, instead, to jump the conversation back to the more constructive track he'd originally had in mind.

"I've figured out how to get Trevor off his ass finally."

"Let me guess. Our home is now a county landmark, and Trevor has been named Head County Preservationist."

"And you want me to go back to insurance? I couldn't get our home declared a county landmark if I was in insurance."

"You said if you got into politics there would be perqs."

"There are perqs."

"There are no perqs."

"There are."

"There aren't."

"There are."

"Name one."

"You wouldn't get dinners with the governor if I were in insurance."

Dahlia had fussed for weeks before her last dinner at the governor's mansion.

"I don't see how our home can be declared a landmark, Bo. It was built in 1996."

"It's not a landmark. Who said it was a landmark?"

"You did."

Bo was pretty sure he hadn't, but now that everything in their conversation before the bit about Dahlia being wrong about the perqs had gone all fuzzy. He gave up. "Either way, it doesn't matter. I'll have the bathroom thing settled for you tomorrow. Friday at the latest."

A bold statement. Perhaps rash. But he was going for the effect.

It didn't seem to be working. Dahlia picked up the remote. She'd missed part of the show, now she had to rewind to watch that bit again. "Like I haven't heard that before."

Bo's eyes drifted to the screen as the figures on it began to move again. This episode had apparently been shot in a desert somewhere. A woman wearing a robe that looked like it had been fashioned possibly from a tent fly. She was watching a man similarly dressed, who hacked a piece off of a cactus with what appeared to be a sharpened stone. He handed the piece to the woman who eyed it warily, then suddenly dropped it, shrieking "it's got THORNS," plus a string of bleeped-out words.

"Look, I know this has been stressful for you."

"That's an understatement. How, exactly, are you going to get him out here now, when for the last year you haven't even been able to reach him on his phone."

"I'll—he'll—"

"Make it good, Bo."

"I'm going to go talk to him in person. Reason with him."

"Ah."

Kill or Be Killed had come to an end. Dahlia switched off the television and picked up her notebook. Bo knew where she'd be for the next several hours. She maintained a vigorous online presence on a number of reality T.V. forums and blogs, where she posted as RealMe21 and frequently bested other fans in arguments hinging on minutiae as astonishing for its granularity as it was for its insignificance.

Bo stood for a moment to see if Dahlia was going to switch from conspicuously ignoring him and resume the conversation. But she didn't, so he said something about not yet having had his lunch, and left the empty cola can on the table in the foyer when he retrieved his car keys.

# O'ER A PLATE OF LASAGNA

*"People say they hate politicians. But they don't really. I mean, try to get anything done without us. Can't. Can't do it. We're the grease that keeps the city from falling to pieces."*

—Bo Valgus,
New York State Assemblyman

Some people choose particular careers because of a calling. Others are motivated by something that more closely resembles an itch. Bo fell into the latter and no doubt more populous category. Not that he was particularly conscious of this. He believed, as was his prerogative, that he'd gotten into politics to be of service to his community, thereby framing his motivations at a more endearing angle. In reality, he was a politician because he loved to truck in the business of favors. It resembled almost an addiction. His intellect was almost entirely devoted to a kind of favor tally sheet which was, by the way, perpetually unbalanced, perhaps even since childhood—perhaps his father or mother had bargained in favors, perhaps the deals they struck weren't always quite fair, maybe they too often left little Bo—"Stewart" back then—a bit off kilter, always either indebted or burdened by another's debt.

Whatever the origin, instead of resisting he had embraced it, cultivated it into a kind of gift, albeit a gift over which Bo had little control. He collected favors from people, he bestowed favors on people. No prospective trade was too momentous or too insignificant. In one moment, he would intervene on a slight acquaintance's parking tickets—not only to help the acquaintance, but to render himself slightly beholden to particular local bureaucrats. The next moment, he'd be on the phone, brokering a multi-million dollar state grant to fund some constituent's retail development project.

His addiction was so complete that even when favors weren't necessary, he bestowed or requested them. He overtipped. He maneuvered for little freebies—at the car wash, the dentist, the farm stand near his home.

It was his gift. And no matter how tangled and intricate his inner ledger became, he never lost track of any entry, ever. And at times he found himself inexplicably fallen into a kind of favor-trading zone, a cascade of favor transactions would suddenly tumble through the ledger, multiple parties would almost simultaneously find themselves recipients of favors or called upon at last for repayment. At these times, like no other, Bo was a happy man.

He now parked his car in front of yet another restaurant.

The rumble in his stomach had returned with a vengeance.

This particular restaurant was an Italian place, and was slightly larger than Dahlia's walk-in closet. It was only open Wednesday through Saturday and had no liquor license, although patrons could bring in their own bottles if they wanted, and there wasn't even a cork fee. It smelled of garlic and tomato sauce and slightly rancid fat. The walls were lined with framed prints of travel posters. Venetia, Italia, Napoli—the posters had probably conveyed a bit more cheer before they'd faded so badly. The tables were cloaked in the inevitable pizza parlor red and white check plastic.

The owner's daughter, a large middle-aged woman with scraggly whiskers on her neck, slouched on a stool at the far end of the room between a counter and the pass-through window leading into the kitchen, the cash register positioned on the counter in front of her like the top of a lectern. Her name was Dora and Bo greeted her and waved, but it was Ralph that he was there to see.

Ralph was the owner's nephew and a generation older than Dora. He was seated with two other gentleman his own age in the restaurant's only booth.

They'd finished eating some time ago. Their plates were stacked on the end of the table, gluing themselves together as their remnants of tomato sauce slowly dried.

He waved Bo over and Bo squeezed himself heavily into the booth.

Finally. Lunch.

Dora came over and Bo ordered the lasagna.

Ralph's two companions were retired. Ralph was as well, in any practical sense of the term, but his name was still listed as owner of D'Signario's Contracting and would be until the day he died, at which time his four sons would own in name what they already owned in sweat. Not that they were in a particular hurry. The D'Signario family was hardly wealthy, unless you accept the standards of Washington political rhetoric, but there was plenty to go around. Everybody was content and that was all that mattered.

Now Ralph and his buddies were talking sports. Bo joined them until he was halfway through his lasagna, and Ralph asked him if there was anything else he needed. Bo's cue.

"I have some news," Bo told him.

Ralph waited.

"The arts center deal." Bo swallowed another hunk of lasagna. "It's a mess. Been a mess. You know that. So we're going to re-do some things."

"How's the lasagna?"

"Good. Good."

Since Bo would not be paying for the lasagna, Ralph's words marked Bo's receipt of the meeting's first favor.

Time for the real trading to begin. "So with these changes," Bo said, "you guys—we wanted you guys involved, here, we want you guys to be on top of everything that is going on."

He meant, of course, that D'Signario would be, ahem, well-positioned to be selected as the project's general contractor. But Ralph, of course, made no response. Because the statement amounted to a wash. D'Signario had been well-positioned to be selected as the general contractor for FairARTS. D'Signario—and for that matter, Ralph personally—did not contribute generously to Bo's general election campaign funds with any other expectation.

"This is strictly confidential, you understand." A glossing over. To give everybody time to adjust to the favor re-set.

Bo was nearly done now with his lasagna. He took a pull from his diet cola, leaving a greasy lower lip smear on the rim of the pebbled plastic glass. And then he sketched out Rocco's cannery idea.

Ralph was outwardly non-committal. He'd been around too long, he no longer needed to affect emotion. On the inside, of course, he was logging every detail, not to mention calculating D'Signario's potential profit margins. But all he said at the end was, "Bo, that's very interesting." He pronounced all four syllables of the word "interesting." This was one of only a handful of verbal indicators of Ralph's ethnic heritage. For he might have been 100 percent Italian American, but don't imagine for a second that he talked like a Soprano. In the genial and hearty community that is Borschtchester, a single generation is plenty to dissolve forever any overt evidence of one's ethnicity. Not that there aren't ethnic groups—there are plenty—but their distinguishing characteristics are primarily which houses of worship they frequent and to some extent their dietary preferences. Ralph's enunciation of the third syllable of "interesting" was an exception. Most of Bo's constituents pronounced the word "intersting."

Bo, of course, switched back and forth, depending on who he was with. So now he agreed, "yes, interesting" using Ralph's pronunciatory tic, and then went straight on to further enumerate the cannery project's virtues, the primary one being, of course, DipTych's forthcoming investment of cash.

Ralph's inner calculation of how much D'Signario might bid ticked up a couple of notches.

Dora shuffled over, collected the stack of plates from the table, and shuffled them back to the kitchen, smacking her lips as she did so in some private conversation with herself.

Bo drained the last bit of his cola.

It was time.

"Ralph, one other thing."

Ralph nodded.

"A buddy of mine could use some work. Trevor Mancely."

Ralph lifted his chin in a half-nod. "Very sad, his wife ditching him that way."

"Terrible."

"He took it real hard."

"It was rough for a while. He's pulling through."

"And a fellow with his . . . assets, too."

Ralph's buddies chuckled. "Assets," one of them repeated, then said, "You know I once saw some babe tailing his truck."

"Naw!" said the other Ralph buddy. He thrust a hand between two buttons of his shirt to scratch his belly.

"Swear to God. I seen her park across from JJ's and wait for him. Some babe in a yellow Camaro."

JJ & Son was a plumbing supply outfit. Not a usual destination for a babe in a yellow Camaro.

Apparently Ralph hadn't heard the story before. He guffawed appreciatively. "Did he know she was following him?"

"How could you miss it."

Politicians must, of necessity, be highly patient individuals. So Bo smiled as if he were enjoying the story. He'd heard several like it. Trevor's good looks were legendary. Bo chalked it up to an odd sort of urban legend, not that he'd know, since Dahlia had hired Trevor, the bathroom re-do was Dahlia's project, Bo had never laid eyes on the guy.

It seemed like the story had wound down, finally, so Bo cleared his throat and tugged the conversation back to the business that needed settling. "So, as I was saying."

Ralph nodded. "His divorce, he's let his jobs slide some."

Bo was ready for that. Because of course Ralph knew Bo had hired Trevor. Ralph knew every major job any plumber, electrician, roofer, or insulation installer, or window-and-door guy was doing in Borschtchester. "He'll be wrapping up my bathroom very soon now. Assuming my wife doesn't change her mind again. She's been driving the guy crazy. This tile, no that tile. I want sconces, no make that pendants. Turns a one holer into the Taj Mahal, that woman."

Ralph's friends snorted in manly sympathy.

Ralph wasn't really fooled, of course. He knew damn well the job was a major botch. He had probably already guessed what Bo was going to say next.

"Anyway. Him being a bathroom man," Bo said, "I'd like to see him come in for the cannery johns."

Ralph had already mentally rejiggered his calculations. "He does nice work."

"Yes, they say he's an artist." Bo smiled on the inside as he drained the rest of his cola. He stood up. "Gentlemen," he said, and they all shook hands. Then, to Ralph: "I'll keep you posted."

Ralph nodded, then waved Dora over to ask for a cannolo.

Bo dropped a five on the table so Dora could see he'd tipped her.

When he got to his car, he dialed his office.

"Kelly. Need you to look something up for me. Address. Trevor Mancely. Find out where he's staying now. And what time am I supposed to be at the shoot?"

"You have ten minutes."

He closed his cell.

The cannery bathroom transaction left Bo one down to Ralph. But that was okay. And you never know, when the time came to pay him back, the favor might well add up to more than 20 toilets.

# AND A DREAM DIES

*"What can I say? We live in an activist community. I'm actually proud of that, myself."*

—Borschtchester resident,
interviewed at FairARTS rally

"Oh gawd. You must be kidding me!"

The street was closed. Unbelievable.

And was that a film crew? Really? In downtown Borschtchester?

Taylor sighed and watched her mirror for an opening in the left lane. She'd try Millennium Street. Assuming she could make a left on Millennium Street, which was questionable.

Not that Taylor really wanted to be here anyway. Truth be told, now that she was pushing 45 hours or more a week at DipTych, Taylor's appetite for attending protests had waned considerably.

It's not that the causes didn't matter to her any more. She was just damned tired. Mentally. Mentally exhausted.

She watched the wind blow scraps of paper up the sidewalk as she waited for the light at Millennium, then checked her mirror again for cops before making her illegal left turn.

Despite being a bit late, Taylor was still the second protestor on the scene. The other was a woman whose name she should have known, but didn't.

"Where is everybody?" Taylor hunched her shoulders against the cold. She'd forgotten her hat and gloves when she'd left home in the morning. Figures.

"I dunno."

"Have you seen Aimee?"

"Nope."

Taylor sighed. Then tried again. "Who's bringing the signs, do you know?"

"No idea."

They stood for a few minutes.

"Why is Premium Street all shut down? Was that a film crew?"

"Tourist Board thingy."

"Filming a tourist spot? In March?"

The woman shrugged, then pointed down the street at a small cluster of people carrying signs. "Who's that now? Is that us? They don't look like us."

"I dunno." Taylor squinted at the approaching group. She noticed that they didn't appear to be anarchists. Possibly the average anarchist knew better than to attend a protest with the wind chill pushing temps into the low 20s.

Where was Aimee? It was damn cold. Damn it.

A pigeon landed, walked around a bit in a series of tight circles, pecked at something on the sidewalk, flew off again.

"They're coming this way," the woman said. Narrating the obvious. "I'm going to see what they're up to."

Taylor stood and watched as the other group drew closer. She couldn't make out what the woman said to them but their leader—slightly overweight, clean shaven man in a leather bomber jacket—was facing her, so she could hear his answer. "No. No. We're NOT counter-protestors." He shook his head vigorously as he spoke. "No way."

They were closer now, and the woman was walking beside them, arguing. "I told you. You're the ones who are AGAINST the FairARTS Center. Counter. Against. Counter. Against."

"But we were here FIRST. You don't even have any signs."

"We've had our protest scheduled for WEEKS. And our signs will be here any minute."

"So what?"

"What do you mean, 'so what'? We scheduled a protest. PROTEST. You show up to COUNTER our protest. That makes you the COUNTER protest."

"Oh, look," Taylor said. "I think I see the people with our signs." She blew on her hands.

But the woman didn't hear her. Because she wasn't done with the anti-FairARTS Center guy. "That's all beside the point. We support FairARTS.

That's why we're here. You can't possibly call anything this positive and supportive as a 'counter' anything."

"Well. You're an idiot."

Taylor flipped open her phone and dialed Aimee.

"Hey. Where are you?"

"Oh. Yeah."

"Oh, yeah," Taylor mimicked back. "Aimee, it's freezing out here."

"Something came up."

Taylor guessed, then. "Jenna."

"Yeah."

"So is this a good thing or a bad thing."

"It's nice to be needed."

"I'm not sure that answers the question. Are you going to have time to get over here at all before work?"

Someone was trying to get Taylor's attention. She looked up.

It was a pro-FairARTS person, the one who'd brought the signs. He held out a sign to her that read "SAVE THE ARTS. SAVOR THE ARTS." It had been deployed, apparently, at previous rallies. The top right hand corner was folded over.

She took it, which meant that both hands were now outside her pockets. One for the sign, one for her cell.

"Yeah, I'll be there," Aimee was saying. "I'll leave now."

"Do me a favor. Bring me some gloves or something, will you? I forgot mine and I'm freezing."


Aimee got there about 20 minutes later. With gloves. That she'd put on her dashboard on the way, so they'd be warm. Heavenly.

"Where is everybody?" Aimee handed Taylor's sign back to her when she'd finished buttoning her coat back up again.

"I dunno."

"This is almost as bad as the Stand Up for Gay Marriage protest."

"Not really." Taylor had counted the protestors. "We've got eleven people."

"No anarchists."

"No." She nearly said "anarchists are too smart to attend a protest in sub-zero weather" but she stopped herself. Aimee teased her about Miles enough as it was. Better to avoid any reference to him if she could.

"I don't even see the counter-protestors."

"If they were, in fact, counter-protestors. I don't think they ever agreed to that. Anyway, they all split right before you got here."

"They did?"

"Yeah, and what's weird is, they were cheering."

"Oh really."

"Yeah."

"I'm calling Lou."

Lou was the founder of the Save FairARTS movement.

Taylor listened to Aimee's half of the conversation. Yeah, yeah, okay, all right, I'll tell them, keep me posted.

"What?" said Taylor when Aimee hung up.

"I guess there's a rumor going around that it's over."

"What's over?"

"C'mon." Aimee started walking toward the rest of the protestors. "FairARTS is over, I guess. They're going to put something else in here instead."

"You must be kidding me. I'm out here, freezing my—"

Taylor waited while Aimee relayed the news to the other protesters, then handed her sign to the guy who had brought them.

"Hungry?" Aimee asked.

"I need hot soup."

"And a couple shots of whiskey."

"But mostly hot soup. So we lost? FairARTS is done?"

"I guess."

"Does Lou realize that we were out here protesting . . . nothing?"

"As a matter of fact, that seemed to kind of dawn on him while we were talking. Let's see if I can remember what he said. Something about how being on the battlefield you can't always know how the battle had turned."

"Oh, frickin great."

"We can go hunt him down and give him wedgies after dinner if you want."

"You'll have to manage that alone," Taylor said. "I think it might be a couple of days before I can move my fingers again."

# ROCCO'S TRIUMPH

*"There's a rumor that Scally's high school sweet heart broke up with him because he had some kind of thing for Tippi Hedren. They say he asked the girl friend to dye her hair blond. And it pissed her off so she dumped him. His wife dyes her hair, not a lot of people know that. I saw her roots, once, when I had to drop some documents off at his house."*

—Amber Overhold, Executive Assistant,
DipTych Corporation

"Mr. Scally will see you now."

7:20. Not bad for a 7 a.m. meeting.

Rocco stepped through the door into Scally's office.

It was, of course, the largest office in DipTych headquarters, and gleamed, and smelled of wood and polish and Scally's cologne. Nearly everything in the room that was not carpet or leather or oak was gold, or gold-plate, or (discretely) gold-tone. The desk was nearly as big as the table in Conference Room 3A. Scally's chair was also enormous, its gleaming leather back framing Scally himself in thronish splendor.

There was no computer in the room.

Scally was looking downward, intently, at something in his top desk drawer when Rocco walked in. Rocco stood inside the door, waiting. After a moment Scally pushed the drawer in and looked up.

"Rocco. What can I do for you."

He didn't invite Rocco to sit, but Rocco didn't expect it. He stood facing the desk, holding his leather portfolio in his hands, one finger tucked inside so that when the time came he could quickly produce all his required props. For Rocco had been practicing. And he knew a bit about pitching an idea to Paul Scally. He knew, for example, just how long to preamble.

"Paul," he said, "I've known Bo Valgus for a long time."

Pause.

"He went to school with my cousin. University of Iowa. Many times in those days I drove out, the three of us would go to Hawkeyes games. Good times."

Only a single shred of truth in that bit, but not likely Scally would ever have occasion to chat with any of Rocco's cousins, so it was a nice safe lie.

"I'll never forget the 1984 shutout against Michigan." Another line chosen with excruciating care, as anyone who was anyone anywhere above the second floor was aware of Scally's fanatic devotion to his alma mater, Ohio State. In fact, it was a terrible pity that Bo Valgus hadn't attended Ohio State. What a sweet lie it would have been to place himself at an Ohio State win over Michigan? But Bo had chosen Iowa, and all things considered, praising a team for beating Ohio State's arch rival was a decent back-up. And it seemed to be working. That seemed to be a satisfied gleam in Scally's eye.

"So last week, I got a call from Bo."

Rocco paused again and drew a breath. Here goes—

Something thudded. Against the window at the far end of the room.

Scally looked over.

Rocco looked over.

There was a pigeon walking back and forth on the window sill.

Scally leapt up. "GodDAMNit." He ran to the window, windmilling his arms wildly.

The bird flew off.

Scally turned, straightened his tie, and started back.

He sat back down and cleared his throat. "Go ahead, Rocco."

Rocco drew another breath.

But Scally had turned around. And the bird was back. "GodDAMNIT!" He leaped waving at the window again, then rushed back to his desk, to his phone this time, and jabbed its keys.

"Amber!"

"Yes sir." Scally's admin, on speaker phone.

"Tell Maintenance those goddamn birds are back!"

"Yes sir."

"If they have to stand up there all day with that hose—"

"Yes sir. I'll tell them."

Scally jabbed the speaker phone button again to shut it off. Straightened his tie. Settled himself back down into the chair.

"Go ahead, Rocco."

"Um. I believe you can mount spikes on the sill to repel them, sir."

"Excuse me?"

"Spikes. You mount them on the sill."

Rocco tried not to peek as he spoke but he couldn't help himself. And the pigeon was back on the sill. Only this time it had friends. One was a male. It chortled and cooed and paced back and forth.

Scally heard the cooing. "GodDAMNIT!" He snatched the faux fountain pen and holder from his desk and rushed the window. For a moment Rocco thought he might hurl the fountain pen holder at the window but at the last second, he checked himself and instead simply rapped the window with it.

The birds had flown off.

Scally turned around. "What did you just say to me, Rocco?"

"I got a call from Bo Valgus—" Rocco knew as soon as he spoke that he'd answered the wrong question. Damnit.

"No! About the birds."

"You can install spikes. On the sill. To repel pigeons."

"Pigeons? Those goddamn filthy birds are pigeons?"

"Yes sir."

"Someone told me they were Rock Doves. Rock Doves. Goddamnit, Rocco, pigeons? Pigeons?"

Scally stumped over to his phone and hit the speaker button gain. "Amber!"

"Yes sir."

"Those goddamn birds, Rocco here says they're pigeons!"

"Yes sir, I believe they could be, sir."

Rocco was watching the window. And the pigeons had returned. Only now, suddenly, a stream of water jetted down from somewhere above the window.

The birds, startled, flew off.

"Maintenance should be on the roof with the hose now, sir," Amber said.

Scally turned and saw the stream of water. "About goddamn time."

"Anything else, sir?"

"I want spikes on my windowsills."

"Sir?"

"Tell maintenance. Spikes. S-P-I-K-E-S. Rocco here tells me spikes will keep the goddamn things off my window."

"Yes sir.

Scally sat down again. The stream of water had stopped. The window dripped. Water dripped from little icicles hanging from the top of the window frame.

"Go ahead, Rocco."

Now Rocco couldn't remember where he'd left off. Reflexively he went back to the beginning. "I've known Bo Valgus a long time."

"So I've heard. You played college football together, right?"

"Sir," Rocco answered to buy time.

"You're a bit small for college ball, aren't you, Pinnoccho?"

"But quick, sir."

"Ah, running back?"

"Mainly, sir. So, as I was saying—"

Scally looked at his watch. "How much time you need, Rocco?"

"One more minute, sir." No more time to finesse things. "Bo and I go a long way back, so this will be no surprise to you, Paul, he reached out to me last week, picking me to reach out, to look for some support, sound you out for support for an issue he is addressing relative to our community—" Way off script now. Damn it.

Scally's brow furrowed. "Not a dime to that goddamn arts center, Rocco."

Rocco smiled. "Exactly right, sir."

"Then what does he want, Rocco."

Time for the props. Rocco whipped open his portfolio, pulled out a newspaper clipping, and laid it on Paul's desk. The headline read "WE NEED MANUFACTURING."

"The Performing Arts Centre is toast, as you know," Rocco said. "Bo needs an out, and he's got an idea that is one of the best I've ever encountered during my entire tenure with our company."

"What manufacturing, Rocco? What are you saying?"

"Paul, as you know, I've believed for some time that our digital business has a huge opportunity. A strategic opportunity to expand our business vertically from can opening to canning itself. So when Bo started chatting about how much Borschtchester needs jobs, the light bulb went off."

"I don't follow you, Pinnoccho."

"I propose we build a cannery operation right here in town."

"Bo wants a DipTych cannery. Instead of an arts center."

Rocco nodded.

"How much."

"Sir?"

"How much can Valgus bring in. If we do this."

"Conservatively, 10-20 million in combined state and federal funding, and of course we could expect some substantial tax breaks."

Scally looked down at the newspaper on his desk.

Behind him, the pigeons had returned. But the jet of water streamed down again and chased them off.

He looked up at Rocco again. "What else does Bo want. Besides a way to get out of the arts center deal."

"His name on the Enterprise Zone."

Scally frowned, then said, "My name goes on the building."

"Yes sir."

"What else."

"Nothing else."

"Who knows about this."

"You, me, Bo."

"What about Van."

Rocco licked his lips. The last thing in the world he wanted was to give any of the company's Executive VPs a role in the cannery. They'd take it over. They'd take credit. They'd edge Rocco out. "Actually, Bo asked me to keep things quiet for now, Paul. Until he can get the agreements on the funding."

Rocco held his breath.

He needn't have worried. Apparently, Scally didn't have a problem with keeping Van out of it for now. He'd moved on to the next tick on his mental list. "And the press?"

"Suggest we let Bo lead it. We can take a more . . . behind the scenes role. Just in case the federal money doesn't come through."

"Hold them to the deal." Scally nodded. "Good thinking, Rocco. You're a thinker."

"We'll be the heroes in any case. Media catnip." He hadn't really found a way to work "media catnip" into his script, so he was glad to have done it as an improv.

"Media catnip." Scally repeated it, meaning he liked. "What else. What do you need from me."

"Your go-ahead to pursue this as a special ops."

"Name?"

"Betta Fighting Fish."

"Good name."

"Thank you, sir."

"One other thing, Pinnoccho. The last time you presented on your cannery idea, you said you were looking at a plant in Mexico."

"Yes, sir."

"We haven't committed to anything there yet."

"No. We've got until April to let them know, one way or another, if we want the facility."

"That's not much time. Pin Bo down, Rocco, and pin him down fast."

"Give me three weeks."

The pigeons had returned. A jet of water hit the window, rattling it.

"You can't do it in three weeks."

"Give me three weeks."

Scally jabbed his phone. "Amber!"

"Yes sir."

"Put Rocco on my calendar. Same time. Three weeks from today."

"Yes sir."

Scally stood up.

"Do it or lose it, Rocco."

"It's done, sir," said Rocco, and he placed his props back into his portfolio and zipped it shut.

# TAYLOR A-TWITTER

*"Sherry Snells sells seashells at the seashore."*

—Miles Chacuderie

Sherry Snells, E-Commerce and Web Portal Developer, DipTych Digital Can, wanted an update on the DipTych Digital Can Twitter initiative.

Because she was ready to put a Twitter feed on the DipTych Digital Can landing page.

It was Darryl's daily staff meeting in Conference Room 3B.

Taylor pulled out her manila folder labeled Twitter. "Yeah, I got it going a while ago—let's see, two weeks ago."

"You worked with Corporate on that, right?" Basil. Ready to pounce if any of Darryl's reports failed to abide by DipTych rules.

"Yeah, they set up the account for me."

"What's the name?" Sherry asked.

"Diptychdigital."

Sherry made a note.

"Is that all one word?" Basil was looking over Sherry's shoulder.

"Yes," said Taylor.

Basil frowned and glanced at Darryl. "That doesn't follow our branding guidelines."

"Corporate approved it."

"And how many followers do we have?" Taylor noticed that Darryl wasn't really paying attention to how she answered Basil's questions. Which,

70

unfortunately, didn't get her off the hook. "Last I checked, we had 23."

"That's not very many."

*No kidding.*

"What do you twitter about?"

*Tweet, not twitter.*

"You don't twitter anything about Britch, I hope."

Britch Openers Ltd. was DipTych's major rival in the can opener space. They held only 5.2 percent of the global can opener market but were nonetheless an object of heartfelt loathing within DipTych's walls. Which didn't stop DipTych from exercising the utmost caution in making public statements that mentioned their rival by name—Legal was adamant that DipTych scrupulously protect itself from potential lawsuits, even when the potential could be measured in nanometers.

"No—no, I went to a training. We're not allowed to tweet about competitors."

"I've got a question." Miles was seated across from her at the conference table. Cute Miles, with the hair curling over his ears. Fortunately Taylor had gotten used to the idea of being around him now. Yeah. She'd talked herself down from that little crush she'd had on him for a while there. So she was able to respond to him with professionalism and composure.

"Yes?"

"Who are these people—our 23 followers?"

Was he deliberately trying to make her look bad? She glared, but he met her glare with a quick flash of a smile that suggested something else—that he was inviting her to join in on a joke of some kind. But on whom?

In any case, the question was out there now—Basil, for one, was looking at her, probably wishing he'd been the one to ask.

Sherry's pen was poised, waiting.

Taylor pulled a printout from her folder. "Let's see. It's kind of hard to tell who they are. But . . ." *Damn it. No getting around this . . .* "I've got their names here . . ."

"Let's take a look." Basil took the paper from her. "Mmmm. Who is 'hotdeals'?"

"It's hard to tell—"

"'Borschtchesterrealestate?'"

Miles answered for her. "Someone trying to sell real estate in Borschtchester, obviously."

Did he just wink at her?

Basil frowned. "So our followers . . . all seem to be people who want to sell things *to* us, rather than buy things *from* us."

"From what I've been able to tell so far," Taylor said, "most people are on Twitter to sell things to other people on Twitter."

"But I thought there were celebrities on Twitter. Are any celebrities following us?"

"Celebrities?" This was too much, even for Taylor. "How do celebrities help us, I don't understand."

"They're our demographic." Basil held his mouth in the prim lines he used when he was in teaching mode. "Affluent professionals. I've read that John Mayer and Kayne West are both twitter users. Have you tried engaging them with some twittering? Ask them about their albums."

"I'm not sure Corporate would approve of—"

"How about Stewart Cink?" Miles said. "He's a big tweeter."

Why was Miles egging Basil on? She glared at him again. "Who is Steward Cink? I don't even know who that is."

"He's a golfer. I've heard golfers eat canned food. On occasion."

More nods around the table.

"Taylor."

It was the first time Darryl had spoken since kicking off the meeting.

She braced herself.

"What are you tweeting? When you tweet?"

She pulled another document out of her folder. A 32-page printout of a PDF document from Corporate, stapled together in the upper left hand corner. "I'm following Corporate guidelines on that," she said, opening the document and turning it around to show Darryl the page that explained how to get tweets approved. "I submit a list of suggested tweets for approval. I'm waiting on my last submission. They're a bit busy so it's taking them four or five days to respond on approvals."

"Ah," said Darryl. He looked up from the text Taylor was pointing at, looked at her face. "And how much time would you say you've spent on this altogether?"

"Well, counting the Corporate Twitter training seminar, I'd say maybe six or seven hours?"

"And you are also working on—what?"

"Kich-N-World press kit, press interviews, website copy—"

"Sherry." Darryl cut Taylor off. "Take over the Twitter business, will you? Thanks."

He handed Taylor's Twitter folder across the table to Sherry.

Just like that.

Basil snorted his disapproval. But, Taylor realized with a twitch of satisfaction, there wasn't a thing he could do about it.

And Miles, across from her, had caught her eye again.

And this time it was a wink. No doubt about it.

Her reprieve lasted only a few seconds however.

"So what's next on our agenda?" Darryl. Moving the meeting along.

"What are we using for our booth giveaways?"

It was the sales manager who had spoken. So now he was looking at

Taylor. Along with, again, everyone else.

Booth giveaways?

"I—I'm not sure," she said.

"You haven't ordered them yet?" Basil's voice rising, rising to the full height of his towering incredulity.

Thank heaven the meeting was nearly over, so that Taylor could dash to her cubicle and start Googling trade show tchotchke companies. And making phone calls. And finding herself the New Best Friend of no less than 16 trade show tchotchke sales reps, each of whom began to fertilize these blossoming friendships immediately with multiple phone calls and emails.

Taylor was a polite young woman, and well brought up, so at first she gave each of her new best friends ample time to describe the uncountable value of patronizing their respective businesses. But as panic began to set in, she did what any rational person would do: she made a decision.

She chose pens.

She gave an update on the booth show giveaway the next morning, at the next morning's Kich-N-World status update meeting. Passed around a print-out from a web page. "I've ordered pens."

Nobody said anything for a moment.

She looked around uneasily.

Basil, once the room's response was sufficiently obvious, was only too happy to get the discussion going. "I'm not sure about pens," he said.

She looked at him. He didn't appear to bathe very often. Or maybe he put something in his hair to grease it.

"I'm not sure what 'pens' says about DipTych."

There were murmurs of agreement.

"Basil has a point." Truth be told, Darryl didn't give a crap. But now that it was in the open, his managerial dignity required him to acknowledge the sense in it. Taylor's relative likeability notwithstanding. "It's better if our giveaways are consistent with our branding."

"I've already ordered them." Taylor's voice cracked slightly.

"When?" Basil taking up the attack again.

"Yesterday."

"Uh, you'd better cancel it."

So she did. Dove back into her cubicle seat as soon as the meeting adjourned, and delivered the news to one of her new best friends, who immediately became a former new best friend.

Back to the Interwebs.

This time, she spent more time. First, she combed again, but more thoroughly this time, through webpage after webpage, printing out anything that looked remotely promising, daubing sticky notes to keep track of why particular items evoked, to her thinking, something related to the DipTych brand identity—

How many new emails? Sixty? How was that even possible? Better look at this one, though, it's marked urgent. Darn it, the Homebuddies editor wanted to reschedule her interview. What to do, what to do . . . maybe move the *Greenie Does It* interview? Eco-home living website, no big deal if *Greenie Does It* doesn't feel like DipTych wanted to do it. Heh.

Yeah, she was feeling a bit punchy.

Email to *Greenie Does* It, email to *Homebuddies*, make a note in the press interview schedule file, quick update to Darryl . . .

Back to the tchotchke hunt.


This wasn't easy. Foil covered chocolate coins, because DipTych products are worth their weight in gold? No . . . how about refrigerator magnets. Can openers are more or less in the food business. Is there a refrigerator magnet shaped like a can?

Her phone rang.

Randolph Schilling, DipTych Digital sales manager. Asking would Taylor please order reprints of the "behind the scenes" profile of EasyCan that had run in *Housin' It*.

Sure thing, sure thing.

What was the email address for *Housin' It*? Ah, there we go. Quick email to *Housin' It*. Pricing for 100 reprints of EasyCan profile please.

What? Another twenty emails? Did people do nothing else but send emails all day?

Mustn't look at them now or she'd never finish this other thing, wait, what was the other thing? Oh yes. To her Kich-N-World tchotchke spreadsheet, keyed in descriptions of the coins and the magnets. And pricing. She'd present a bona fide report, with budgeting, at tomorrow's meeting.

Back to her web browser—and whoa! A breakthrough.

Key chain trinkets shaped like little hand can openers.

Taylor stared at the thumbnail image on the screen. This was too good to be true.

She didn't even hesitate, picked up the phone and made a new favorite best friend, who better yet had a southern accent and sounded motherly and sympathetic. And best of all offered Taylor an incredibly good price. A big plus, because Taylor, in addition to being polite and well-brought-up—or perhaps because of it—was also instinctively frugal, especially when it came to other peoples' money.

So she nearly skipped, the next day, on her way to the conference room.

She passed out her spreadsheet with all the different options and their pricing.

And on top of it, a print out of the jpeg her favorite new best friend had emailed the afternoon before. Of the key chain trinket shaped like a can opener.

Perhaps the response was somewhat more muted than she'd hoped.

"So?" she said nervously.

"Do you think," Basil asked thoughtfully, "that it looks a little too much like a Britch can opener?"

Taylor froze.

Of all the things that had never crossed her mind—she'd never thought to compare the trinket to a photo of a Britch can opener.

Taylor waited in agony.

Randolph came to her rescue. "I think it's okay. Britch has the little bend, right here." He pointed, in the photo, at a place on the can opener trinket's toy handle. "And they're wider near the cutter."

She let out her breath.

"But—"

She stopped letting out her breath.

"I have another question. It really says 'analog' to me."

Thoughtful nods around the table.

Taylor was thinking about her deadline. Her new favorite best friend had mentioned that she had to place the order today or there wouldn't be enough time to have them in for Kich-N-World.

"It sends the wrong message," Basil said, settling the issue for good. "We'll undermine our entire branding effort."

Murmurs of agreement.

"Can you find something digital-y?" Darryl asked. "A computer chip refrigerator magnet or something?"


It had become hard for Taylor to detect when her stomach twisted into a knot, since it was pretty much always in at least half a knot.

And her newest best friend wasn't sounding so friendly any more. "Well, honey, that's the hahrd pahrt," she was saying. Motherly and sympathetic as always, but right now, it was like hiding the point of the thumbtack on your seat with a daub of whipped cream. Sweet and fluffy, but wasn't going to do jack for the pain. "You have only, what is it? 'Til the show?"

"A month." Taylor's voice cracked slightly.

"That doesn't leave us many options, sweet hahrt."

Taylor had yanked open the file cabinet drawer of her desk and was pawing through the hanging folders, looking for the tchotchke company's catalog. "What do you mean?"

"Well, I've been doing a little research for you. It looks like we can get you, let's see. We can give you a good deal on mouse pads shaped like a mouse."

"I dunno."

"They're very clever. Everybody loves them, a mousepad, shaped like a mouse. Very clever. I could email you a picture, would you like that?"

"No, no—I don't think—is there anything else we could do?"

"We could do pens."

Pens again!

"No. No, I'm sorry, that's just not . . . what else? Is there anything?" Her voice had developed a bit of a whimper.

"The problem, honey, you see, we hardly have any time."

"I realize that."

It was that moment, of course, when Basil's slumping frame appeared in her cubicle doorway.

Taylor's hand on the phone receiver lost all feeling.

"We have Band Aid dispensers," the woman was saying.

"I'm sorry?"

"They're plastic. If we place the order today, we'll just have time to get your logo on them."

Basil had stepped into the cubicle and was now inches from the front of Taylor's desk. His stomach pouched out at her, directly at face level. He looked annoyed. She should have hung up immediately when she'd seen him. Busy man.

"Taylor," he said. "A word with you, please."

"We really don't have much else we can do at this point, except the pens," the tchotchke woman drawled into Taylor's other ear.

"Okay, okay." Taylor gave up. She was going to get fired eventually anyway. It might as well be over trade show tchotchkes. "That will be fine." She avoided Basil's eye.

"The Band-Aid dispensers."

"Yes."

"Do you want me to send you a quote?"

Taylor had been adamant about seeing quotes in the previous round of tchotchke shopping.

"Yes, please."

"Problem?" Basil licked his lips.

Taylor returned the receiver to the phone base.

"No, no, not at all."

He didn't believe her. He wanted a confession. He stood, waiting.

A couple of weeks ago, she might have crumpled. But Taylor was learning. Better to inform the entire group in their next Kich-N-World status meeting, where Basil's response would be diluted by the others.'

He eyed her suspiciously but gave up, and instead turned to his other business. "How is the press kit coming?"

"Almost done," Taylor said.

"And the press interview schedule?"

"Getting close."

He eyed her suspiciously some more. Then: "Good. I've got something else for you."

Oh no.

"We've got a hole in our PR program, a gaping hole. We need an e-newsletter to communicate with our channel partners."

More people to chase down. More schedule juggling. It was enough to make a grown woman cry.

Only she didn't. Of course. She waited until Basil had left and then sat in her chair, clenching and unclenching her hands and staring at the undone rewrite of the EasyCan press release until the screen flicked suddenly and her screensaver, a ricocheting can opener, began its predictably random trek back and forth across the display.


It was chilly, but still gorgeous out later, when Taylor walked through the half-empty parking lot to her car. The sun had just gone down, and overhead toward the west sky two contrails formed a gigantic pink X in the otherwise crystal clear sky. A flock of starlings swirled overhead, making their last turn through the air before settling in to roost for the night, the sound of their wings just audible above the background noise of the city's evening traffic.

She sat in her car a moment before turning the key in the ignition.

She glanced down at the passenger seat. Stack of folders. The work she was bringing home that night.

And instead of turning toward the expressway ramp, she made a left.

It was 15 minutes before closing when she got to Orwin's.

The air inside was humid as paradise and smelled green and earthy as a bed of moss.

The marked-down holiday ornaments that had been in a basket inside the door were gone now. In their place, a stack of boxes, kits for forcing paper whites indoors.

Taylor wandered slowly toward the back of the store.

A women she didn't know walked from the back room to the cash register counter, looked at Taylor, said "hi, be with you in a sec," took something from behind the counter, and returned to the back room.

"Take your time," Taylor answered. "I'm just looking."

She'd reached the cut flower display. A galvanized metal bucket stuffed with tall sprays of blood red hollyhocks.

She touched a bloom.

"May I help you?"

Taylor looked at her. That might well be Taylor's old Orwin's apron she was wearing.

"Ma'am?"

Ma'am. Taylor was no longer the girl in the Orwin's apron. She was now a ma'am.

The bell on the entrance door jangled and the woman's eyes left Taylor to see who had come in.

It was a man in a suit, tie loosened. He came straight to the back of the shop—so not a browser, he knew already why he'd come, he'd probably ordered an arrangement from work and was picking it up on his way home.

"I'll wait," Taylor said.

She slipped back outside while the woman was waiting on the man in the suit.

# IT'S ALL IN THE PLAN, MAN

*"Don't believe them when they tell you all it takes is brains. It was hard work. Damn hard work."*

—Rocco Pinnoccho

When the sun goes down, windows switch sides.

All day long they reflect the outer world back on itself.

But when nightfall comes, they reflect a room's innards back within.

So that if you'd been able to hover in the air outside Rocco's seventh floor office window, he wouldn't have been able to see you, but you'd have no trouble whatever seeing him, framed within a fluorescent shimmer, there in front of his computer screen, hands on the keyboard, typing.

He was still at work because he loved loved loved his job.

And was taking near-orgasmic pleasure in writing the DipTych EasyCan Cannery business plan.

Sitting there at his desk, his legs kicking and swinging off the edge of his faux-leather executive swivel chair, blue computer screen light glancing off his slightly lopsided face, sneaking up on the plan section by section and always with perfect cunning.

Of course his assumptions dwelt unchallengeable in their platonic isolation, but that hardly worried him. He simply wrote, building his new kingdom as he went, his fingers flying over the keyboard.

The building itself was now four stories high. There was a warehouse to the west, and on the east, facing the most-trafficked of the bordering streets, a modest entranceway flanked by modern statuary. Now comes the ribbon-cutting ceremony—Paul Scally standing with the state governor, a dutiful media phalange which would bristle with gigantic cameras and microphones dangled from booms, speeches, Rocco himself nodding decorously as he was publicly noted and thanked.

In the next of the many mansions, a sales and marketing plan. And oh! What a plan! Plans within a plan! The lead-up publicity, the cultivation of channel partners, the signing of contracts, the consumer ad spend, the great splash of the factory opening itself, and then the ongoing pulse of communications afterward as the product began at last to flow.

The operational plan laid itself out almost without requiring Rocco at all. Locals, dazzled by the prospect of genuine manufacturing jobs—with benefits? Are you kidding?—lined up to be sorted, from such a vast pool of potential workers it was easy to be selective, to pick only those too dutiful and grateful to ever consider anything messy, unionization or such. Switches were tripped, machinery hummed, semis pulled up, and as demand for EasyCan canned goods grew—whoa! Add a second shift! Now a third! And—what's that? Plans for a new factory? Rocco jetting about, scouting for a suitable site?

A cursory look and swift dismissal of competitive threats. There were none to speak of. How could there be? This was DipTych, new titan of the canning industry. Who would dare?

And then, finally, the numbers, several pages of them, artfully coiling and uncoiling onto the screen from their embedded formulas.

He had never worked such long hours. When he left, the parking lot was empty save that disabled Ford Focus that someone had left off in the far corner for weeks.

Rocco's laptop was in its case. He clasped it against his waist. He'd boot it up as soon as he got home, swallowing his take-out in the glow of the screen, too intoxicated to stop.

Perhaps it was luck. But he preferred to think of it as a kind of serendipity bleed-through—the writing of the EasyCan Cannery plan had gone so well, Rocco was zipping along within his own personal career enhancement zone.

So he opened the Word file where he had stored all the notes he'd compiled to prepare for the Kich-N-World Chips and Clicks panel.

It was a huge honor, being invited to sit on that panel. Huge. Oh well, not quite as huge as being invited to be the show's keynote speaker—but that would come soon enough, by next year no doubt, when the kitchen trade finally accepted the fact that DipTych Digital Can was the future of kitchen gadgetry—no—when the trade grasped the fact that the EasyCan Digital Canning System was about more than opening cans, but was the entre into a comprehensive digital kitchen management system—

Rocco felt a little shiver of pure bliss waver through his body.

Quite the vision. And right there, in his notes, because what better place to drop that little bombshell than in this panel—where it would come straight from Rocco's lips, unfiltered by the DipTych PR machine, unattributable to anyone but he, Vice President Rocco Pinnoccho?

He opened a web browser and, without really thinking, went to the DipTych home page. Then clicked on the DipTych Digital Can landing page. And noticed for the first time a link to—what was this? A blog?

He frowned and followed the link.

It took only a few seconds to figure out what was going on. This was an R&D thing. Okay. Very technical, looked like. Andy Spittleton's guys, engineers, blogging about engineering minutiae—not many comments, who reads this crap anyway? Teenage kids probably.

Then Rocco noticed one post that had quite a few comments. Something had sparked quite a bit of interest?

Hmmmm.

He scrolled back up to the top of the page to reread the post.

Sucked in his breath.

Who was this?

*I call it "Tangential Integration." And yes, it's challenging to architect products that support it, but obviously it's the wave of the future. Call it a crowdsourcing of product co-integration, as solutions we build individually start to connect within consumers' homes, share information, leading ultimately to a seamless digital experience revolving around disparate yet related user needs . . .*

"What the—"

Rocco's stomach twisted with the sharp nausea of pure envy. Then his fingers exploded across the keyboard. Highlight, copy, switch to his Chips and Clicks panel document, paste. Back to the blog again—

Whose blog was this?

George Bonmont?

Rocco knew who the guy was, although he couldn't picture his face at the moment. One of the Spittleton's senior engineers.

"Tangential Integration." Rocco's tongue wrapped itself around the words. "Tangential Integration."

Brilliant. No question. Appallingly so.

He had finished.

He leaned back, his face reflecting the blue hues favored by the DipTych website color scheme.

He knew what he had to do.

He flipped open his cell and hit one of the numbers on his speed dial.

Voice mail—he'd expected it, it was, after all, nearly 10 p.m., and barring some major litigation crisis, nobody at the DipTych Legal Department would be at the office that late.

"Hi," he said into his phone.

"This is Rocco Pinnoccho over at Digital Can. I need to speak to you immediately—please call me at home tonight if you pick this up. We have a serious issue on our hands—someone is disclosing intellectual property online. Through one of our corporate blogs, I'm sorry to say."

He closed his phone and grimaced.

By the next day, that post would be gone or he'd know the reason why.

By this time next week, a new opening for a Head Systems Engineer, DipTych Digital Can, would be listed on Monster.com.

# SUCH A PLUMP MORSEL

*"With a combined 75 years' experience in marketing, marketing communications, and public relations Hedy Fusee and Archibald Madelaine know what it takes to take your firm wherever you want to take it."*

—from the Fusee & Madelaine web site About page

"It's utter bullshit."

There were two individuals in the entire Fusee & Madelaine organization who were permitted to utter, at any time, words that were both perfectly truthful and brutally blunt.

One was Archibald "Switch" Madelaine.

He'd just finished leafing through Rocco's fine business plan.

The other was Hedy Fusee.

Hedy was not in the room. They were conversing by phone. And although until a moment ago she had been on speaker, just before Switch pronounced his truthful and blunt words, he'd picked up the receiver and put it to his ear, making those words and even more important Hedy's response a private exchange between the two of them. Not that any Fusee & Madelaine staffers would deliberately eavesdrop outside his office door. But Switch never left anything to chance if he had any choice in the matter.

So when Hedy answered her voice was close, up against his ear.

"Absolute bullshit," she agreed.

Switch paused a moment to savor her response. Hedy's voice was liquid, the vulgarity it had echoed back to him all the more striking when spoken in such tones—her voice so molten, pure as precious metal. He was not in love with her—had not been for many years—but how she still thrilled him when their minds moved, as they were now, in such liquid symmetry.

"And he's offered us Digital Can," Switch continued after the pause had run its course. He was not telling Hedy anything she didn't know—just running down the list of talking points that they both drew, naturally, from the document.

"Quite the plump morsel." Hedy laughed.

"I stopped by the Tourist Board shoot the other day."

Hedy waited.

"Bobo looked like he had a bag of Werthers Originals up his ass. I'm surprised he didn't spill the beans."

"Rocco's not stupid."

"Not smart—"

"But not stupid." Hedy laughed again. "He probably told Bobo we're in."

"No doubt." Switch's upper lip curled slightly as he said the words. Few people earned his contempt faster than poor liars.

"It's a plump morsel," Hedy said. "The only question is what will happen with our city retainer."

Fusee & Madelaine, as Borschtchester's PR and Marketing Firm of Record, had a monthly retainer to cover all FairARTS!-related marketing programs. It also owned, through a discrete network of subsidiaries and partnerships, interest in a number of marketing- and advertising- related ventures that stood to gain by public spending on FairARTS! public awareness campaigns. Like big ads painted across public buses, things of that sort. But of course that money was subject to politics. Whereas the Digital Can business was somewhat less vulnerable to the vagaries of the mob.

"With the thing styled as a jobs creator, the mayor should jump on board with a complementary program of some kind," Switch said. "He'd be foolish not to. I'm having dinner with him Saturday."

"Then, Archie, it's a go."

Switch pushed back against the leather of his vintage Eames chair and crossed his slippered feet on the top of his desk. "Enjoy New York," he said. "See you Monday."

"I'll have good news for you by then on the Be-licious account."

"I love start-ups."

"Mmmm. Start-ups with VCs."

Switch laughed. "Ciao, dear."

"Ciao."

# SOMETIMES IT TAKES
# A LITTLE MAN-TO-MAN VISIT

*"Men get depressed, too. They just hide it. But we have to admit what we're feeling, because otherwise you never ask for help, and then you just stay depressed for, I don't know. Years, maybe."*

—Trevor Mancely

Trevor's digs were in a rather scruffy part of town, outside of the city proper, in a neighborhood where all the north-south avenues had been snubbed off in the 1960s by a grand and mighty branch of the state highway system.

Bo parked at the end of the street, his front bumper resting inches from a concrete sound barricade separating it from the highway.

He and his State Assembly colleagues had funded that barricade, shortly after Bo was elected—and some 20 years after the four-lane beyond it was built. It was a belated nod to human decency, and in some respects a feeble one, considering the outrage of the actual act—the land grab, the bisection of the neighborhood. But Bo and his colleagues felt very good about themselves nonetheless. After all, they'd made the neighborhood so much quieter.

Today, the barrier was covered in a tangled mix of feral English ivy and wily saplings, preparing now to leaf out, and no doubt hoping to one day grow roots mighty enough to upend the entire structure. Bo would be retired by then, so it wasn't his problem.

Trevor's address was listed as 117B.

Bo had found 117 easily enough.

It took a while to locate part B however. The place was a modest cape, it hardly looked large enough from the front to have been broken into apartments. But there were two utility meters mounted on the exterior wall facing the driveway. And in the driveway, a truck with Mancely Kitchen and Bath printed on the doors. So Bo walked down the driveway and sure enough the backside of the cape telescoped outward. An addition. 117B.

He pressed the 117B doorbell and waited.

Nothing.

He pressed it again.

Still nothing.

He knocked.

Then he tried the knob, and it turned in his hand.

He shouldn't have gone in.

But Bo had to do what he had to do.

His marriage was no doubt at stake.

He opened the 117B door.

He stuck his head inside.

The door opened directly into a kitchen. Small, but spotless, and in the cheery light of the pocket lights in the ceiling, every fixture, every tile, every appliance, every cabinet pull looked hot-from-the showroom new.

"Trevor?"

That might have been a noise. Coming from somewhere beyond the kitchen, beyond the hallway that stretched away beyond the glistening stainless refrigerator.

But Bo wasn't sure. He listened a moment. Nothing.

"Trevor. Trevor Mancely. You here?"

Now *that* was a sound. Paper rustling. And then footsteps.

And then the hallway was filled with a fellow who had to have been at least 6'5". Shirtless, shoeless, stretching now like he'd just woken from a nap.

Bo wasn't a small man, plus he had his belly. So it wasn't fear that filled him when the man stepped into the kitchen and into the gleaming light. It was something else, although it gripped his guts exactly like fear would.

It was awe—a great gripping primordial stunning awe.

Bo nearly staggered, but forced himself back under control and instead straightened up, instinctively making himself as large as he could as if in self-defense.

"Can I help you?"

"I'm looking for Trevor Mancely." But Bo knew it was Trevor standing before him. It had to be. For this man—Bo had never seen anyone like him. Those eyes. Enormous, luminous, sapphire blue. The cleft chin. The impossibly thick mop of dark hair. Those shoulders, that chiseled chest frosted with curls of sweetly scented hair, the way his torso tapered gracefully to the beltline of his jeans—

"I'm Trevor," Trevor said. "Are you okay?"

A bead of sweat broke and ran down Bo's forehead. "Uh," he said.

"You're Bo Valgus."

"I'm . . ."

"I recognize you from your mailers."

"I'm . . . I'm not . . . g—gu—I'm not—"

"Gay? I know. I get it all the time." Trevor shrugged. "I'm not either, or I guess I coulda gone into modeling or something instead of becoming a plumber." He shrugged again. "I suppose you're here to fire me."

Bo was breathing again. "No, no, that's not . . . it." He tore his eyes away at last. There was an empty dish rack next to the sink. The only other object on the counter was a coffee mug, black, with *JJ & Son Plumbing Supply* printed on it in gold lettering. "Look." He forced himself to breathe. "Can I get a glass of water or something?"

"Sure, yeah."

Trevor padded over to the sink. Bo forced himself to look away as the other man filled the black coffee mug from the tap.

"You want to siddown?"

Bo nodded and took the coffee mug, but he'd forgotten he wanted a drink.

"C'mon in."

Bo followed Trevor down the hallway.

"There's not much room," Trevor said. "You mind the ottoman?"

The room was not large, and the only other piece of furniture in it was a sofa, which was heaped with a toppling pile of newspapers, some of which fell to the floor as Trevor pushed them aside to make room for himself to sit.

No way was Bo going to sit next to that man on a couch. He lurched to the ottoman.

"So. I suppose you're here about your bathroom." Trevor's beautiful eyes shone with shame and sadness.

"Uh, well . . ." Bo had rehearsed himself on the drive over—rehearsed himself into a bit of a temper, to tell the truth. But now that he was here, he couldn't bring himself to scold this . . . creature. "It's more like, you see, me and your other, uh, friends, we're worried about you, and we'd really like to see you, you know, able to get back to work."

"I dunno." Trevor leaned over and picked up the newspapers that had fallen onto the floor.

Bo considered him a moment. The dark hair falling down over his forehead. The broad hands. He forced himself to breathe, and realized as he did that, thank heaven, the shock of beholding a specimen of manhood so unthinkably perfect had begun to wear off, and to be replaced by something else . . . "Look, Trevor, we know what you're going through."

Trevor raised his head, wincing. "No, you don't."

The fact was, Bo had no idea what Trevor was going through, having never been through it himself, but that didn't stop him from pursuing his chosen course of logic. "Things . . . don't always last. We have to, uh, start a new dawn."

The other man didn't look up. "You don't understand. I'm still processing the grief."

The new feeling nudged itself back into Bo's attention. He recognized it now. It was . . . impatience. Because this man—how could this man . . .?

"You know grief has 34 stages. They've figured that out, now. I'm only on eleven."

"Thirty four?"

"Yeah." Trevor raised his head, fixing his gorgeous eyes on Bo's. "Eleven is 'preparation for letting go.' I've been in eleven for about a month now. It's a tough one."

"Good God," Bo said.

"I know. I never thought eleven would take this long."

"No! That's not—Trevor. Look at yourself."

Trevor didn't, he looked again at Bo. A note of wariness had crept into his luminous eyes.

"You're . . . you're . . . you're quite possibly the hunkiest heterosexual male on the planet . . . Good God, I'm not gay, but you make George Clooney look like . . . like the Elephant Man!"

"Excessive good looks are a kind of disability, you know."

Bo stared. "Are you joking?"

"Of course not."

"Trevor, you could have any woman . . ."

"I want only one woman, and she won't have me."

"Who freaking cares! If I had half your looks—"

"It wouldn't matter. You'd still be in love with your wife."

That was not the way Bo had planned to completed the sentence.

"If you loved your wife, no matter how you looked, you'd still love her."

Bo stared at Trevor again.

"Right?"

"That's not the point. We're not talking about Dahlia."

"You would be, if she'd left you. She's a beautiful woman."

A beautiful woman? A beautiful woman who . . . who . . . who had been alone with Trevor Mancely for hours on end while Bo was out serving constituents or meeting with officials. Bo shook himself slightly and his voice came out a bit louder than he expected. "Damn right a beautiful woman, and, uh, also out of your league." He watched Trevor as he spoke.

"I told you, there's only one woman I want. But look, Bo, I'll be okay. I just need to get to stage thirty two or so."

"Jesus, Trevor, you got to man up, here."

"Man up?"

"Get over it."

"Excuse me, but are you invalidating my wound?"

"Uh, no! No, of course not. I would, uh, never—'"

An image of Dahlia . . . she was watching Trevor, admiring him as he muscled away at a pipe wrench wrapped around a stubborn Valgus bathroom plumping fixture. Bo pushed the image aside. "Look." He thrust his arm out of his coat sleeve to check his watch. "I've got to go." It was the first thing he'd said that he actually meant. He really really needed to get out of there. He stood up.

Trevor stood up too. "So, uh—"

His face looked suddenly very mournful.

"Look," Bo said. "I wish I could help you. But I can't get, uh, your wife to, uh—"

"Nobody can," said Trevor.

"But, uh, your friends are worried about you and—the one thing I can do, if you're interested, which is why I wanted to talk to you. There's this big job coming up, a public job, know what I mean?"

Was that a spark of interest in those big luminous blue eyes?

Bo could only hope. "And so I'm here to, uh, to see if maybe you might be interested in, you know, moving on to some bigger type deals than, you know, the whole home bathroom sort of job."

Trevor sighed.

But Bo trusted his instinct and gave the line a little tug. "Of course, if you're not interested—"

"I . . . I could check with my therapist."

"You could afford your therapist."

"The bills are getting a bit out of control. It's so hard . . ."

"The only thing is, Trev, you gotta finish my bathroom first. You know. Clear the slate."

"Understood."

"So you in?"

Trevor sighed heavily, looking down at his hands.

Bo waited.

Trevor nodded. "Yeah. My therapist actually mentioned that, you know, if I got out some, it might help me move on to twelve."

"Good deal, then. I'll tell Dah—I mean, I'll see you at my house Monday morning then, say 9:00."

"Okay, Bo, and thanks."

"Yeah, no problem."

Bo only appreciated how claustrophobic Trevor's apartment was when reemerged into the cold late winter air, and walked back up the driveway and onto the street, where his car waited and the highway traffic rumbled by, invisible behind the concrete wall.

# "THIS IS IT, DARRYL"

*"When Mom died . . . maybe that's what happened. Things just weren't the same after that. A guy gets lonely, you know. Work isn't everything."*

—Darryl Fiegit

Darryl was sleeping. He was dreaming. He was hungry. Ravenous. He cracked an egg and dropped it into the frying pan. Grease splattered and crackled. He needed to flip the egg. The egg seemed suddenly rather large. He slid the spatula under the egg. The egg was growing. He lifted the egg, its heavy slick egg white edges draped pendulously off either side of the spatula blade. He flipped the egg over. It spread now across the entire pan. Then it began to puff up. The puffing caused it to reach the top of the frying pan, and then to breach it. Egg was spilling over the sides of the frying pan, onto the burner, smoke was rising, is there a bigger spatula, this egg will be ruined—

The alarm on his cell phone was beeping.

He opened his eyes. The blanket had slipped off his couch. He shivered. A thin rectangular beam of sun was striking the television screen at just the right angle to illuminate a trapezoid shape in its thick coating of pale dust.

Darryl was not a morning person. His circadian rhythms were, truth to tell, still lodged in the pattern they'd found when he was 17. Four in the morning was a perfect bedtime for him. Two in the afternoon was the perfect time of day to wake and get his jump on the day. Working a corporate job was, therefore, a particularly exquisite form of torture for him. He was perpetually sleep deprived. Among other consequences, this exacerbated his native clumsiness. He stumbled a lot, ran into things, mottled his shins with bruises. And no woman stayed long with him. Bad enough the pouching belly protruding midway down his pole of a frame, his nostril hair, his perpetually sweating palms. He was no specimen of manliness, our Darryl. But women will look past such things. Women will find sweetness in the oddest of corners. And women had found sweetness in Darryl. What they could not look past, however, was the cold deprivation of their nights. It was too much a shock to discover the man you've found so uncannily alluring sleeps not in his bed but on his couch, to find your rival is a parade of late-night cable shows.

A woman might stomach his homeliness, but she'd have no stomach left afterward for sleeping alone.

Of course, there had been One . . . there was always One. But oh! Perversity! She was too good, too high above him, a goddess, pure light, a goddess of light and intelligence and humor and surety—Darryl knew his place, he knew better than to trust himself with her, his body failed him in her presence, his lust failed him—he knew better than to even try to touch her, however much he wanted to—however many times she had invited him to somehow overcome himself and reach out to her and take her into his arms . . .

He groaned and resolved for the billionth time to never think of her again.

Sat up. Groaning again as his body separated itself from the crude embrace of his couch.

Showered. Shaved. Looked for something to wear. The only shirts with sleeves long enough to cover his wrists were men's XLs, which were too large through the shoulders . . . and today, as it happened, all of his altered shirts were at the cleaners. Which meant he'd have to wear a jacket all day to hide the bagginess. Darryl bowed to his fate, his shoulders bowed around his slight chest. He dumped three spoons of instant coffee into a travel mug, filled the mug with hot tap water, and headed to his car.

He backed out of the driveway.

It had snowed in the night, a slushy snow that would be melted off by noon.

This morning was the big staff meeting. To announce the cannery.

Which meant a wasted morning, because first Rocco would tell everyone about the factory, and then they'd watch the press conference. It was bound to consume his staff's attention for hours.

Rocco sat down in one of the two plastic seated chairs wedged between Darryl's desk and the cubicle wall.

"This is it, Darryl." Rocco grinned, looking almost happy. He slicked his hair back and stroked his moustache. "It's going to be big. For both of us."

"You say so, Rocco." Darryl kept his voice down so nobody could overheard him. "I'd feel better if we were . . . a little further along . . . if we had a—" He cleared his throat. "—an actual product."

Rocco smiled. "Of course we have a product."

Darryl touched the knot of his tie nervously. "Last time I talked to R&D—"

"You've got a prototype lined up for the booth at Kich-N-World. That's what you said."

Darryl cleared his throat again.

Rocco scowled.

"Uh, no, like I mentioned, the original firmware spec had to be scrapped." Darryl shifted, then spoke again, more confidently as he went along. "They wanted to let individual users save their can preferences, market research said it was a top functionality preference, we were going to position it as family friendly—"

"Yeah, yeah, so we went to single user for v. 1. I knew that already. You don't need that for a prototype."

Darryl didn't answer.

"Why are you telling me all this now, anyway? It's not really relevant, is it?"

"I guess not."

"Let's get to business, then." Rocco wasn't smiling any more.

Darryl waited.

"So I'll start things off by breaking the news to the team."

"Right."

"Then you can tell them about the other bit, about transitioning the launch announcements over."

"Not just the launch announcements," Darryl muttered. He wasn't happy that Fusee & Madelaine were now running his entire marketing and PR program. Not happy at all.

"It's just for now."

"Right."

"Oh, come on. You didn't want the headache, Darryl. With Kich-N-World only three weeks away? Really?"

He had a point.

Darryl sighed. "Look. Rocco, about this prototype."

"Aw Jesus, the prototype again."

"They've run into a materials issue of some kind. They did a new set of stress tests and some doohickey keeps snapping—"

"You don't need a working doohickey for a prototype."

"They're sticklers, those guys. They say the doohickey might have to be completely reengineered. That will mean changing the size and shape of the chassis again."

"You don't need a working doohickey for a prototype. Prototypes are fakes, Darryl."

"You can't open a factory until you've got a product to factory with."

Rocco's scowl lines blackened. "Look, Darryl. Two things. Number one. We're getting federal funds because this project is shovel ready. We break ground next month or we lose the money. And losing the money is not an option. Got that? Number two—"

"Shovel ready? How can it be shovel ready?"

"The arts center is shovel-ready. We just need to work a little switcheroo."

"A switcheroo? You're crazy. You can't go from an arts center to manufacturing, just like that."

"You'd be surprised how easy it is when you have the right people on the team." Rocco stroked his moustache contentedly.

"A switcheroo." Darryl dropped his eyes. A naïve man would have wondered if perhaps Rocco's chair was missing a castor. But Darryl knew his boss too well.

"We can't let this get knocked off the tracks because R&D is . . . a bunch of dicks. You know that, Darryl. You know the only reason they're dicking with their doohickeys is that they have money and Scally's too big a pussy to come down on them. But once this sinks in. They'll realize their assholery will be out there for everyone to see. Then we'll start to see some action."

Darryl tried one last time. "What about our number?"

"What number."

"You know what number. The 100 million."

"What about it."

"They going to push out the timeline at least?"

"Hell no. This doesn't affect the number. If anything, it helps. This gives your guys the world's biggest baseball bat. Who's going to pass up a chance to migrate to EasyCan once they see how serious we are—once they see we're so committed to this business model?" Rocco's lip curled. He was thinking about the way consumer goods manufacturers had, until then, declined to embrace EasyCan Dimpling Technology. "Wait until the food guys find out we really are going into the canning business. This is going to turn their world upside down."

Darryl wiped his hands on his pant legs. Any private doubts he had about the wisdom of the cannery idea were immaterial. He knew that now. Against the firm momentum of a DipTychian executive on a mission, he had no choice but to yield.

"Oh, and did I tell you. The project name is Betta Fighting Fish."

"Betta Fighting Fish."

"Good name, eh? When's your next meeting with R&D?"

"Tuesday."

"Move it up."

"Kich-N-World . . . I don't see how we get a prototype in three—"

"Aw. FUCK the prototype," Rocco snapped. "You're way too hung up on prototypes, Darryl. Think outside the box for once. Plan B. Artist rendering for the back wall. Virtual demo, computer screen, 3D rendering, lots of movement so people can't see things too closely. Cutaways, rotating objects. You've got Fusee & Madelaine now, remember? Just toss it over to them. They'll do it. They'll put in so much splash nobody will notice there's no fucking prototype."

"Got it. Artist rendering."

"Plaster the walls with it. Tell Fusee, style it like a work of art. A da Vinci drawing." Rocco stood up and thrust his hands straight out from his sides. "Renaissance it."

"Da Vinci. Got it."

"There. See? Problem solved. I've solved your problem. Next?"

"Got it."

"What do you say, eh?"

"Thank you, Rocco."

Rocco glanced at his watch. "Time to tell the troops."

# PRESS CONFERENCE, INTERRUPTED

*"No. I didn't see it happen. I heard the sirens, and for some reason I looked up, and I could see something dangling—I think it was his leg. But it wasn't moving."*

—Eyewitness

Dementia affects the body last. Long after the last dregs of rationality have drained away, the body clings to a kind of  intelligence. It smiles in the presence of love, it tenses when it perceives a threat. It can carry on this way for years, so that from a distance—from across the street, say, or if you happened to glance into the living room window after dark—you might even think, at first, that nothing is amiss.

So it is with dysfunctional corporations. There's a staff meeting. An announcement is made. The person making the announcement—he's an executive, a Higher Up—smiles widely, sweats a bit in excitement, and then leaves the room, striding with exaggerated force off to the elevator.

He's on his way to a press conference.

Leaving the body of people in attendance to react as if what had just happened were a rational thing that merited a rational reaction.

 For a minute they were unable to muster any reaction at all. They looked at each other. Then Basil dropped an f-bomb that managed to be both under his breath and audible to everyone in the room, and the questions began to fly, alternatively accusatory and pleading. "How are we supposed to handle this, with Kich-N-World in three weeks?" "Can't you get them to hold off until after the show?" "I will definitely need more staff. Can we get more help, contractors even?" "What about budget?"

Darryl raised his hand.

"Hold your questions for a minute, guys," he said.

They quieted, looking at him.

"The corporation . . ." He stopped, looking at the eyes looking back at him.

He cleared his throat.

"What I mean is . . . I hired you to, uh . . . to do a job."

Nobody moved a muscle.

"And that job was to launch a new product. A revolutionary product, one that will change the canning industry forever."

"Oh gawd," Basil said. "Get it out, Darryl, whatever it is."

"I'm trying, Basil."

"Shut up, Basil," said a woman in the back of the room.

"Thank you, Karen. So, as I was saying, I hired you to do a job, but now as Rocco explained, things have changed—we're no longer launching a product, we're now opening a new ch-chapter, which means we need to make some organizational changes as well."

Poor Darryl. He was trying. But it was a poor choice of words.

"Oh GAWD," Basil screeched. "We're all laid off. We're ALL laid off."

The room erupted. The woman in the back burst into tears, Basil let go with a string of curse words, everyone turned to the next person and said "oh!" or "I saw this coming" or "I never saw this coming" or "did you see this coming?"

Taylor looked around for Miles. He was standing a few feet away from her, just the other side of Sherry Snells. His face wore an expression of bemused nonchalance.

She looked back at Darryl. "Stop it!" His voice was rising. "Stop it, stop it, I never said that, I NEVER SAID THAT."

Everyone stopped it. Except the woman who sniffled away quietly into her Kleenex.

"Nobody is getting laid off. You are all keeping your jobs." He looked around the room. "Look, you guys. Rocco felt that—for strategic reasons—because this now will have a higher profile locally and politically and everything—that we should engage an outside agency—"

"Fusee & Madelaine," Basil guessed.

"Correct."

"Great, now we're working for them."

"You're working for DipTych. Fusee & Madelaine are working for you."

Basil rolled his eyes.

"There will be some re-shuffling of responsibilities, obviously." Darryl was no longer looking directly at anyone in the room. He was looking at a point on the wall above the door. "I'll be meeting with you privately over the next few hours as we sort it all out. Okay?"

Silence.

"The press conference should be starting."

There was a television in the corner of the conference room.

Someone took the clicker off the shelf on the television stand, and pointed it at the television and flicked through the channels to one of the local stations.

They looked at the screen.

The image was the exterior of the DipTych building—so at first, nobody realized there was anything wrong.

But there was something wrong.

The anchors were narrating excitedly. And where was Paul Scally, and the mayor, and Bo Valgus, and Rocco?

The camera panned the scene—hey, those were emergency vehicles!

Their blue lights and red lights swung and flashed.

"Shhh!" Everyone said. "Whoa, what's going on?"

They crowded to the television.

An anchorwoman's face appeared.

"Breaking News" scrolled across the screen.

"So again, we're showing you scenes, this is live, live on the scene at DipTych headquarters, where eyewitnesses report are that a man has jumped or possibly fallen from the roof."

"Wow."

Taylor hadn't realized that Miles had moved so close to her. His breath, as he spoke, tickled warm air right into her ear. "Someone did it. Finally."

"So much for Scally's press conference." Basil snorted. "Pre-empted by a jumper."

Had Miles deliberately maneuvered so that he'd be near her?

She turned her head to see if he was still there. But he was two people away already, looking at someone else, shaking his head.

# PLATE OF TAYLOR, BASIL
## ON THE SIDE

*"People wonder why I work in a tattoo parlor. Well, try talking to someone with one of these fat cat corporate jobs. You think they're happy? Hardly. So you know what. F—k that shit. That's what I say."*

—Aimee Hume

"So let me get this straight," Aimee said. "You're still PR Manager or whatever."

"Officially, nothing has changed, as far as my job description or anything."

"But everything you used to do, has now been turned over to whosamacallit."

"Fusee & Madelaine."

"And you are now working for Oregano."

Taylor laughed but not heartily. "Basil."

"Who's an asshole. And he's now your boss."

"Until after the trade show anyway. Since I've got zero experience at product launches, Fusee & Madelaine wanted to simplify our department's management structure. They say it's easier for them to just have to deal with one person."

"I see."

They were ferret-proofing the couch. Under the light supervision of

Aimee's two ferrets, Hermes and Daemon.

Ferret-proofing the couch consisted of hammering pieces of mason board to the bottom frame so the ferrets couldn't burrow up inside.

Taylor was holding the mason board, Aimee was hammering, and the ferrets were playing with plastic wrap.

Aimee put down the hammer and reached for another nail.

"Quit," she said.

"I can't quit."

"Why not?"

"Brenda will find out."

"Brenda may not show up again for another 15 years."

"Let's hope not," Taylor giggled. "She didn't like the plants, I doubt she'll be too happy with the ferrets, either."

"Hey, appreciate you letting me move in with you."

"I told you, *mi casa es su casa*. Always, Aimee."

"Yeah, right up until you and Miles start doing the light fandango, then it'll be 'see ya round, Aimee.'"

"No danger of that."

"Sure there's not, look at you, I say his name and you're suddenly leaving palm sweat prints all over my mason board."

"I'll admit he's cute."

"Hand me a nail. You're into him and you know it. And I bet he's into you, too."

Taylor shook his head. "He's into women period, I'm sure. Just like you-know-who was. And we all know how that turned out."

"Taylor, that was yesterday. You have to move on at some point." Aimee held the next nail in place and hammered for a moment.

"I am moving on," Taylor said as she held out another nail. "Now that I've got this job—it's changing things. I have new priorities now."

"What do you mean?"

"It's hard to explain. But the company . . . it's really a community when you think about it."

Aimee rolled her eyes. "So is a lunatic asylum."

"I spend more time now with Basil Bane than I do with you."

"That," Aimee hit the nail with her hammer for emphasis, "is kinda the point."

"There's nothing wrong with devoting my life to DipTych—to my career."

"So you're saying you want to be like Brenda."

Brenda?

Taylor waited until Aimee had finished hammering again. "What do you mean?"

Aimee set her hammer down and pushed her hand through her Cupie-doll hair. "I mean, you'll be perfectly happy if your life is one endless business trip?"

"That's different. I don't have a kid. All I've got, now, is my job. You know my boss?"

"The skinny one with the pathetic home life?"

"Darryl. Yeah. We don't know he has a pathetic home life. That's pure speculation."

"I know the type. Pathetic home life. Wouldn't get a tattoo if his life depended on it."

"Yeah, anyway, every time I saw him today he was drinking from a bottle of Maalox. Wiping the back of his mouth after every swig, like a cowboy at a bar."

Aimee laughed. "He's the one I feel sorry for."

"Yeah, me too."

"And your honey? How'd he take the news?"

Taylor made a face to make sure Aimee knew the "honey" bit wasn't passing without comment. "I guess he's kinda in the same boat as me."

"Only not reporting to Dillweed."

"No, that was a special treat for yours truly."

"Well. Things could be worse. Like for the guy who fell off the roof."

"Are you kidding me?" Taylor said. "He falls from at 14 story building and lives? He's, like, the luckiest guy on the planet."

"I guess if you're going to fall from the roof of a skyscraper, pick one with a big wide ledge partway down."

"It's actually not that wide."

"Wide enough." Aimee picked up another nail. "So what was he doing on the roof, anyway?"

"What I heard is he was spraying pigeons with a hose."

"Weird. But they do say pigeons are dirty birds," said Aimee, and tipped back her glass to finish the last of her Bacardi and orange juice. "I wonder how much DipTych pays its pigeon-washers?"

Taylor rose and threaded her way around the overturned couch to the kitchen. The living room was, like all houses of this sort, impossibly high-ceilinged, framed enormously as if intending to make the house look empty even if it were crammed full. The walls and molding were all painted blindingly white. The carpet and drapes were beige. The overall effect was one of profound sterility. At least it had been. Now it was livened by the faint scent of ferret.

Daemon followed Taylor to the kitchen, and Hermes followed Daemon, tackling him on the tile while Taylor refilled two glasses from the carton of orange juice in the fridge.

"All done. You take that end," Aimee said when Taylor got back to the living room.

They flipped the couch back over.

Hermes and Daemon leapt up and restarted their game of tag along the sofa back.

"I guess what I don't understand is why you stick with a job you hate."

"I don't exactly *hate* it hate it."

"You hate it." Aimee would not let her confidence be shaken. "You don't think you hate it, because if you let knowing how evil it is enter your awareness, you'd run from the place screaming."

"I'm not sure it's really evil, more like . . . I dunno. Misguided."

Aimee laughed. "It's evil. Shall we order a pizza?"

"Yup."

Aimee put her feet up on the coffee table and opened her phone. "Speaking of hating DipTych—hey, I'd like to order a medium pie."

Taylor waited until Aimee had hung up. "You were saying?"

"About what?"

"Something about hating DipTych."

"Oh yeah. We're going after them."

"Who is?"

"A coalition of anti-de-globalization activists, in solidarity with Mexican Americans."

"Anti-de-globalization?" Perhaps the Bacardi was fogging Taylor's brain.

"Right." Daemon had climbed onto Aimee's lap and she stroked the ferret's tail. "You see, by putting the factory in Borschtchester, DipTych is depriving Mexicans of the jobs they could have if the factory were in Mexico."

"I see."

"Typical behemoth corporation. Like I said. Evil."

"I dunno if I should join this one, Aimee."

"We're going to have TV. crews there. You'd get fired for sure. But if you didn't want to get fired, you could always wear a disguise. What's the matter?"

Taylor had put down her drink.

"What's the matter, Taylor?"

"I don't know. DipTych. It's not like I love my job or anything. But—"

"Oh geez. Look, I said, you don't need to do it. I understand. I don't want you to get fired. You've invited me on an all-expense-paid trip to the Caribbean next winter, remember?"

"No. It's not that. It's worse."

"Worse?"

"Well. In a way."

"C'mon. Out with it."

"When you doing this?"

"Two weeks from Monday." Aimee stood up. "Another rum and OJ?"

"In a minute." Two weeks from Wednesday. So . . . the day before Kich-

N-World.

"Geez, Taylor, you're going all weird on me." Aimee set her empty glass back down and studied her friend's face.

"I feel kind of sorry for Darryl, that's all."

"Ah."

"Don't you believe me?"

"Nope." Aimee shook her head. "Nope. I don't. Why would you care that some DipTych lifetimer has another bad day?"

Taylor sighed. "I dunno."

"You know what I think? I think that job is getting to you. You need to quit."

"I can't quit. Not yet. Mom—"

"How is Brenda going to even know?"

"She keeps track of me, Aimee. You know that. Somehow."

"Darryl is probably her paid informant."

"I think Darryl is a genuinely nice guy."

"So help him out. Tell him about the protest."

Now it was Taylor's turn to do the face-studying. But after a minute she said, "I couldn't do that."

"Why not?"

"I'm on your side, not DipTych's side."

Aimee shrugged. "It's not like they can do anything to stop us."

"Still." Taylor stood up, restless. Where had she put her purse? Money, to pay the pizza guy. "It wouldn't feel right."

Weird, to find her loyalty divided like that. But of course the job was changing her. How could it not?

# GREAT PLANS GONE AWRY

*"Taylor? Well, you know. She was pretty young, pretty inexperienced. Would I have hired her? Probably not. But, you know, we're all professionals. And mentoring is part of the job. So I showed her the ropes, I made sure she had what she needed to, you know, succeed in her job, because that was my job."*

—Basil Bane

It was a non-problem, Taylor decided the next morning.

She was wearing a new suit she'd bought over the weekend. Well, not a suit, exactly. The pieces were separates—a pinstriped taupe jacket, a black skirt with a little flair at the bottom.

She washed her hands, smelling the chemically scent of the industrial grade soap DipTych used in its bathroom soap dispensers, then bent toward the mirror to re-tie the scarf around her neck—it was new, too, paisley, mix of blues and taupes, added a bit of color to her ensemble.

I'm a chameleon, she thought to herself as she straightened back up and smoothed a lock of hair back behind her ear. I'm here lounging in the DipTych environs, blending in, but loyalty? Nah.

Heck, she just might join that anti-deglobalization protest after all. They had a point—it was a disappointment, DipTych pulling those projected jobs away from Mexico like that.

But the thought of being caught at the protest made her nervous again . . .

She pushed the nervousness away. She had a lot of work to do. She needed a cup of coffee.

"You're here early."

Taylor started. She was pouring water into the top of the coffee maker to start the first pot of the day, she hadn't heard Darryl walk up.

Damn, she was jumpy.

"Yeah," she said. "I have so much to do."

There was a stack of Styrofoam cups upended on the little table that served as the department's coffee service. Darryl took a cup now from the stack. "It's a real grind, leading up to Kich-N-World. Always is."

She glanced over. He had dark circles under his eyes. Did the man ever look rested?

"This will be my fifteenth." He dumped a spoonful of non-dairy creamer into his cup. "My fifteenth Kich-N-World."

Taylor took a cup from the stack herself. A stream of coffee hissed down into the pot.

"But knock on wood, the cannery deal will be our last big surprise."

Taylor put the cup back. Wait, what the hell was she doing? She picked it back up again.

She could smell the coffee now.

"So what are you working on this morning?"

She looked over at him again. "The, uh, press kit. Legal said they'd get their changes to me."

He nodded, then pulled the pot from the burner and nodded at her to hold out her cup so he could fill it. "Room for cream?" He smiled, one corner of his mouth high because of course it wasn't really cream.

"Darryl. There's something that . . ."

Oh cripes, what was she doing?

He looked at her—and it was already too late, she'd already given too much away—he still looked exhausted but she'd alarmed him, she could see it in his eyes.

She winced, miserable. "I heard a, uh, rumor."

Darryl set the coffee pot down without filling his cup.

Taylor, you're an idiot. But it's too late now, isn't it. Idiot. She drew a breath. "It might be nothing. But over the weekend, I heard from someone that, uh, well, there's a protest, being organized, about the cannery."

"Oh. What sort of protest."

"Some people are upset, the way I heard it, because DipTych is bringing jobs back into the U.S. that were going to be in Mexico."

Darryl looked at her, blinking. "Do you know who is involved?"

"I hear it's partly Borschtchester's Hispanic community." She drew another breath. "I heard it's part of a growing anti-de-globalization movement."

Darryl's thin slumpy shoulders slumped even further.

"When?" he said.

She told him the date.

"So right before the show."

"Yeah." The DipTych coffee was never exactly tasty, but the smell of it now was turning Taylor's stomach. She looked back up at Darryl, and he met her eyes as if searching in them for what to do next.

"Okay," he said finally. "I'll look into it. Hey, Taylor."

"Yeah?"

"Keep this quiet for now, would you?"

"Sure."

He glanced around, but it wasn't even 7 a.m. yet, they were the only ones there. "I have some challenges . . . with some of the staff. Morale issues."

She nodded, but he wasn't done. He leaned slightly toward her and caught her eyes with his again.

"Certain individuals tend to panic and upset the others."

Basil. She nodded again.

"So if you wouldn't mind—"

"No worries," she told him, and watched as he walked off with that wobbly gait of his.

She felt positively sick.

And yet . . . it wasn't all bad, was it? To have done poor Darryl a bit of a favor?


She was back at her desk, waiting for her computer to boot, when her phone rang.

Darryl.

Was she was free at 10? Because he was going to meet with Rocco, and they wanted her to join them.

She looked at her online calendar.

"I have a meeting with Basil then, to review Legal's input to the press release."

"Damn it," Darryl said.

She knew why. Because if she cancelled, Basil would ask questions. He'd want to know what could possibly be more important than her meeting with him.

"Taylor, I know this is unusual. But Rocco—Rocco was pretty clear he wanted you there. Do you think you could figure out a way to . . . could you make some excuse?"

What could she do? "Sure, yeah, Darryl, I'll figure something out."

"Do you know where Rocco's office is? Seventh floor."

"Okay. See you at ten."

She hung up the phone.

Eighteen new emails—this was since she last checked right before she left yesterday at 6:30.

She scanned them, and good news—there was the email from Legal. With an attachment—good. This would be their input into the EasyCan press release.

She opened document.

She stared.

Line after line of document text had been slashed out.

She scanned the text bubbles in the margin that explained the edits. Apparently there were serious legal ramifications for using many of the vocabulary words she'd incorporated into the release. "Cannot say 'innovative' unless substantiate with data." "Cannot say 'revolutionary,' see above." " "Do not make comparisons to competitor products." So much for the paragraph suggesting that consumers were frustrated by the limited functionality of conventional can openers. "Might be construed as reference to Britch."

Was there not a single paragraph untouched?

Taylor began hunting for the words that had been left untouched.

There were three of them.

And.

The.

Can.

Basil was going to throw a fit.

Basil! Oh crap, that's right. She had a 10 o'clock with him. That she needed to skip . . .

The little clock in the right hand corner of her computer screen read 8:12.

How was she going to pull this one off . . .

Her coffee was untouched. And tepid.

Voices wafted over the tops of the cubicles. People were starting to arrive, greet each other. Sounded like there was a group of them at the coffee service table.

She looked at her clock again. 8:15.

Basil generally got there at 9 or 9:30. She had an hour, maybe, to figure out what to do.

If she didn't replace her coffee now, the pot she'd made would be empty. And she'd no doubt be the one who would have to make another.

She stood up. Then cocked her ear. Was that Miles' voice she heard?

Maybe he could help her come up with a plan to dodge Basil?

Then she remembered the other thing—that this whole mess had started when she'd snitched on the anti-deglobalization people . . . no! Not snitched. Hadn't Aimee said it was no big deal?

But remembering that she knew she couldn't say anything about it to Miles. What he would think, if he knew . . .

Ugh.

What a mess.

She looked sadly at her tepid coffee.

She listened again.

Then she pushed back from her desk and stood up.


Too late.

The coffee pot was empty.

It smelled like burnt grounds.

"Aw sheet. Gone already?" Marsha Wainwright, US Sales Channel Manager.

Taylor nodded.

"You making another?"

"Yeah."

"Guess what I just heard." Marsha grinned. She had a little daub of lipstick on her front right incisor. "You know that guy who fell from the roof?"

"What about him."

"Million dollar settlement."

Taylor's eyes widened appreciatively. "No kidding."

"Out of court. But I wouldn't be surprised if that's what he got. At least."

"So then it must be true." Taylor shut off the coffee pot burner. "That they made him go up there to chase off the pigeons."

"Yep. And guess what else." Marsha leaned toward Taylor and grinned again.

"What?"

"You know the first person that got to him after he fell, Amber somebody?"

Orsen, the pudgy guy who worked for Marsha, had walked up. "Hey, is there any coffee?"

"Taylor's making it," said Marsha. "So you know who I'm talking about, right? Scally's admin?"

"Oh, I heard about this!" Orsen laughed.

"They're getting married," Marsha said. "Amber and million dollar settlement guy."

"You're kidding me."

"He 'fell' in love that day. Get it?" said Orsen.

"No, he 'fell' in rich, she fell in love," Marsha said. "She quit her job. She quit her job, and she and the maintenance guy are flying to Vegas to get married."

Taylor shook her head. "Isn't he still in, like, a body cast?"

"Nah, it's a walking cast. And anyway, so what? Love will find a way."

"One minute, was inches from a grisly death," said Orsen. "Next minute, rich, and on his way to Vegas to get laid."

"Almost makes you want to play around on the roofs of tall buildings, doesn't it," Marsha said.

But Taylor was no longer paying attention. She'd heard a noise, coming from the direction of Basil's cubicle. It couldn't be him, yet. He was never in this early. Right?

It was the sound of a chair creaking—the sound a creaking chair makes when someone is rousing himself, standing up . . .

She put the coffee pot back on the burner.

"Something's up with Taylor," Marsha said as they watched her disappear around a cubical corner. "She's all stressed." She looked at Orsen and lowered her voice. "The Basil Effect. Hey, I think it might be your turn to make the coffee."

Okay. So she'd do it by email. Right?

Sure! She'd cancel the meeting by email. That way, she wouldn't have to actually speak to Basil about it. So she wouldn't have to lie.

Easy, right?

Sure!

She clicked "send."

Done.

It was 9:02.

She pushed her chair back from her desk again.

Yeah, that had been easy.

But the next part would be anything but.

Because now she had to stay out of Basil's way for the next fifty eight minutes.

She couldn't stay in her cubicle, that was for sure—that would be the first place he would look.

But if not her cube, where?

Hmmmm. Ladies' room . . .

But she didn't make it.

In retrospect, it was a timing error. If she'd waited until Basil was settled into his office, it would have been simple.

But she was nervous, not thinking clearly. And being there in her cube—it made it worse, she felt trapped.

She needed to make a break for it.

So she did.

And practically ran into him—she rounded a corner, and there he was, at the other end of the aisle, headed right toward her.

He'd seen her. He was lifting his hand, he was gesturing!

She whirled, ducked back the way she'd come, back toward her office, past her office—there was an empty one two cubical openings down. Nobody in sight. She slipped in and crouched against the wall.

Noises. Rustling. Footsteps. Someone coughing in the next aisle down. More footsteps.

Then Basil's voice—very close. "Sherry, did you see Taylor come by here?"

They were just outside Taylor's hiding spot.

"Nope," Sherry said.

"Do me a favor, if you see her, let her know I need to speak with her before our ten o'clock."

So he hadn't gotten the cancellation notice yet.

She let her breath out, easy.

Great. So now she had to avoid two people—Sherry and Basil.

Could this get any worse?

She slumped against the wall.

Desk phone ringing. Close by. Nobody picked up. Know why? Because that was Taylor's phone. And she knew who it was—it was Basil. He'd gotten her meeting cancellation and was calling her to find out what was going on.

Well. She couldn't sit here much longer. It had to be nearly 9:30 by now.

Which meant it was no longer merely a question of hiding.

She also had to figure out a way to get to either a stairway or a foyer, without being seen, before 10 o'clock.

The stairs were closer.

But they were right next to Basil's office.

And the elevator was on the other side of the building from where she was hiding.

She cocked her head to listen again.

Things sounded quiet out there.

She poked her head out into the aisle.

And then she noticed Conference Room 3B, down there at the end of the aisle. It was dark. And it gave her an idea. The conference rooms were located around the perimeter of the floor. So all she had to do was leapfrog, conference room to conference room, and she'd be free.

She darted down the hall and stepped into the waiting darkness of Conference Room 3B.

But she was not the only one in the room.

"Hey, protest girl. Who you running from?"

# TAYLOR MEETS A CEILING FIXTURE

*"Yes, if you want to put it that way. We are against the stoppage of the exporting of jobs."*

—Diamond Menendez, Leader,
Borschtchester Anti-De-Globalization Movement

It was Miles, of course—on the other side of the room, sitting in one of the conference table chairs.

"What—" She remembered, then, that she was, in fact, hiding, and said the rest in a whisper. "—are you doing here?"

"Meditating. Maybe. But you still haven't answered my question. Only I bet I can guess."

"Shhh, please—not so loud!"

He laughed.

"Miles, really, please?"

"What's ol' Baz after you for?"

"It's not funny, Miles. I had a meeting with him and I can't make it."

"Here's an idea. Tell him sorry, Baz, I've got better things to do than listen to your fat lips flap this morning."

"I can't tell him that. He's my boss."

"Then you could just dodge him until he forgets about it."

"Hello? That might be why I'm here, instead of in my—oh my god, what time is it? do you have a watch?"

"Who wears a watch?" Miles flipped open a cell. "9:39. Take the day off, then, if you don't want to keep your appointments with the Baz man."

"I've only been here six weeks. I can't ask for time off."

"Who said you should ask?"

"Anyway, I can't. I have another meeting."

"Really."

"Really. And the problem is . . ."

"Go ahead, you can tell me."

She shook her head. How could she tell him? It was too . . . mixed up.

"Taylor, really. It's okay. I specialize in solving damsels' problems."

"I just . . . I need to get to the elevator foyer in about fifteen minutes, and Darryl—I've been asked not to discuss the purpose of my next meeting with Basil. That's all."

Her stomach had twisted up a bit again.

"Ah, we can only hope that means that Baz is about to get the ax, and you're going to ascend into his notch on the DipTych bedpost."

"That's a very weird metaphor."

He grinned. "Like it?"

"Shh!"

Footsteps, talking—it was Sherry, talking to someone.

They passed by the conference room door.

"So what's the plan, protest girl."

"To go from conference room to conference room, I guess."

"Bad plan."

She looked at him. "Why?"

"Because there's a meeting of sales reps going on right now in E.

She understood instantly what he meant. Conference Room 3E was in the corner of the building—the last corner before the elevator. Without it as an interim hiding spot, she'd have no way of reconnoitering the area around the elevator foyer before she made her final dash.

"I could go the other direction?"

But that would take her past Basil's office.

"There's another option."

She looked at him again.

"C'mere."

She didn't move.

"I won't bite."

"I don't understand."

"Trust me, Taylor."

She circled around the conference room table, unknotted her scarf from her neck and handed it to him.

"Why do you wear these anyway?"

"I don't know. Miles—"

"They're silly."

"Thanks."

"I mean it. With a beautiful woman, less is always more."

"Stop it. And give me back my scarf, please."

"All the way down to skin, in fact, if you ask me."

"Stop it, Miles. What are you doing?"

Miles was holding both ends of the scarf and spinning it to wind it into a rope. Then he snapped it upward, at the corner ceiling tile over his head.

"What exactly are you doing?" Taylor hissed to keep her voice from becoming too loud.

Miles snapped the ceiling tile again. "Jelly!" he whispered loudly. "Jelly, you there?"

The ceiling tile moved. Then lifted away and slid off to the side.

A face appeared in the hole. Thin face, thin moustache, dark eyes.

"'Sup, Miles?"

"Can you transport something for me from here to the hall outside the elevator, delivery time 9:57?"

"Yep."

Miles pushed his chair over so it was beneath the hole in the ceiling. "Taylor."

"What are you—"

"Up."

She stood on the chair. A wiry arm reached down and clasped hers, and Miles cupped his hands to make a footstep.

A moment later she was lifted up and was inside the ceiling.

"Here's your scarf." Miles balled the scarf and tossed it up into the hole. The wiry man grabbed it out of the air and passed it to Taylor.

"Miles! I can't just—"

"You want to dodge Bane, don't you? Don't worry. Jelly will take care of you. Jelly?"

"I'll scope things and let you know when coast is clear."

"Sure thing, man."

The wiry man replaced the ceiling tile.

It was pitch black for a second, then he switched on a flashlight.

It was mounted on his forehead, like the kind of light spelunkers use.

"Follow me," he whispered. "Stay on the boards. You don't want to fall through the ceiling."

Then he turned away from her—which made the flashlight point away from her as well.

"Wait! I can't see!"

"Here." He pulled the flashlight off of his head and handed it to her. She put in on. "You go first."

Ahead of him, and with the light on her head, she saw a makeshift catwalk. 1x4s. Big gaps between.

There was maybe four feet of clearance between it and the subfloor above. She began moving forward on her hands and knees.

The boards were rough. She was glad she hadn't worn nylons.

"See the cushions," Jelly said.

Couch cushions. Lined up against a wall. Taylor climbed to the last cushion in the row and sat.

Jelly sat on the other end.

"I was taking a nap," he said.

The cushions were still warm.

"You can turn that off."

She felt around for the switch on the flashlight and flicked it.

It was pitch black again for a minute. Then she could start to see. Some light from the room below—were they over cubicles now? Must be—seeped in between the ceiling tiles. Just enough that she could make out a tangle of beams and pipes and wires.

They sat.

"Do you think I'm strange?" the wiry man said in a low voice.

"I—uh. No." It wasn't really a lie. Hiding up above the ceiling, now that was strange. The wiry man was rather normal, given the context.

"I think I'm strange," he said. "But then, I've never seen faces come out of the rain. Are you going with Miles?"

"No."

"Are you available?"

"No."

"You say 'no' a lot," he said. "Shh. Someone's coming."

"Hey Basil." Miles' voice—almost directly underneath them.

And then Basil's. "Have you seen Taylor? She's not picking up her phone."

"About 5 minutes ago. She was looking for you."

"Was she."

"Yeah. I think Darryl is, too."

"Darryl? What could he want. I just spoke with him."

"Dunno. But I heard him talking to himself while he was walking by my office not five minutes ago. 'Where is that fat ass,' he said."

"Shut up, asshole."

"Oh, sorry, you're right. He didn't say 'fat ass.' It was 'lard ass.'"

"Go to hell."

"Meet ya there."

Silence.

"Miles, he's funny," Jelly said. "He don't take no shit."

Taylor's legs were getting stiff. She shifted her weight, taking care to keep her skirt tucked tightly around her thighs. "I don't see how I can hide up here like this."

"Don't worry about it. Miles comes up here all the time. When he needs to get around without talking to people."

"Do you live up here?" Now that her eyes were fully adjusted, she'd seen a coffee maker on some boards across from the cushions. And some plastic supermarket bags with stuff in them.

"Nah. I have an apartment."

"What—why . . ."

"I'm a maintenance engineer."

"What do you mean?"

"What do you mean, what do I mean?"

"You're a maintenance engineer for DipTych?"

"Fifteen years next spring. Pay's real good."

"Doesn't anybody realize you're up here instead of working?"

"I get my work done. Enough. It's cool."

Jelly pressed the button on his watch to light it up, so he check the time.

Ha, so much for "who wears a watch." Miles might not, but the maintenance guy who lives in the ceiling—different story.

"C'mon, we better get going." Jelly pointed. "That way."

Taylor switched on her light and began crawling again. "Can you get anywhere in the building?"

"Pretty much. Wanna go spy on Scally?"

"You can get to other floors?"

"Yep."

"How?"

"Elevator. Wanna go spy on Scally?"

"No!"

He laughed. "Turn right."

She turned right.

Her hands felt gritty and her knees hurt.

"Okay, stop."

"What time is it?"

Jelly checked his watch again. "9:55 on the button." The light from his watch shown upward and blue against his thin face. "Miles should give us the all clear any second."

And sure enough, he'd barely finished whispering when they heard Miles again. "Okay, Jelly. Let's get her down."

Jelly moved a tile and she peered down.

Wow, the floor was a long way away.

Miles was looking up at her. He had a little beard stubble, like he wore sometimes—she hadn't noticed when they were together in the conference room, with the lights out.

"I'm . . . I'm wearing a skirt," she whispered down to him.

He made his arms into a cradle shape. "Oh well—better hurry, protest girl, Basil's looking all over for you."

Ugh. Better to break her neck jumping down from the ceiling than be caught by Basil.

She turned and let her legs through—absolutely no way she could be ladylike in this position, damn it—felt Miles hands now, on her calves and then her thighs and then he was catching her by the hips as she dropped, easing her to the floor as neatly as if she were a dancer.

She smoothed her skirt back into place.

"You've picked up a bit of dust." He brushed her jacket with his hand and she bent over, brushing the dust smudges from her skirt.

Then she looked up. The ceiling tile was back in place.

"I didn't get to thank him."

"I'll let him know. You'd better get going."

He was right. Standing there, they were out of the line of anyone walking that way—but it wouldn't do to linger too long.

Plus her meeting upstairs was about to start.

"What floor you need?"

"Seven."

Miles pressed the up button.

"Is he really a DipTych employee?"

"Jelly? Sure."

"He kind of put a move on me up there."

"And?"

"What do you mean, 'and.'"

"Hey, don't be too hasty, he's loaded."

"He's not loaded."

"He is."

"He's a janitor."

"He shorted Bear Stearns."

"He what?"

"He borrows books on stock trading from the exec offices. He's a kind of stock trading savant."

"You're joking."

"He can't just sleep up there in the ceiling all day. So he reads."

"Nobody notices when books are missing?"

The elevator doors slid open.

"He returns them. And anyway, people don't notice things that don't make sense. If there's no logical way a book could disappear one day and reappear the next, blip. Your mind just blips it out."

Taylor stepped into the elevator. "How did you find him up there?"

"Oh, I didn't meet him here." Miles reached out an arm to keep the elevator doors from closing. "I bought him a drink once at Loopy's. He's also a bit of an alchy. I see him in there all the time. He rides a bike to work year round and stops at different bars on his way home. I run into him there once a month or so."

"Only now he buys you drinks."

"Oh no, I still buy."

"But he's loaded, you said."

"We look out for each other."

"He hides you too sometimes. He said so."

"Sometimes."

"A rich alcoholic janitor that lives in the ceiling."

"He doesn't live there. He just hangs out during his shift."

"I don't understand how he's never been caught."

"I told you. People don't notice things that don't make any sense."

Miles let go of the doors so they could shut, and waved.

"Give my best to Rocco," he said.

# DAMAGE, CONTROLLED

*"DipTych Corporation Announces New Scholarship for Latinos"*

—Press release headline, DipTych website

The ceilings on the seventh floor were easily twice as high as they were on the third, which served to midgetized Taylor, and the thickness of the carpet soaked up the sound of her footsteps so even that was diminished as she walked down the hallway.

The name of each occupant's office was engraved on a removable gold-tone plate mounted on a slotted housing next to each door. Taylor peered at them as they walked.

Then came to the plate with Rocco Pinnoccho on it.

She tapped on the door's dark faux oak.

"Come in."

She stepped through the door.

It was Rocco who had spoken, and as she stepped inside the office there he was . . . and how small he looked behind his desk—she stopped herself, horrified. Because if she noticed such a thing, her noticing might leak out and it was the sort of observation you would not want your boss's boss to detect.

Fortunately Rocco was standing, gesturing at her to sit.

There were two chairs in front of his desk. Darryl was in one of them.

"So," Rocco said when she was seated. "Why don't we start again at the top."

Darryl repeated what Taylor had told him, lifting his arm when he was done and passing his shirtsleeve over his brow.

Rocco didn't look at Darryl as his director spoke. His eyes were flicking back and forth across his computer screen.

"It doesn't look like anything has been picked up on this locally," he said. He glanced at Taylor. "Tiffany, right? So tell me, where did you find out about this, what is it?"

"Anti-deglobalization," Darryl said.

"Anti-deglobalization," Rocco nodded.

Taylor forced herself not to squirm. "It's a rumor I heard—I can't recall exactly where—one of my friends had heard about it."

Rocco frowned. "It could be nothing."

Taylor glanced at Darryl. This was her out, then—to say sure, it's probably nothing. Yeah, nothing, I've gone and wound up my boss and my boss's boss over a big nothing . . .

"What kind of media attention do you suppose it would get, if it turns out to be more than just a rumor?" Rocco switched now from his computer to his Blackberry, and was studying it, thumbing through his emails.

Taylor wasn't sure who was supposed to answer the question—but then she realized that Rocco was no longer looking at his Blackberry.

He was looking at her.

"You're our PR person, right?" he said. "So? What's the risk."

She cleared her throat. "Well. Worst case . . ." She considered for a moment how Aimee might view the issue. "Worst case, it will look like DipTych has ruined the lives of hundreds of poor working Mexican families"

Rocco scowled. "You think the media—we're creating jobs here, for cripesake."

"You asked for worst case," Darryl reminded him.

"Right." Rocco set his Blackberry down. "Remember the freaks smashing windows at the WTO protests in Seattle?"

Taylor moved uncomfortably. "Maybe it'll just . . . die down. These things don't always take off."

She glanced at Darryl again.

Then Rocco's phone rang.

Darryl and Taylor sat, listening to half a conversation.

"Where have you been? No. No . . . Sunday morning. Well it would have been—. Fine. Right . . . the Hispanic vote, I know . . . that's exactly what we're doing. 7:45. Right."

Rocco hung up.

"That," he said, "was Bo Valgus. Who, as you know, has been a staunch supporter of the cannery." He looked at Taylor. "Apparently, your intelligence is accurate, Tiffany. They're planning to form a human chain across Beet Street."

"That will do it," Darryl said.

"It's time to call Hedy."

Taylor saw Darryl out of the corner of his eye. He was swallowing rapidly and the color had drained from his face.

Taylor had Darryl react similarly to that name before. The man definitely had some sort of problem with Hedy Fusee.

Rocco stood up. "Darryl, you'd better stay."

Meaning Taylor had better go.

She stood up.

"Appreciate all your help here, Tiffany," Rocco said as she let herself out of the door.


"Well?"

"Well, what?"

"How'd it go?"

Taylor glanced over her shoulder.

They were standing by the coffee service table—for the third time this morning, Taylor was trying to get a cup of coffee.

There was about a half cup left.

It looked like it had been sitting in the pot for at least an hour. Meaning it was slightly more viscous than warm tar.

She poured it into a cup, took a sip, and wrinkled her nose.

"Hey, you're not being very forthcoming, protest girl."

She avoided Miles eyes. And not only because they were so disarmingly cute. "I'm not supposed to talk about it," she said.

"Basil's still looking for you."

She sighed.

"The good news is, he has an eleven o'clock. So if you elude capture for the next fifteen minutes or so, you're safe until after lunch."

"Where is he now, do you know?"

"Back at his desk. He'll be there for at least the next five minutes."

"You're looking a bit of the devil now, Miles. What did you do?"

"Oh, nothing much. Just forwarded some documents he needs to review ay-sap."

She sighed again. "I just wish I could check my email. You can't believe how many emails I get."

"Come on. You can check from my computer. This way."

They were back by the elevator.

"Wait a minute, where do you sit?"

"Fourth floor."

That explains why she'd never seen his office.

"Why don't you sit with the rest of us?"

"I don't work just for Darryl. I'm a floating asset."

The stepped into the elevator.

"Miles?"

"Yeah." He pressed the button for the fourth floor.

"I have a question."

"Shoot."

"What's the big deal with Hedy Fusee?"

"Ah. You haven't met Hedy."

"No."

"Hedy Fusee is the PR brains behind the DipTych empire. Also spectacularly hot."

Taylor decided to let the last remark pass. But also wondered what sort of woman Miles would consider spectacularly hot . . .

"This way," he pointed to the left outside the elevator.

The fourth floor looked exactly like the third floor, only the color scheme was grays and blues, instead of grays and greens.

They got to Miles' cubicle.

"Make yourself at home."

She looked around. "Your office is . . . neat."

"Yeah?"

"More neat than I would've thought for, you know. An anarchist."

"Shows what you know about anarchy."

"What do you mean, about Hedy Fusee being the brains behind DipTych?"

"How long do you have?"

She probably had seventy five new emails. But they could wait . . . "About five minutes."

"Okay, short version, then. Throw away everything you ever thought about DipTych, or for that matter Borschtchester. This town is nothing more than a toybox for Fusee & Madelaine."

"Oh, come on."

"Hear me out. First, there's not a politician or business in this town that doesn't owe Hedy Fusee something. Second, she's got the master blueprint of all Borschtchester's dirty laundry chutes. You look skeptical."

"I am extremely freaking skeptical."

"Okay. The Performing Arts Centre. Where did that come from."

"The arts community wanted a better venue for theater productions."

"Wrong. It's a sloppy old-fashioned threeway. D'Signario's Contracting, the city, and our very own Bo Valgus. And guess who gets paid every time any one of them moves a muscle."

"Fusee & Madelaine?"

"Bingo."

"So don't tell me, Miles, Fusee & Madelaine were doing the marketing campaign for the FairARTS! Centre—"

"You're catching on."

"So the billboards, the stuff painted on the sides of the city buses—"

Miles nodded. "See, if you were my girlfriend, I'd kiss you now."

Best ignore that one, too. "Wait a minute. If Hedy's so good, why would she let the FairARTS! Centre get scuttled for the DipTych cannery?"

"Okay, I'm not going to kiss you. What did I say about her making money?"

"Oh. Right. She handles DipTych PR."

"Exactly. So what does she care if FairARTS! goes down? She's just trading in one gig for another."

"So that's why they didn't let Digital handle the cannery."

"Exactly. Of course, you have to do all the work. But the strategy, the creative—the project management. All the big bucks stuff, that's what Fusee & Madelaine does."

Taylor looked around the cubical again. "Geez, Miles. Your pencils."

He had a row of pencils on his desk.

"What about my pencils?"

"They're in a perfect line. And they're sorted. Shortest to longest."

"So we're done with the Fusee & Madelaine discussion, I take it."

"The only thing I still don't understand is why Darryl gets so upset whenever anybody mentions them."

Miles shrugged. "He probably thinks Rocco will fire him and just let Fusee & Madelaine do his job."

"Makes sense. More sense than—" She grinned. "An obsessive compulsive anarchist."

"You seem to be under the wrong impression about anarchism."

"Oh no, I know exactly what anarchism is. It's a political theory that espouses a stateless society."

"Nothing there about being neat. Anyway, I became an anarchist mostly as a way to meet chicks." He grinned again. Disarmingly. "So you looked it up, huh?"

"Don't change the subject. It occurs to me that your life is a mass of contradictions."

"Isn't everyone's?"

She shook her head. "Not mine. Mine doesn't rise to that level of organization. It's more like barely controlled chaos."

"Your problem is you're taking your job too seriously."

Taylor shrugged.

"You probably spend more time with Basil than you do with your best friend."

She started. Wasn't that pretty much what she'd said to Aimee the other day? Pretty much word for word?

"Am I right?"

Taylor didn't answer.

"You don't have to, you know."

"Have to what?"

"Take it seriously."

"It's not like I have a choice."

"You always have a choice. Want to check your email?"

But she didn't. At all. She wanted out of there. So she shook her head. "You know, it's nearly eleven, now. I'm going to head back."

"Taylor. What was your meeting about, with Rocco?"

If she told him, he would know what she was.

And what was that?

Someone who had no idea what she stood for.

But guess what. He was bound to find out sooner or later. As soon as this afternoon, in fact—as soon as Rocco and Darryl and Hedy Fusee figured out what they were going to do for anti-deglobalization damage control, Miles would easily figure out that they'd found out about it from Taylor.

Confess and get it over with.

"I didn't really mean to," she whispered. "But I feel sorry for Darryl."

"He seems to have that effect on the chicks."

"And I let something slip."

"You betrayed The Movement." Stated as a fact, not a question.

"Aimee told me they're planning an anti-deglobalization rally."

She looked at him.

"Protest girl," he said. "I was wrong about you."

"How so?" she whispered.

"You don't take your job too seriously."

"I don't?"

"You take it waaaaaaaaaaaaaay too seriously."

"I'm just trying to . . ." But she couldn't finish the sentence—she wasn't really sure what she was trying to do. "Look, I'd better go. Thanks for helping me hide this morning."

"Any time, protest girl."

# A WOMAN'S PLACE

*"He did my kitchen and yeah, what they say about him is true. Oh, I don't mean his looks! Although that's all true too! I mean the quality of his work. I live in an older home, you know? Built in 1912. When I moved in, there wasn't a 90 degree angle in the place. But the kitchen today—it looks like something out of a magazine, if you know what I mean."*

—Bailey Summerbun, Borschtchester resident

"What is this? What is this?"

Bo looked around the kitchen, aghast.

It was in a shambles. No. "shambles" didn't begin to describe it. The island was a pile of rubble half-covering a gaping hole in the floor. The cupboard doors were hanging open—exposing the interior of the cupboards, which were empty. Beneath his feet—he stood in the hallway leading to the kitchen entrance—drop cloths.

The chalky smell of dust powdered the inside of his nose.

Dahlia was standing with her back to him, plugging a food processor into an outlet that had been stripped bare of its cover plate.

"Oh, I've hired Trevor to re-do our kitchen."

"What?"

Dahlia turned toward him, shrugging. "You said he has a couple of months before he'll have to start working on the cannery, right?"

Bo stared. "But you—the bathroom."

"Oh, he'll get that done too, he says he's got plenty of bandwidth to handle both. You can close your mouth now, Bo, you'll breathe flies with that thing hanging open like that."

"Dahlia. Are you sure this was a good idea?"

She shrugged again. "I've wanted a new kitchen for yeeeeears."

Bo swallowed. What could he do? Really. What could a man do.

"And you said he'll work out just fine, now that he's got that cannery bathroom deal."

"But what if—I thought you were sick to death of our home being a construction zone." If he lived to be a thousand, he would never understand that woman.

"Oh. It's fine! I'm fine with it."

Bo staggered back, turned, was about to leave the room, leave Dahlia to her—and then another thought struck him.

What if this wasn't about a new kitchen?

What if it was about . . . Trevor Mancely?

He turned back again to face his wife.

She was at the refrigerator now, opening the door, and humming.

"I'm going to make a salad," she said. "Want one?"

"Dahlia?"

The tone of his voice caught her attention, this time, and she shut the door and looked at him.

"What's the matter, Bo? Are you okay?"

"Dahlia."

Her brow creased and she crossed the room to him.

"What is it?"

"Dahlia, I have to ask you a question. And I want you to be one hundred percent honest with me."

Was that alarm in her eyes?

But it didn't matter.

He had to know.

"It's about Trevor Mancely."

He studied her face as he said the name.

"What about him, Bo?"

Bo cleared his throat. No turning back now. "Look, Dahlia. We're both adults. Trevor Mancely is a very . . . good-looking man. And as we both know, he's—he is single."

Dahlia looked at him blankly for a moment.

Then she burst out laughing.

"Bo!"

He felt his face redden.

"Bo Valgus. Do you think—"

But she couldn't get the words out. She was laughing too much.

He cleared his throat again. "He's a very good looking man," he said. "And he's here, with you, in the house, every day."

Dahlia put her hand in front of her mouth to force herself to stop laughing. "Oh, Bo," she said, and put her arms around her husband's fat waist.

"I'm a happily married woman," she said. "And way out of Trevor Mancely's league."

"Dahlia," Bo said into the hair on the top of his wife's head, and they stood in the smashed-up kitchen, smelling drywall, in each other's arms.

# DARRYL CROSSES TO
# THE DARK SIDE

*"Should we have been more careful? Yes, of course. But it was a pressure cooker. Mistakes happen."*

—Darryl Fiegit

To Andrew Spittleton, the corporate world was divided neatly into two categories. On the one hand you had reality itself, a place where science, mathematics, and logic rendered rational any object or event a mind could contemplate. This was Andrew's world. The other was one he summed up, with visible disgust, as "puff." There, objects weren't really objects. They were illusions, tricks. Events had no status in an objective sense, they were elements of some narrative over which players fought for control. It was a world ruled by capriciousness and instability. One day, a thing was described one way; the next, it was called something else. Motives were always suspect and were rooted—naturally—in the desire to make money.

The more he saw of the world of puff, the more hardened he became in his admiration for his own world, his world of data, of the rational. His staff he hardened as well, armoring them, for they were after all the knights assembled around his righteous table. Take The Number, for instance—the $100 million sales target supposedly set by Corporate for the Digital Division. Andrew dismissed it with a contempt so immediate and persuasive that it never even arose, not once, as a topic for discussion in his department, not even as gossip. It didn't exist.

In this way, he maintained his world as a kind of heaven.

Not that the other world didn't intrude sometimes. Which was why, today, Andrew was in a foul mood.

He'd been forced to fire one of his best men, his Head Systems Engineer.

And for a transgression that nobody could articulate with anything approaching clarity. Sure, George had blogged about the team's development progress on the EasyCan project. So what? How could Legal possibly claim he'd disclosed DipTych corporate secrets? It was absurd. Indefensible. Andrew had pressed them, pressed them until his face was crimson under his salt and pepper beard, and they were unable to describe a single, objectively verifiable bit of information that, in the hands of say Britch, would give Britch a measurable competitive advantage.

He'd even considered appealing to Scally. He hadn't, in the end. He wasn't quite sure of how much influence Legal had with Scally. There was the risk, always, that Legal might get its revenge by suggesting that Andrew, too, was culpable for George's questionable blog posts.

And what help could Andrew offer George if his own name was dragged into the mess?

So instead he withdrew, sulked. And focused his energy on helping George find a new job. It wasn't hard. George was a brilliant engineer. He could probably double his salary out on the west coast somewhere.

Andrew finished writing his latest letter of recommendation and hit "Send."

And looked up. Darryl was there. He looked unwell. Disheveled. The third button of his dress shirt was inserted into the fourth buttonhole, and there was an ink stain on his right sleeve.

Andrew considered telling him about the buttoning issue. He rather liked Darryl in a way, knowing full well that the man was too much a misfit to be truly one of Them. But Andrew's mood was foul. Let Darryl make a fool of himself, what did Andrew care?

Darryl sat.

He was there for one reason. They both knew what it was. Darryl wanted Andrew to tell him he'd have a working prototype of EasyCan ready in time for Kich-N-World.

Andrew's lip curled slightly behind his beard. "Our best estimate," he said, "is that we'll have a working prototype in eight to ten weeks."

"Eight to ten weeks." Darryl had heard it. But he needed to say it himself, out loud.

"That's right."

So. The pronouncement was a relief in one way. The trade show, at this point, was just about upon them. It was going to be hard enough to finalize the print materials without also having to dummy up a simulated EasyCan, to finish the nips and tucks and costuming that would be needed to make it pretty enough, dressy enough for such a grand and dramatic entrance. And Darryl was glad as well that he'd no longer have to worry about whether the thing would actually perform at the show, under the scrutiny of potential buyers or the press.

Nor was this the first time that it occurred to Darryl how pleasant it was when his utter powerlessness assumed its rightful place in his life. Powerlessness is only unpleasant when you're expected to fight against it. When the fight is over, and you're forced to succumb—ah, there is a kind of peace. No more choices to make. The worst of the worst has come to pass.

"Fine, I understand," he said. "I discussed this possibility with Rocco, and we agreed we'll go to Plan B. We'll build a virtual demo."

"A virtual demo of what?" Andrew's eyelids fluttered as he spoke.

"EasyCan."

Andrew was too overcome to respond. The best he could do was pull a face depicting his barely suppressed exasperation.

Darryl didn't need to see his expression to know how Andrew was reacting. He kept his gaze fixed on its usual spot—somewhere in the neighborhood of Andrew's shirt pocket. "We can use the schematics."

Andrew shook his head.

Darryl plodded ahead. "The back wall will be an artist's rendering."

"What?"

"An artist's rendering."

"An artist's rendering of what?"

"EasyC—the EasyCan schematics. The concept is da Vinci sketchbook, we'll use a winged flying machine analogy to evoke how EasyCan marks a dramatic Renaissance in canning technology."

Andrew was confident enough there, with his knights assembled just outside his door and the secret patronage of his cousin-in-law's wife that he permitted himself a luxurious snort. "There are no 'schematics.' How can there be schematics when we haven't even solved the LSR quadrant issue."

"They don't have to be—you know. The final schematics. They can be whatever you have now, the working schematics."

Andrew's mouth dropped open so far the end of his carefully trimmed beard nearly touched the tip of the pen in his short pocket.

"Surely you must have something."

"This is engineering, Darryl. It's not . . . fiction. You can't just . . . tell whatever story you feel like telling this week."

"Andrew—"

One of the fluorescent tube lights overhead began to flicker, making the already sickly light strobe vaguely across Andrew's face. "Next," he said, "you'll be telling me you're ready to start manufacturing. Without a design."

He was touching on another sore point. Andrew had not been consulted before the decision to build the cannery in Borschtchester. Another slight, like being made to fire one of his best engineers. Such things add up over time. They make a man wonder if he perhaps has less influence than he thought.

"Believe me," Darryl said. "I'm no fan of the cannery idea either."

"I don't object to having the cannery here. I object to your boss announcing that it will be operational by December."

"Look, Andy, I am with you on this," Darryl said, trying to move himself over to R&D's side of the boundary. "They should have been a little more careful—"

"An understatement." Andrew stood up. "I'm getting a cup of coffee. Do you have everything you need?"

Darryl shook his head, the look of slight panic returning to his face "About Kich-N-World—"

"Fine. I'll be right back." Andrew stood up and left the office.

Darryl slumped back into his chair. Andrew was never easy to deal with, but today—he must be pretty roiled about the cannery thing. Which meant that Darryl might well have to go back to Rocco and tell him there was no schematic.

It was not a conversation Darryl wanted to have.

He hit his chest several times in rapid succession, hard, his hand flattened, like people do when they've swallowed something too dry and irregularly shaped to go down all the way.

He stood up.

He needed water.

Then his shifting and panicked eyes lit on Andrew's briefcase, which was spread open on the desk. There was a sheaf of papers inside.

One sheet in the stack was sticking out.

Darryl could see just enough of the words across the top to read them.

They said RESTRICTED USE.

He leaned forward and pulled at the piece of paper.

It was a drawing, a diagram.

EasyCan.

Darryl jumped up and carefully lifted the papers above the sheet marked RESTRICTED USE. Was there only one drawing? He lifted some more papers to check the page above.

Apparently the answer was yes . . .

He looked at it again. It was crude, a hand drawing rather than a CAD piece. But it was enough.

After all, all they needed was conceptual inspiration, right?

Darryl pulled the sheet free, folded it in half, and slipped it quickly between the last page of his notepad and its cardboard backing.

He sat back down. His heart thudded painfully. He took a breath and wiped his palms on his pant legs.

Footsteps. Andrew's voice, speaking to someone a couple cubicles away.

Then he was back.

Andrew sat down.

Darryl stood up. "We've known each other a long time, Andrew," he said.

"Yeah, right."

"They tell me what to do, I don't have a say in it."

"Ask them if they want a technology that works, or if they'd prefer to spend the next five years running a multi-million dollar product recall."

"I'll pass along your feedback," Darryl said, his voice cracking, as he drew his sports coat back over his narrow shoulders and hustled himself out of there.

# PANTONE AND PARCHMENT

*"You'll never look at cans the same way again."*

—EasyCan brochure copy

She ought to have called in sick.

Classic symptoms. Two days ago, the scratchy throat. Yesterday, the first real wave hit so that by the time she left work she felt like a piece of limp fruit embedded in a gelatin dessert, the world around her rendered bleary, she was unable to breathe naturally, unable to move her arms and legs without an extraordinary effort.

She stopped at a drug store on the way home and stumbled to the pharmacy counter to beg for advice.

A plump twenty something in horned rim glasses came out from behind the counter and escorted Taylor to the aisle paved with over-the-counter cold and flu relief concoctions. She rattled off the pros and cons of different concoction's constituent chemicals.

The plump woman's personal preference seemed to be remedies designed to promote sleep.

"It's going around," she told Taylor when she'd finished, as if knowing that countless others had been struck by the same malady was somehow a comfort. "Knocks people right out. It would be a good idea to get lots of rest." She thrust her hands into the pockets of her white smock and left Taylor to make her decision in solitude.

Back in the drugstore parking lot, Taylor waited as car after car nosed behind hers, blocking her in as they jockeyed for the last remaining spots close to the door. It was quite possible she'd be stuck there forever.

And of course, the lurid purple liquid didn't really do anything. When her alarm's obnoxious beeping roused her again in the morning, she felt vaguely feverish.

She sat on the edge of her tub, soaking tissue after tissue until finally, finally, the contents of her nose petered out.

She stood wearily under the shower and told herself that of course she was fine.

Because the truth was, she couldn't miss a day of work. Not one. She had too much to do.

And especially not today.

Big meeting with Fusee & Madelaine on her schedule that morning.

"Taylor, you are now a full blown DipTych martyr," she muttered as she poured a dose of the second variety of cold medicine she'd bought. This was not the purple, make-you-sleep recipe. This was opposite on the color wheel, a lurid orange. She dumped it down her throat, grateful that the fogged mirror hid her face.

She had no illusions about how she must look that morning.

By the time she got to work the orange colored concoction had kicked in, possibly abetted by her coffee, and the gelatin salad encasing her took on a jittery and surreal quality, as if it had been spiked by accident with something from the cleaning cabinet.


If Taylor had expected to meet any of the Fusee & Madelaine luminaries, the legendary Hedy perhaps, or the terrible Switch—she was sadly mistaken. They were the strategists, the minds behind the revamped EasyCan-plus-cannery launch campaign.

Whereas today's meeting was purely tactical. Today's meeting was conducted by a Fusee & Madelaine lieutenant, one Lawrence McNabb, whose job it was to project manage the launch, to coordinate the efforts of Darryl's staff with those of the agency's.

"So given that we don't have a working prototype to demo at the show, we're taking a conceptual approach," Lawrence told them.

He was running a PowerPoint presentation. The slides were projected on a screen on the conference room wall. Taylor's neck was already cramping because from where she sat, she had to turn her head about 30 degrees to see. The cold medicine had kicked in as well. Her tongue felt sandy. And Miles had looked at her funny when he'd walked in. She must look worse than she realized.

"Our next slide is of the schematic that will be the basis for the visuals."

Lawrence pressed the Enter key on his keyboard.

"Excuse me," Miles said. "What did you say that was?"

Lawrence looked back at the group around the table to figure out who had spoken. "That would be a working schematic of EasyCan," said Lawrence.

"Really," said Miles. "Interesting."

"Let's get on with it," Basil said.

Lawrence put up the next slide. "We've picked a new color scheme based on Pantone 723. We've redone the back wall in parchment-y oranges. The booth vendor is handling production for that—it was tight but looks like they'll be able to make it."

The next slide showed blocks of Pantone color swatches next to a scan of a Da Vinci drawing.

"Very nice," Basil said.

"So Miles," Lawrence said, "now it's up to you to get us some conceptual renderings of the schematic for the press kit collateral and the presentation we'll loop in the booth kiosk. Think we can see something by noon?"

"We've got everything ready for the press kit except the brochure," Basil said.

"Miles?" said Lawrence.

Miles shrugged. "Okay, I guess."

Lawrence looked back at Taylor. "You're planning to distribute the press materials electronically on Monday, right? The day before the show?"

"Yes."

"Should be doable, if Miles comes through for us. I've got a team at the agency on call over the weekend. Basil, you're available, right?"

Taylor stole a look at him.

Ha.

Basil had to work over the weekend and she did not.

There was some justice in the world after all.

The presentation was over.

Darryl was sitting next to Taylor. His head looked large to her, and was lolling slightly like a puppet's when there is no hand inside.


They filed out the door.

"Hey, protest girl," Miles said in Taylor's ear. "You okay? You look funny."

"I'll live." They turned down an aisle and she glanced behind them to see if anyone else was in earshot. "Miles, you know what looks funny to me? That schematic."

"Funny doesn't begin to describe it. It's shit. It doesn't make any sense."

Lawrence had handed out printed copies of the schematic. Now they reached Taylor's cubicle, and Miles held his copy at arm's length and shook his head. "What's this even supposed to be?" He pointed to a section of the device's cutaway.

"Don't ask me." Taylor pulled a tissue from her jacket pocket and pushed it up against her nose. "All I ever wanted to be was a florist."

"It's shit. I can't do shit with this." He looked at the paper again.

"You have to. Otherwise—no Kich-N-World." Taylor giggled suddenly. As if this momentous stupendous world-shaping event could be made, suddenly, to disappear.

"Careful, you're losing it. Are you sure you're okay?"

"Why don't say something to Darryl?"

"I'm thinking about it."

"He respects you."

"Darryl knows more about what's going on than you'd think. He respects you, too, you know."

"No, he doesn't." She sighed. "Although he respects me more than Basil does."

"Basil's a lower life form. He'll be capable of feeling respect in approximately 2.2 million more years of evolutionary advancement."

"Darryl . . . he didn't look very good this morning either."

"How could you tell?"

"He looked even whiter and wobblier than usual."

Miles studied her a second. "If I'm not mistake, you might be the one who is whiter and wobblier than usual. Do you need to sit down?"

"So other days I'm just partly white and wobbly?"

"No. Most days you are cute as a button. Maybe you should sit down."

Taylor sat. "Miles, can't you do something with it? Just to get this damn trade booth stuff done?"

He picked up the paper again. "It makes no sense. It looks like a child drew it."

"But they're just asking for 'artistic rendering.' So you can take some license, right?"

"All I have to go on, here, is license."

"What choice do you have, though?"

"What's going to happen is that the 'rendering' will be completely different than the product, if there ever is a product, and ya know who's going to be dealing with that mess?"

"Oh. Me?"

"PR. You're PR, right?"

The gelatin thinned again slightly, letting Taylor's thoughts come back into focus a bit. "Yeah—"

"Well, you'll be PR in a sling. Look at this. Does this look even remotely like a can opener to you?"

"Well. It's a digital can opener. Maybe they don't look like standard old-fashioned can openers. And Fusee & Madelaine—"

"The minute the sharks show up, Fusee & Madelaine will be tossing you and I overboard as chum, to give them time to swim away."

"Ew."

Their eyes met.

And suddenly he was looking at her in a way that cut right through the thick wobbling gelatin lens.

She stood up, alarmed. "I think I've, uh, got another meeting now."

"Not so fast, protest girl." He grinned at her. Damn it.

Her face felt warm all at once. It would be easier if he wasn't so damn cute.

"If I'm going to get this done by noon I'm going to need your help."

"But I—"

"Meet me in the parking lot after work."

"After work? What does after work that have to do with—"

"Unless you're too under the weather."

"What's this about?"

"Top secret."

"I need more specifics than that."

"It's nothing evil, I promise." But his grin was decidedly devilish. He was enjoying this way too much.

"I can't make a bargain unless I know what I'm agreeing to."

He grinned again.

She swallowed to control the faint tickle in her belly.

"Okay, fine." She pushed the tissue back up against her nose. "But promise me it's nothing I wouldn't want to do."

He laughed. "Oh, I promise."

She sat down. She couldn't hear his footsteps, but a moment later his voice, faintly, greeting someone in the vicinity of the elevators.

She turned to her email.

Basil. Subject line: *Another Priority*.

Wow. Could there even be a such thing as "another priority"? Wasn't a priority, by definition, a lone thing, the tip atop one's slippery-sided pyramid of trade-offs?

The thought jiggled koan-like around Taylor's brain.

Why was she doing this, again?

And then, as if her defenses were finally broken down enough to permit the notion to enter, she got it.

Humans are hardwired to market.

Because marketing is, at bottom, nothing more complicated than the need to arrange one's face for presenting to others—and the desire to dress up that face to its best advantage.

So maybe there is another layer in there, somewhere—a self that is formless, its wellbeing dependent on factors that have nothing to do with one's odds of survival or ability to procreate or to claw one's way up the pecking order. But for the first time, Taylor realized why ascetics believed it takes such great sacrifice to make that formless self—if it even existed—assume anything like primacy. It would take a battle, years of friction to sandpaper away one's instinctive faith in externals. And in the meantime, DipTych hadn't dirtied her. Not at all.

She was already mundane, a thing of the earth, by definition.

Spraying fixant on flowers so they'd retain their scent, then, wasn't an evil idea per se. It was an expression of Taylor's humanity.

The revelation propelled her, groggy as she was, from her seat, and she stumbled out into the DipTych Marketing Department to find her next meeting.

The parking lot smelled of gas fumes and tires. But she was outside. Somehow, her head cold didn't feel quite as oppressive in the fresh air.

Miles had seen her and made his way between the rows of cars to where she was standing.

"Where are you parked?"

Taylor pointed.

"Okay. And I hear you know a good florist."

"Orwin's. The place I used to work."

"They're good?"

"Yeah."

"Okay. Let's go."

"To Orwin's? Can I ask—"

"I need your help picking out some flowers. For a girl I know."

Taylor felt a tug of disappointment. Because yeah, of course she'd secretly hoped the favor might be something else. A . . . date. She shifted the shoulder strap of her purse and felt around in her pocket with her other hand for her tissue. Like anyone would want a date with Taylor the rednosed PR girl. "You know, you don't really need my help for that. Ask for Georgie. He's really good."

"No go." Miles shook his head. "First of all, people named Georgie scare me. Second of all, this was our deal, remember? You help me, I help you."

She sighed. "Okay. I'll meet you there in fifteen."

Georgie was standing with a customer looking at a seven-foot potted banana tree when Taylor walked into the store, but he excused himself and came over to give her a hug. He seemed oblivious to how bedraggled she looked. "Taylor!" he cooed, "more beautiful than when we saw you last!"

Then he went back to the customer and the banana tree.

The air smelled lush and rich as a forest floor.

The antique sleigh bells dangling from the door jangled.

Miles was there.

"The flowers are this way," Taylor said, and they wove through the displays of potted plants and chic vases and shabby chic furniture and upscale bric-a-brac to the rear of the store.

The cut flower display was enormous. Galvanized buckets stuffed with flowers, more buckets stuffed with sprays of greenery. The common things like Gerber daisies and roses, and things only Orwin's carried. Maidenhair fern. Calla lilies such a dark shade of purple they were nearly black. Delicately tinted ornamental kale with all the leaves stripped away except the centers, so that when you first looked you'd swear they were peonies or roses. Stripey spiked leaves from variegated flax plants.

"Well, what's she like?" said Taylor. Her nose felt like it was going to drip again. She bowed her head to hide it, digging for a fresh tissue in her purse.

"What do you mean?"

"If she's, you know, the sort of laid back, hippy chick type, you might want to go with something casual, like these Shasta daisies." She found a tissue and turned away from him to blow. The daisies were one of the frilly Shasta varieties. Their petals were long and narrow and gloriously unkempt.

"What about those little lily kinda things?"

She pushed the tissue into her pocket. "Freesia." Her voice was so nasal! "A classic. She'll love them if she's into retro 40s stuff. Art deco, that kind of thing. Same with the callas."

"How about roses."

"White for purity, pink for admiration. I'd stay away from yellow."

"Why?"

"Traditionally sent to say you're jealous."

"Oh. I suppose red means love."

"Yeah. That's the . . . uh, passionate love one. Do you know where she'll be putting them? The bouquet, I mean?"

"No idea."

"So palette's not a factor."

"Palette?"

"You want them to match her décor if you can."

"No, palette's not a factor. Which do you like?"

"Well, I can tell you what I like, but she might not like the same things."

He shrugged. "She's not that fussy, really. And I have to start somewhere. If she doesn't like them, I'll know what not to get her next time."

"Okay." Taylor considered the display again. "Well, let's start with . . . I love the color of these ranunculus." The outer petals were peach, the inner pale green.

"Sounds good." Miles pulled three sprays from the bucket. Water dripped from their stems onto the floor's stone tiles. "What would you put with them?"

"You could pick up the same peach, a little deeper, with these foxgloves."

"What do peach roses signify?"

"Sympathy or gratitude."

"Well, she's way above needing sympathy, and I can't say I have much cause for gratitude."

"Sounds complicated."

"Very. Let's skip the roses then. What else do you like?"

"The architectural stuff is nice." She led him over to the foliage section. "Oooh, I love these ferns. Don't they look like feathers?"

He picked out some ferns. "By the way, did you hear about the new scholarship fund DipTych created?"

In her cold medicine-induced fog, it sounded like the first line of a joke. "No, what about it."

"On the advice of Fusee & Madelaine, DipTych created a nice fat scholarship fund for Borschtchester Latinos."

"Yeah?"

Miles looked sideways at her.

"What?" she said.

"That anti-deglobalization movement seems to have suddenly lost a bunch of members."

"Really?"

"I expect your same sex marriage movement has more supporters, at this point, than they do."

Taylor sighed. "It's my fault."

"What's your fault? That DipTych's giving scholarship money to high school kids?"

She considered this.

"See? It all worked out just fine. So, do I need anything else, here, or am I done?"

She looked at his bouquet. "Depends. I tend to favor a more minimalist look. But if she likes things fancy we should add more."

"This is probably plenty. You think it's okay?"

She pursed her lips. "No. Not quite."

She led him around to the Gerbera daisies. "We have to think flower shape, too. You have two that are trumpet shaped and pretty small." She picked out three daisies that were dark orange and another few that were lighter, more melon. "There."

"What do I do now?"

"It depends on if you want to give them to her yourself, or have Georgie make them into an arrangement for you and deliver them."

"Hmmm. Guess I need to think that over."

"Okay. See you tomorrow."

She left him in the store and went to her car. It was pouring rain, and she needed to run the AC to keep the windows from steaming. So she was shivering by the time she got to the expressway, and the traffic was dismal. Simply dismal.

She wondered how long Miles and his girlfriend had been together.

# THE CURE

*"Your pigeon pest control experts."*

—From the Bye-Bye Birdie website

"I can't believe you took this stuff." Aimee was holding the lurid orange colored cold remedy in front of her nose, perusing the ingredients.

"I had to do something."

It was late Sunday afternoon. Taylor had spent practically the entire weekend in bed and was still in her pjs. She sat on the stool next to the kitchen island, holding one bent knee next to her chest.

"I'm throwing this out." Aimee tossed both bottles into the garbage can under the sink. "I can't believe you'd take that stuff just so you could drag yourself in to a job you hate."

Taylor sighed. "We've been over this before. I don't hate it. Is the soup hot yet?" Aimee had brought chicken noodle soup, takeout, from a little restaurant on Polk Ave. that called its soups "better than Mom's."

"Right. You love it, my mistake. Bowl or mug?"

"Mug. I don't love it, either. I'm like a little mouse running in a wheel. It's exercise for the sake of exercise."

"I think you just stick around for love of one of the other mice."

"I told you. He's taken."

"Right." Aimee took two mugs from the cupboard and opened the drawer next to the stove and rattled around in the contents looking for a soup ladle.

Taylor watched, hugging her knee tighter.

Aimee ladled out the soup. "Hey, I meant to ask you, what's with all the scaffolding?"

Taylor knew what she meant. The scaffolding that had been erected along one side of the DipTych skyscraper. "Yeah. They're putting some sort of pigeon-repelling spikes or something on the windowsill outside Sally's office."

"Ah, so they don't have to make their maintenance guys stand on the roof with hoses. Since they might slip and fall. Good thinking."

Taylor swallowed a spoonful of soup. "Thanks for doing this. I woke up ravenous."

"It's good and good for you. You up for a pay-per-view tonight?"

"You don't have to work?"

"Nope. Night off."

"Cool. Let's watch something scary."

The doorbell rang.

They looked at each other.

"Speaking of something scary, who's that? At 6:00 on a Sunday?"

"Not sure," Taylor said.

"Okay. Don't get up, I'll defend us."

Taylor listened to Aimee flick the deadbolt.

Man's voice at the door.

"Thank you," Aimee said. "Sure thing."

Sound now of the door shutting, deadbolt again.

Aimee rounded the corner from the foyer.

She was carrying a bouquet of flowers in one hand. A little card in the other.

The flowers looked familiar. Ranunculus. Foxglove. Gerber daisies. Nestled in a cowl of green feathery ferns . . .

"So. He's taken, is he?" Aimee said as she handed the bouquet to Taylor.

# MUST BE L-L-L...

*"Hell, I knew they'd end up together. I kept telling her. They were into each other from the first day they met."*

—Aimee Hume

Her cold was much better this morning. Much better.

She turned her head, watching in the mirror as the blow dryer tossed her wet curls, drying them into soft waves around her cheeks.

The bouquet was waiting for Taylor when she came downstairs. In the vase she'd taken down from the cupboard, and filled with water.

It was a beautiful bouquet.

Her favorite flowers, there on the kitchen island.

She looked at them as she sipped her coffee.

Would she see him today, at work? Of course she would. She wouldn't be surprised, in fact, if he sought her out. He'd want to know how she liked the flowers. And what would she say?

That she loved them, of course.

She set her coffee cup down—coffee unfinished, although she didn't notice it was unfinished—and floated across the room, dipping down only long enough to pick up her coat and briefcase and car keys.

Sitting in her office.

She had so much to do! Last day before she flew out to Kich-N-World! So much so much so much.

Press interview schedule finalized. She printed it out. She must call Fusee & Madelaine sometime before lunch to let them know the *Homebuddies* interview had been moved. Oh darn, had one of the emails with the press kit attached bounced? Yes. The one she'd sent to *Digital Gadget*. No biggie, *Digital Gadget* wasn't a key book for them. She scanned the MAILER DAEMON message. Looked like the guy's mailbox was full. No worries, she could resend later. Was Miles in his office now? He must be. What did he do all day? Graphics stuff. He might be sitting at his desk now, would he be thinking of her? Should she email him?

"Pssst."

She knew it was him almost before she heard the pssst.

"Hey," she whispered.

"Hey," he whispered back.

Her face felt warm and she was about to thank him for the flowers but he put his index finger to his lips to tell her to shush.

"What?" she whispered.

"Up for a little fun?" he whispered back.

Her eyes widened and she nodded.

"Okay." Still whispering. "But we must be vewy vewy qwiet."

He gestured at her to follow him.

They crept up the aisle. Around the corner.

Basil's cube.

She could smell him. Ben Gay and mildew and Lean Cuisine.

Miles pointed, and Taylor moved closer to the cube entrance so that she could see.

Basil's back was turned to them.

He looked like he was on the phone.

Taylor looked back at Miles, head tilted in a silent question—what . . . ?

Wait. Was that . . . snoring?

Was Basil . . . asleep?

Miles grinned as she saw she'd figured it out. Then he gestured at her to follow again.

They tiptoed back to Taylor's office.

Whispers. "He sleeps sitting up. Does it all the time, the freaking slacker."

"He does?"

"He's got the phone receiver to his ear, right?"

"How'd you know?"

"He tapes down the pegs on his phone base so it won't ring up to tell him his phone's off the hook. Then he naps holding the receiver. Genius, really. If Darryl Hannah or Rocky Raccoon or somebody walks by, they'll just think he's deep in the middle of some important confab."

"Darryl Hannah?"

"I'm trying to be funny. Do you think I'm funny?"

"Sometimes."

"Okay, I'll show you funny. C'mere."

More tiptoeing. This time to a cubicle one row over Basil Bane's. Miles turned to Taylor and put his finger to his lips, mouthing "sh."

"Hey, Sherry," he whispered it, leaning into the cubical.

Sherry turned and Miles repeated the "sh" gesture.

She nodded.

Miles waved Taylor into the cubicle and signaled that they should both stand on Shelly's desk so they could see over the top of the cubicle wall into Basil's.

Then Miles opened his cell phone and tapped in Basil's number.

It's hard to believe so much flab could bounce that high. Basil's knees knocked his keyboard off its tray. Sandra and Taylor both slumped down quickly out of sight as Basil picked the receiver back up and peeled the tape hastily off the base and barked his hello.

"Basil, my man, Miles here. Just checking in on you. Everything okay? Nice and rested?"

"Asshole," Basil answered.

"Same to you, Basil. Now you have a good rest of your morning, ya hear? 'Rest,' get it?"

He shut his phone, carefully, so that Basil wouldn't be able to hear it, and Taylor was by now nearly sick with trying to hold in the laughter, and Shelly had a shocked look on her face that suddenly began to melt into something else—

"Asshole," Basil was muttering to himself. They listened as he rearranged his keyboard, his chair creaking, and then they heard him mutter "asshole" again as he left his cubicle.

"Oh gawd," Taylor whispered. "He's probably going to come looking for me now."

"You can always hide," Miles said, winking at her.

"You guys had both better get back to your desks." Sherry, still trying to pretend she didn't think it was funny.

"C'mon, Taylor, back to work."

This day, she thought. It couldn't be more perfect.

She could feel the warmth of him, walking next to her, standing aside as she stepped back into her cubicle.

It couldn't be more perfect.

But perfection is not a thing that holds its perfect form for very long in this world.

Just ask Andrew Spittleton.

Who was, under normal circumstances, a patient man. He had to be. He could not have managed a department thick with engineers unless he was patient to a nearly preternatural degree. He could not have withstood his own intellectual standards—this man who so valued detail, certainty, and the need to check one's work not twice, not three times, but over and over and over— were he not so supremely equipped with supremely masterful patience.

Yet some things call not for patience but for outrage.

This new email in his inbox was one of those things.

It had rolled up his inbox queue the day before, as cutesy and beguiling as a Trojan Hamster, warm and furry subject line ("Subj: final marketing collateral for Kich-N-World"), chitchatty open ("Hi, all, here you go!") and promises of minimal care and feeding ("Forwarding as an FYI so you can all see the terrific campaign design we're using in our Kich-N-World booth.")

The day before. But he'd postponed even looking at it. So lulled he was by the marketing department's all-too-habitual inanity, in fact, that even when he did open it he very nearly skipped opening the attachments.

Press release blah blah blah. Backgrounder blah blah blah.

Third doc. This one was a PDF. Some kind of four-page brochure.

But—what was this?

Andrew stared at the screen.

Grabbed his mouse. Scrolled down in the document.

Scrolled back up again.

It was—surely this could not be—was this—had they really presented this . . . garbage . . . as some sort of representation of his baby? His EasyCan????

He suppressed a scream.

Re-opened the cover email, hunting for a sig line.

Found it.

Picked up his phone.


"So," Miles said.

"So."

"You got the flowers."

Taylor melted now into a full blush. "Yeah. They were—that was—"

"You can say it."

She laughed. "Okay. That was one of the really sweetest gestures . . ."

She dropped her eyes but he'd seen what she thought.

"So what are you doing later?"

"Tonight, I—"

"Naw, like, later meaning right now." He grinned.

"Well, I have to—"

"Jelly's found a way to get up on the roof. Want to go?"

"I hear it's dangerous."

"Only if it's wet. Want to go? The view is amazing."

Taylor's phone rang.

She looked down at it.

"Come on," Miles said.

The phone rang again. The display showed a DipTych number. She didn't recognize it.

"I'd better just take this," she said.

"Okay."

Taylor picked up the phone.

The person on the other end didn't introduce himself.

On the contrary, when she said "hello" the person on the other end of the line snarled, "Who the hell is this?"

"I'm sorry?" Taylor said.

Miles was watching her.

"You heard me," the voice snarled. "Who the hell are you?"

During her orientation Taylor had been trained in procedures for contacting Security. She glanced now at the file cabinet on the far cubical wall. She'd filed her DipTych New Personnel Training Guide there. If she remembered correctly. Now she just needed to quietly stand up and—

"This is Andrew Spittleton, Director of R&D. You sent me a file this morning."

Taylor dropped into her chair. Her alarm gave way to the earthier emotion of wild dread. Director. A director, a furious director. This was bad, whatever it was. Very bad.

"I want to know who you are."

"Taylor—"

"Not your name. Your name is on the goddamn email. Who do you report to?"

"Darryl Fiegit."

Click.

Taylor looked at Miles.

She set the receiver back onto the base.

"Some kind of trouble?"

"I'm not sure." She realized she was shaking. "I think so. Look, I'd love to see the roof view and everything but—"

He waited. But she didn't know how to finish her thought.

"Okay," he said finally. "Let me know if you change your mind."

Taylor hadn't moved yet, five minutes later, when Darryl appeared in her cubicle door. His was wobbling slightly and the skin of his face looked slightly blue.

"Andy called you?" he asked. His voice was barely above a whisper, and cracking.

She nodded.

"What did he tell you."

"Nothing. He asked who I was—who I report to."

"That's it."

"I gave him your name and he hung up."

"Okay. Okay, then. Thank you."

She waited a second, then got up and peeked around the corner of her door. Darryl was wobbling still as he made his way down the aisle.

He turned in the direction of the elevators and was gone.

# RUMBLIN' TROUBLE

*"The illuminative angle on any engineering problem may also be considered its apex. You derive the angle by considering the matter from multiple vantage points, and once you've determined what it is, you set about to build collaborative consensus that is consistent within the political temperament of the organization."*

—Andrew Spittleton, unpublished manuscript,
"The Art of Engineering"

Rocco had the desk. Andrew had the outrage. Darryl had neither, so he sat, shrunken in on himself.

"I would like to know how the hell you even got the document in the first place."

Andrew was six foot two, and he'd refused to take a seat, preferring to stand instead. This rendered him, in his height and outrage, the avenging angel armed with flaming sword and tongue.

Unfortunately, the scale of Rocco's desk protected him, and he showed no sign of being the least bit flustered.

"We agreed that that doesn't matter right now," Rocco said.

"Like hell it doesn't. I never released the document you used for these drawings. I'd like to know how you got it."

Rocco did not look at Darryl. This was not the time to betray any member of the marketing tribe.

"What matters is that we keep this quiet," Rocco said. "What matters is

Kich-N-World."

"I'm not sure Scally would agree with that."

"I'm not sure Scally would be happy to know that the DipTych Digital Can division R&D organization maintains a file of bogus drawings that might get mixed in with product schematics." Rocco's tone was pure triumph. See, if you assume you have the upper hand, you do. Always works. "Andy, if I were you I'd make damn sure nobody else got their hands on these. What if we had commissioned manufacturing equipment based on these things?"

Andrew's avenging flames were immediately doused by this irrational yet implacable spray of corporate logic.

He sat down.

Rocco stroked the glossy veneer of his desk and turned to Darryl. "Darryl, who knows about this?"

"Nobody, I don't think."

"How about your PR girl, does she know?"

"She says Andy didn't say anything to her about why he'd called." Darryl looked over at Andrew, who shrugged in sullen agreement.

Rocco sat back in silence for a moment, running scenarios through his mind.

Andrew guessed first what he was thinking.

"Roc. You cannot be serious." Flames sputtering back to life again.

"We have no choice."

"Look." He hadn't told them, yet, what the original drawing was. He'd figured it out of course—as soon as the shock had worn off, the cold shock of seeing a monstrosity portrayed as an actual DipTych Digital Can engineering drawing, his baby, the EasyCan technology he lived and breathed represented by—it was that kid's drawing. He'd been 99 percent sure, then double-checked with Brad, his contract writer, and yes, that's what it was, all right.

But how had it . . . how had marketing . . . ?

And now he had to tell them. He hadn't wanted to. In the first place, it was none of their business. And in the second place, to be honest, the fewer people who knew the better—because the fewer people who knew, the less likely this was to get back to his staff. He was sure he could keep Brad quiet, but these marketing people . . . And above all else, Andrew Spittleton did not want to get back to his staff—because above all else, Andrew Spittleton could not bear the idea of other engineers laughing at him.

"Look," he wet his lips to try again. "You don't seem to understand."

"Mistakes happen, Andrew," Rocco said.

"The material this is based on—it's a child's drawing."

Andrew had brought a sheaf of paper, a printout of the attachment Taylor had emailed to him. Now he leafed through the pages savagely and yanked one out, the back of a DipTych tech spec, bulleted feature-benefits dripping across a dreamy reproduction of Ethan's masterpiece, as rendered by Miles in the style of da Vinci. "It doesn't even make sense." Andrew jabbed his finger at a cable wrapped around a gear. "It's . . . it's *horrific.*"

"That doesn't matter, though, does it," Rocco said. "We're not saying this is the actual product. It's an artist's rendering."

Andrew stared at him, his jaw working as he tried to find words sufficient to express his indignation. Was it possible that marketing people could be that stupid? That they would stand behind this . . . this grotesque caricature as if it were an acceptable stand-in for EasyCan? "Rocco. Not only does this have nothing, *zero*, to do with actual EasyCan engineering. It's not even—it's not *authorized.*"

"Number one. Kich-N-World is the biggest show of the year," Rocco said. "Number two. It starts in three days. Number three, we've already mailed this out to the press. And number four, we are not going to risk our EasyCan publicity plan over some little snafu—"

"I can't believe you're considering this." Spittle had formed at the corners of Andrew's mouth.

"—that nobody is going to ever know about anyway."

"Like they aren't going to figure it out."

"Figure what out? It's an artist's rendering."

Andrew stared at Rocco for another long minute.

"We tell nobody about this," Rocco said when Andrew finally looked away.

Andrew stood up. "All I have to say, is good luck, Rocco. Good luck. I have another meeting I have to go to."

"Andy."

Andrew turned around.

"Whose kid?"

"Excuse me?"

"Whose kid did the drawing?"

"Brad Tankard. Writer. He's doing our technical documentation."

Rocco frowned in faux thoughtfulness. "Does he know about this?"

"Yes. But he understands he needs to keep that information confidential."

Rocco nodded. "He an FTE?" Meaning full-time employee.

"No. Contract."

"That's good. It might be a good idea to move him off the project."

Andrew's face began to redden again. "My staff is my business, Pinnoccho."

Rocco shrugged. "It's just a suggestion. We want to . . . minimize the risk people will be embarrassed."

Andrew knew what Rocco meant by "people." He meant Andrew. He meant, better get rid of Brad because if he didn't, and word got out that EasyCan was based on a kid's drawing, it would be Andrew who would look like an ass.

Brad wasn't an engineer, so he didn't deserve the same degree of loyalty that Andrew afforded the rest of his staff. Still, he wasn't going to let Rocco think he was taking orders. "I'll consider my options," he said.

"Appreciate your coming over, Andy." Rocco stood up but didn't offer his hand. "We'll set up a de-brief after the show."

Andrew closed the door behind him.

"Okay. So. Next steps." Rocco sat back down, but this time he didn't stroke his desk. Truth was, he was a bit unnerved by Andrew's show of outrage. He looked at the pages Andrew had left on his desk. The artist's rendering of the schematic had looked so satisfying before. Now it looked . . . different. A child's drawing? He had to admit, now that he knew, he could see it, despite the glossy sheen of the expensive paper and the graceful lines and the call-out boxes . . . a kid's drawing. Yeah, he could see it . . . "Darryl. Who knows about this. You, me, Andy, and that's it, right?"

Darryl didn't answer.

Rocco took his answer for a yes. "Well." Time to be a big boy. "Fusee will find out sooner or later. Better make it now."

He lifted the receiver of his desk phone, dialed, waited a moment, then spoke. "Switch. Rocco here. Yes, I know, but something's come up. Hang on, I'm going to have Darryl fill you in. Hang on, he's right here, I'm putting you on speaker." He hit a button on his phone base.

"Who's Darryl?" Switch did not sound pleased, but then he wouldn't. He was not the sort of person who wanted to be interrupted by a conversation that began with "something's come up."

"Darryl Fiegit. You've met. My marketing manager."

"Oh. That Darryl. You know, Rocco, I think maybe you should be the one to tell me."

Rocco pulled a face like he'd discovered a turd under his tongue. "Right. So." He drew an inaudible breath. Turned his face slightly away from the phone console. "It's come to our attention that the EasyCan schematic, provided to us by R&D for use in our marketing literature, is not entirely . . . correct."

Silence. Then, "I'm not sure I follow you, Rocco."

"There was a mix-up, we believe, with the R&D files."

Darryl's mouth had started working. And now he spoke up in a sudden bleat before Switch could speak. "It's my fault, Switch. I take full responsibility."

Impossible to say whether Switch took note of the confession. "How big a mix-up are we talking here? Is this a version issue? What?"

"Just tell him, Rocco."

"Good idea, Rocco."

But Rocco's teeth were gritting too hard in front of his words, so it was

Darryl who said it finally. "The drawing we used . . . it isn't a drawing of EasyCan at all. Apparently it's . . . some kid's . . . drawing."

"I see. Well."

Silence.

"Well. That could be, let's see . . . embarrassing. Potentially."

"If anyone finds out," Rocco said.

"Hang on." Switch's line went silent for a moment. Then: "Okay. I've pulled up the brochure PDF. So this—what are we talking about, here? What drawing?"

"We've . . . used the same drawing—the kid's drawing—in pretty much all of the, uh, graphical elements of all of our marketing literature. At this point." Rocco looked at Darryl as he spoke and Darryl, pinned, nodded in miserable agreement.

"Jesus. A kid's drawing. Yeah. I see it. It looks like a fucking kid's drawing. All right. Has any of this stuff gone out?"

They knew what Switch meant. He meant gone out to the press.

"Yesterday."

"All of it?"

"Yes, a full press kit, pdfs, including the brochures."

"Is it embargoed?"

"Yes." Meaning the press, in theory, was supposed to keep everything under wraps until the first day of the trade show. They could tell Switch was ticking off options mentally, one being to try to pull it back, to swap in something different. Only there was no time to generate anything worthy of a major DipTych product launch in so little time . . .

"Who knows about this—that it's a kid's drawing?"

Rocco told him.

"Are you in your office?"

"Yes."

"I'm going to find Hedy and dial back. Give me five minutes."

Rocco and Darryl sat without looking at each other as they waited.

"Man up," Rocco said finally. "You look like hell." He felt better for making the observation. Somebody has to be the big boy. And that somebody is Rocco. Again. But that's why it was he, Rocco, with the letters after his name—

The phone rang.

"Well, boys," Hedy said. "Rocco and Darryl, right?"

"Right," Rocco answered.

"Hi, Rocco. Hullo, Darryl."

Darryl croaked out a noise that passed as a response. Rocco shot him another look.

"So. Switch and I held a little confab here, right, Switch?"

"Right. So what we recommend, at this point, is that we just lay low and ride this out."

Rocco smiled and leaned back, giving his tie a comfortable pet. "So we'll just act like the drawing is fine. All part of the plan."

"Yes," Switch said. "We do suggest you take a somewhat lower profile at the show."

Rocco frowned.

"You have an internal PR resource planning to be at the show, correct?"

Rocco looked at Darryl, who managed a nod, and then said "yes" at the speaker phone mic.

"Best to have him handle things operationally, then."

"Her," Darryl said. "It's a she. And I'm not sure—"

"She'll be fine, Darryl." Hedy's voice. Musical. Soothing. "Have her refer any prickly questions to us to address after the show."

"Hedy—this girl. She's not the most experienced."

"All the better," said Switch. "The press will pick up on that and give her a pass."

Darryl slumped back into his chair.

"It'll be fine," Hedy said.

"Hang on," Switch said. "I need to put you on mute for a second."

They waited.

Then Switch spoke again. "We've been looking at the press interviews. Rocco, better have your PR person handle all interviews herself."

Rocco's frown deepened. "Okay—but the panel. Chips and Clicks."

"Not advisable," said Switch.

Okay, so there was no way in hell Rocco was going to back out of the Chips and Clicks panel. And miss a chance to showcase his innovative thinking around Tangential Integration? Not going to happen. "Guys," he said. "You understand how bad it will look if I drop out? And I've put a lot of time into prepping for this thing."

"We strongly recommend you maintain a very low profile."

"I can handle it. I'll leave right afterward."

Darryl could feel Switch and Hedy, through the phone, look at each, roll their eyes. But in the end, Rocco was the boss and they all knew it.

Switch ended the call. "You're free to use your own judgment, of course, Roc. Let us know how it goes."


"Well." Rocco sat back again. "Two down, one to go. We need to tell your PR girl what's going on."

Darryl cleared his throat. "Shouldn't we—if she doesn't know the drawing is a fake, maybe we should leave it that way. You know. So she has credible . . . deniability."

"Nope. We need her to be the one who knows, Darryl."

Darryl knew why. So that if it came to it, they'd have someone to take the fall. He pushed his hands down along the crease of his trousers, trying to dry his palms.

"What's her extension?"

It was easier to find Rocco's office the second time.

It should also have been easier to be there. But it wasn't. Because Taylor's gut was churning.

Whatever was going on, it was a very very bad thing.

She tapped on Rocco's door.

"Come in."

Like before, there was an empty seat waiting for her, next to Darryl.

She sat. The vinyl was faintly warm—someone else had been sitting there not too long ago.

"We have a slight issue with the EasyCan launch collateral" was the way Rocco began the conversation.

Taylor could see Darryl out of the corner of his eye, sagging downward into the pool of his own sweat.

"Are you aware of what it is?"

"No sir."

She was going to be fired. Right there, right now, in Rocco's pseudo-posh-filled office. Something she'd done, her press releases . . . no. They'd found out about the booth tchotchkes. That had to be it—

"We want you to know about it, so that if anyone from the press asks any . . . difficult questions, you will be prepared."

She looked at Rocco, forcing herself to comprehend.

"What—what are—what exactly—" She turned instinctively to Darryl, her boss, her protector, who seemed to be trying to smile at her, to reassure her? But poor man, it looked more like a zombie's grimace.

"Tiffany, this information must not leave this room."

She turned back to Rocco, opened her mouth to say "Taylor," then thought it best not to correct him.

"You are under strict non-disclosure. Do you understand what I'm saying?"

"Yes, I guess—yes."

"The schematic used for the collateral was not—it was not an authorized rendition of the EasyCan product."

Miles had said something was wrong. "What was it?"

"A contractor who works for R&D brought his son's drawing to work, and it was released for use by the marketing team. Inadvertently."

Darryl did not try to smile at her this time. He was bent over, rubbing something off the toe of his right shoe.

Taylor's brain began catching up. "I might  get questions. From the press."

"That's why you're here," Rocco said.

"I thought . . . Fusee & Madelaine . . ."

"We've decided, for strategic reasons, to adjust the way we're leveraging Fusee & Madelaine for the launch. We became, ah, concerned that they might be perceived as the face of EasyCan, which is not consistent with our brand."

Taylor looked back at Darryl, then at Rocco again.

"We need you—DipTych—to be the face of EasyCan."

"What do I say to the press, then, about the drawing?"

"Nothing."

"What do you mean?"

Rocco drew his lips back as he leaned toward her over his desk. "You spin. If anyone asks about the provenance of the drawing, you spin and you spin hard."

Taylor's brain stopped making any forward progress, instead pedaled furiously in place. "I'm not sure—"

"Taylor, let's be honest, here. Someone could very well pay the ultimate price for this fuck-up."

She froze.

"It's the kind of fuck-up that stays with you forever. Think about it. Not only is your career here over. Your promising career. But even outside. Who at DipTych would be able to give you a reference?"

"I . . . I see."

"You also understand that if we can't contain this . . . issue, it becomes a matter for the Board of Directors. We're a public company, remember. The Board will become involved if anything happens to hurt our brand. Our stock could take a hit."

Taylor tightened her hands to stop them from shaking. How soon would her mother find out about all this? It wouldn't be long . . .

"I—we—all of us hope to avoid that, because if that happens, we are all in very very very very deep shit. All of us, the whole team. Do you understand?"

Taylor took a breath. Okay. She got it. This was about more than her. It was about DipTych Digital. And Rocco being worried about his own job. Yeah. He was looking a little twitchy himself. So he needed her help—he was calling on her to step up, to deal with a difficult situation. Okay. She could handle it.

She didn't look at Darryl any more.

"You were hired because you are a highly credentialed PR professional. The best of the best—"

Right. No point arguing that. But then again, she hadn't been doing all that badly, had she? Maybe he wasn't just saying that to flatter her . . .

"Your job, at Kich-N-World, is to shine. To bring all your PR skills and make goddamn sure that no matter what questions anybody asks, they leave that show believing that these drawings—" Rocco pointed at the pile of papers Andrew had left on the desk—"are one hundred percent legit."

Taylor nodded.

"There was no accident. There was no child. No mix-up. The drawing is an actual EasyCan schematic, any apparent . . . inconsistencies . . . are due to the fact that it is an artist's rendering."

"Okay . . . that should be . . . that should be doable."

Rocco smiled an utterly charming smile and stood up. "Good girl. We knew we could count on you."

"Yes," she said.

"By the way." Rocco had begun to relax. He sat back and touched his tie. "You'll need to cancel any interviews I had set up with the press. We've decided it's not appropriate at this time to grant press interviews with representatives at the executive level."

And then she was excused.

Darryl didn't join her when she left.

She went back to her cubicle. Opened her file listing press interviews and began composing emails.

Hi. Please forgive the late notice, but unfortunately Rocco Pinnoccho will not be available for press interviews during Kich-N-World this week. Please accept DipTych's sincere apologies, and let me know if you have any questions.

Send.

Repeat.

"Miles."

He looked up from his computer.

"I need to talk to you."

"Any time, babe. Come on into the Miles Chacuderie castle and have a seat."

"No. Not here."

He looked at her more closely. "Wow, what happened, get bitten by a nasty DipTych crocodile?"

She nodded. "You might say that."

"And?"

"I can't talk about it here. I'm—" She lowered her voice. "I'm under non-disclosure."

He widened his eyes dramatically. "And if you talk, they'll have to keeeel you."

"Stop it, Miles, this is serious, I need to talk this out with someone and I don't know who else—"

"Hey, okay, okay. Don't—geez, don't cry. This is DipTych, remember? The joke of a company built with all-joke materials on a foundation of pure jokeness. Nothing can possibly be worth—geez, you're going to drip all over my best pencils."

Taylor dug around in the pocket of her jacket for a tissue. "I'd like to point out that you have the world's neatest pencil collection in your office but you can't be bothered to stock a box of Kleenex."

"I don't normally use my office for crying. Meet you in the parking lot in 15 minutes."

She shook her head no. "I can't—not where someone can hear."

"Wow. Say, if you tell me, will they have to keel me too?"

"You really aren't helping, here."

"That could be kinda romantic, actually. We could die tragically in each other's arms."

"Miles."

"Okay, okay, just no crying. We can go for a walk, okay?"

She didn't answer.

"Don't worry, I won't put the moves on you."

Damnit. Blushing.

"It will be strictly professional. Parking lot. Fifteen minutes."

"Fifteen minutes."


The DipTych Corporate office building was erected by Musgrave himself, of course, and a magnificent structure it was, towering in the splendor of that day's architectural style, brick, sides broken periodically by corniced ledges, arched top floor windows like flourishes along the top edge of a cake, a skyscraper representing all that was best about the DipTych can opener empire.

He'd located it seven or eight blocks from what was, at the time, the midsection of bustling Borschtchester. The location was no mistake. Musgrave had believed the city would continue to surge outward, until, one day, the DipTych Corporate office building would be subsumed by it, enveloped by the warm sleek belly of Borschtchester's ever-growing prosperity.

Thankfully he died, so he never saw what happened in the next few decades—the city's surge reversed, became an ebb that left the DipTych skyscraper isolated, cut off from downtown, a lonely urban outpost surrounded by a patchwork of abandoned lots, the few old homes converted to apartments, the necklace of sidewalks crumbling, cracks filled with ragweed and crab grass.

Taylor and Miles walked away from the office building, toward the city.

They passed Middlins, the last little bit of taxpayer funded gentility in DipTych's immediate neighborhood.

They kept walking.

They stepped around an abandoned grocery cart.

"So," Miles said finally. "Are we safe to talk now?"

It was past 6:30 p.m. There was nobody else anywhere in sight.

"Yeah," Taylor said.

And she told him what she'd learned, that morning, in Rocco's office.

He smiled.

She told him a bit more.

He laughed.

She realizing when he laughed that she'd expected it—and for the first time she felt that yeah, maybe it was a little funny.

"This is perfect!" he said finally. "I knew there was something fucked up about that drawing."

"You said, when you saw it, that it looked like a kid drew it."

He laughed again.

This time she laughed too.

Then she got serious again.

"So what should I do?"

"What do you mean."

"I've never done a trade show before. Fusee & Madelaine were going to send Lawrence, but now it's just me."

"Well, how hard can it be?"

It didn't seem like it would hard at all now, walking there next to Miles. But what about Kyle Shillelagh?

She thought about saying those last words out loud. But maybe she didn't want Miles to know just how scared she was—

"We'd better turn around," he said. "It's going to get dark."


They didn't say anything for a while. They passed a house where there was a party going on. Twenty-somethings slouched together on the porch, hip hop thudding from the open door behind them. It must have been going on awhile, there were dozens of empty cups on the porch steps and railing.

When they got back to the DipTych parking lot the moon had just come up.

It hung, huge, in the sky over the jagged silhouette of downtown Borschtchester.

"Wow," Taylor said. "The moon's bright."

"It's supposed to be bright when it's full."

"You know what I mean. We're in the middle of the city. Here's my car."

They stopped.

She looked up at the moon again. "Do you ever get a funny feeling about it?"

"About what. The moon? What do you mean?"

"It's so old and weird, and sometimes it feels like it's paying attention."

"Well, you know some people believe it's really an alien spacecraft."

"The moon? You're joking."

"I'm not."

"Are these the same people who say we never landed on it?"

"Not necessarily."

Taylor pawed through her purse for a second and pulled out her car keys. "So they think the moon is a big round alien spacecraft made of rock."

"Hollow inside."

She pressed the button on her key fob, and the interior lights of the Toyota glowed to life. "Well, what I was going to say, a minute ago, was that I can almost understand how people could decide to worship it. But, uh, the alien spacecraft thing kind of ruined the mood."

Miles reached down to open her door. "Not *the* mood, I hope."

"Of course not *the* mood. Just a weird feeling about the moon mood."

"I see. I won't try to kiss you, then."

He closed the door behind her.

She rolled down her window.

"Miles. Thank you."

"No worries, protest girl. See you at work tomorrow morning."

"Actually, I'll be on a plane."

"Ah. That's right. Okay. See you around."

"Yeah, see you around."

The moon, or maybe it was the streetlights, lit up the back of his hair for a moment as he walked away, and Taylor sat there, something as great as fear gripping her chest, until she forced herself to start her car and pull away.

# THE FALL OF THE HOUSE OF CANS

*"The biggest kitchen industry trade show in the universe!"*

—from the Kich-N-World website

Trade shows only appear to be contemporary phenomena. They are in fact a contemporary twist on that most ancient of commercial meeting-places, the market bazaar. Only not even remotely as picturesque.

So the Kich-N-World venue was a horrifically ugly building, a convention center located in a Big Distant City to which incidentally there are no direct flights from Borschtchester. The center itself comprised two cavernous rooms connected by an oversized and bleak carpeted hallway. Both rooms were now jammed with makeshift stalls—sorry, booths—staffed by professionally-dressed people who, to the last one, had affixed to their faces pitiable expressions of desperate geniality.

The aisles between the booths functioned as sidewalks.

At times these walkways were rather quiet, but at other times for no apparent reason they surged with pedestrians. These pedestrians strolled from booth to booth. Most carried plastic bags printed with the names of Kich-N-World exhibiters. When they stopped at the booths, they looked for free giveaways to stuff into their plastic bags. Once their bags were full they headed back to their hotels, where they worked out, showered, and then went to dinner and drinks on their companies' tabs.

From time to time, a pedestrian—or perhaps a clutch of two or three— would actually feign interest in more than the free giveaways. It was for this that the people staffing the booths smiled and smiled and smiled. Because there was always the possibility that this next shuffling visitor might be The One, the Real Deal, the connection to that eternally-coveted big sale or perhaps an overdue switch in career paths.

When that happened, the nearest or most ambitious booth staff person would pounce. And the captured pedestrian would nod, and perhaps murmur a few vague promises, and offer to exchange business cards.

Then the pedestrian would move off in search of some other vendor's freebies or deals or contacts, and time would once again slow to a ghastly crawl beneath the ghastly fluorescent lighting.

Taylor's plane landed shortly after 9:00 that morning.

She took a shuttle to the hotel, left her bags with the concierge, and caught a second shuttle, this time from the hotel to the show. This put her at the convention center some three hours in advance of her first press interview. She'd planned it that way. She wanted to get oriented. And like all good business travelers, she'd padded her schedule in case she ran into any snags en route.

The convention center dazzled her slightly at first, like a bumpkin seeing a city for the first time.

She used the map they handed her at the door to find the DipTych booth.

It occupied a corner lot, befitting DipTych's status as a kitchenware giant.

She peered around.

The booth bore an AHa *Take on Me* resemblance to the drawings she'd seen so many weeks ago, on her first day of work, only in the drawings the people were graceful, wasp-thin women in pencil skirts and broad-shouldered men wearing suits and ties.

Whereas in real life, the people were thicker and tended to slouch.

Two DipTych reps approached her. They didn't know who she was so their eyes sought her badge, then slid off quickly as they realized she was of no use to them. They shook hands, then the reps noticed pedestrians pausing and excused themselves.

Taylor explored.

The largest portion of the booth from a square foot perspective was dedicated to U-Ful Utensils. It was designed to look like the interior of an upscale kitchen, with stainless appliances and faux granite countertop. And everywhere, spotless examples of the U-Ful product line. Spatulas, tongs, melon ballers and mango corers, skimmers, ladles, carving knives, steak knives. Utensils hung from pegs along the back wall and lay in lines straight as marching soldiers along the counters—affixed to the counters, Taylor noticed, with metal staples so that nobody could accidentally on purpose mistake them for booth giveaways.

She looked for the other division's displays.

Off to one side, a rack of products featured by DipTych Candy & Nut, set up to look like an in-store end-cap.

DipTych's window and door products weren't an important piece of the booth, seeing as there wouldn't be any window and door buyers at this particular show, so its display was merely representational. A DipTych window was mounted in a partition that separated the U-Ful portion of the booth from the much smaller Diptych Digital Can portion.

Taylor looked through the window and spotted Randolph Schilling, DipTych Digital Sales Manager, standing behind a cloth-covered table that faced one of the show aisles.

She crossed to the Digital side. Like another world. From the cool tones of the faux kitchen into the warm parchment-y costume of the EasyCan artistic rendering. A computer kiosk displayed a looped presentation featuring the many EasyCan features.

Taylor avoided looking at the computer screen.

She didn't want to see the fake schematic, even in its deliberately vague artistic rendered form.

She stashed her purse and briefcase under the table at the front of the booth.

Randolph was smiling and dropping plastic band aid dispensers, trick-or-treat style, into pedestrian's bags.

Taylor wandered back around to the U-Ful side of the booth.

A rep was pitching a captured pedestrian on the Ergogo line. "It's for people who love the kitchen, love to cook, love to make a mess, but care about the ergonomics of kitchenware."

Taylor wondered who the pedestrian was. She edged closer, pretending she was curious about the Ergogo spatulas, until she could make out the pedestrian's name badge. It said, Buyer, Sprylot Corp.

The U-Ful rep had produced a ladle from a box under the counter. He handed it to the buyer who waved it in the air to get a feel for its heft.

"Look," said the rep, taking it back. And he held out the index finger of his right hand, and balanced the ladle on it by its handle. "You couldn't do this with your ordinary ladle."

The buyer nodded and took the ladle back to try the balancing trick himself. "Nice," he said finally. "I'll keep it in mind if we decide to add another line."

"Sure," said the rep. "Did you take one of our band aid dispensers? Here." He picked up the bowl of band aid dispensers from the counter and held it out to the buyer.

"Now, this, I don't get," the buyer said. "Why band aid dispensers?"

He didn't take one.

The rep shrugged as he returned the bowl to the counter. "Don't ask me," he said. "We didn't get to pick the giveaways this year."

Taylor hustled quickly and quietly back to the Digital side of the booth.

The meager layer of carpet underfoot was itself laid on concrete.

Trade show veterans, anticipating the effects standing on concrete would have on their feet and legs, had stuffed the inside of their shoes with extra padding, gel insoles, garishly scented slips of foam.

Taylor was not a trade show veteran. She had worn heels. Not terribly high heels. But high enough, and by noon she was already paying the price. Her calves burned and throbbed. She no longer stood still in one place. She paced. Or shifted from foot to foot to try to keep the blood moving.

It didn't really help.

The clock, meanwhile, paced itself. Running in Trade Show Time.

The flow of pedestrians slowed. Perhaps because it was lunch time.

She drifted back toward the U-Ful counter, where a knot of sales reps gathered the way people at a party congregate in the kitchen.

They were talking about the show, some, and their territories—she gathered that there had been some sort of realignment in the sales channel. Some of them were okay with it, some sounded kind of pissed off.

She scanned the booths across the aisle. There was a drawing over there for a free kitchen makeover. She'd have to remember to enter.

The reps were talking now about basketball. Some of them had placed some bets on last night's Knicks games.

"I lost big on that one," said the rep who had been talking to the buyer earlier.

"Yeah, could have been worse. You could have lost a million dollars."

"Geez, I heard about that!"

"He gambled it away. The whole thing."

"You're shitting me."

"Nope. The entire settlement. Poker tables."

"So it stayed in Vegas then, eh?"

The men laughed.

"His fiancé dumped him too. That admin. She's back in Borschtchester last I heard."

The talk moved back to basketball again, and Taylor decided she might as well get some lunch.

The convention center had an area designated for its food vendors, who operated out of movable standalone mini-kitchens like the kind you see at county fairs. They were arrayed in a makeshift arc around a cluster of tables.

The tables were strewn with crumbs and drying dabs of ketchup.

Several were occupied by small groups of people who talked to each other intently.

She ate alone. Then returned to the booth, drew out her briefcase, scanned her list of press appointments. *Kitchen & Bath Solutions, Kitchen News, Homebuddies Magazine, Kitchen Retailer*, and finally *Greenie Does It.*

Her first press meeting was scheduled for 2 p.m. Her last would wrap up around the same time the following day.

And looming ever closer: the meeting she most dreaded, the dreaded Kyle Shillelagh.

Taylor mentally reviewed her talking points. Again.

If only it were over.

The *Kitchen & Bath Solutions* interview was a twofer, reporter and editor, women, both of them, and matchy matchy as two examples from the same line of dolls. This one's Kristen, this one's Jessica, polished nails, polished hair, no doubt the even soles of their feet has been polished until they shone. They smiled and agreed they were glad to meet Taylor, too, and accepted copies of the press kit and Taylor's business card and left.

Taylor's legs still ached.

*Kitchen News* didn't show up.

The *Homebuddies* editor was thoughtful. She asked Taylor questions like would EasyCan help working women cope with juggling their careers when they were under more pressure than ever to cook healthy meals for their families. Taylor found herself wondering how old the *Homebuddies* editor was. The question proved somewhat distracting. The *Homebuddies* editor's hair was gray and the skin of her face had a papery look. But she dressed like a businesswoman in her prime. Taylor decided that the *Homebuddies* editor would have preferred to be retired, but she hid this by feigning compassion for faceless working women whose lives would be transformed hopefully by a digital can opener.

3:45. *Kitchen Retailer.* This was her first trade pub, which is a whole different animal. Channel pubs are b2b pubs, they are talking to businesses, not consumers. So for this editor what would matter was not so much what EasyCan can do, but whether EasyCan would sell.

Taylor sized him up. Thin, prominent Adam's apple. Thinning hair.

Stubby hands, though, which looked oddly out of place given that he was easily six feet tall.

He'd already read the press release—when Taylor offered him a kit he waved her off. He said he wanted to talk to Darryl. This miffed her slightly—wasn't PR supposed to be in charge of the press? Why wasn't he happy talking to PR?

A kid was hanging around when the *Kitchen Retailer* reporter left. Blue border on his badge, meaning press, so Taylor guessed he was from the online eco pub. Correct. He had some questions about the EasyCan's Energy Star rating that she promised to get back to him on, and whether the mini-printer module would use recycled paper. She promised to get back to him on that, too.

The rest of the interviews would take place in the morning.

She had enough time, now, to get to the hotel and check into her room.

Then dinner. With the rest of the DipTych marketing team, including Darryl and Rocco, who were both scheduled to fly in—she flipped open her cell to check the time—their plane would be landing right about now.

The DipTychians met in the hotel lobby a little before six. There were around a dozen of them, Darryl and Rocco, and Basil, and Randolph Schilling, and a handful of managers from other DipTych divisions.

They stood, waiting for the cabs the concierge had summoned, everyone's body angled slightly toward Rocco because he was the Big Cheese in that particular situ.

Taylor found herself watching Rocco, as well. She'd become increasingly aware of it—how the corporate ley lines organize themselves around their executives, tug you toward them, tug your attention to whatever it is they're attending to.

The cabs pulled up under the hotel's porte-cochere.

Taylor let herself be bumped along as the group walked out to the curb, like a loose pebble bouncing in the current along a stream bed. For a moment she was being carried to the first cab, but Basil cut in like a bigger pebble caught in a rogue eddy and suddenly there was no room for her, so she pulled back and ended up in the second car.

She could see the back of Basil's head in the first cab as they pulled away, and the back of Darryl's head, but Rocco was the shortest of the three and obscured by the glare on the rear window.

"Where is it we're eating?" Taylor asked Randolph as he squeezed in next to her.

"The Oui and Si. Supposed to be awesome. French tapas seafood fusion cuisine."

"Ah."

And with Japanese influenced décor, no less. Black lacquer tabletops bristling with glassware, a long wall of windows uncorrupted by a single thread of drapery, black tiled floor, pendent lights dangling at artfully varying heights.

The maître d' seated them around a long table in the main dining room. It was crowded and deafeningly loud. A young waiter with hair slicked back into a pony tail approached the head of the table and pulled a pad from where he'd tucked it into the rear waistband of his black slacks. His waist was only slightly larger around than his wrists. He leaned over to listen to something Rocco said, then made his way one by one around the table, repeating the gesture.

Taylor noticed people looking at the wine list on the back of the menu so she turned to it, too.

The most expensive glass of white wine was $17.50.

The least expensive was $9.50.

She chose an $11 glass and shouted an approximation of its name into the waiter's ear when he got to her.

The waiter returned to the head of the table and began reading from his pad. Taylor caught the words "braised," "*croustade*," "umber," and "clear infusion." The waiter straightened and smiled and turned away, and she re-opened her menu to look at the entrees.

Behind her the party seated between their table and the window burst again into hearty laughter. The room's bristling glassware thrummed. Someone reached from behind Taylor for her water glass and filled it, and a drip splashed onto her neck. A parade of staff passed holding trays high above their heads, and as they disappeared into a private room Taylor could smell steak and fish. The fish had perhaps been braised. The steak was perhaps swimming in a clear infusion. One of the dishes on the trays had been topped by a tall paper cone, or perhaps it hid some sort of mysterious high end table service.

"WHAT ARE YOU HAVING?" Randolph leaned over to Taylor's ear so that she could hear him.

She had no idea, but since he asked she looked again at a list of tapas flights on her menu and pointed the one called Chalet Dreams that included rosemary crusted puffed new potatoes and salmon cassoulet terrine. Randolph nodded. "I'M TRYING THE 'DAY AT THE BEACH.'" She looked at the description of Day At the Beach. Then the price. It was double the price of Chalet Dreams.

A server—not the one who had taken their drink order—brought their drinks. Taylor watched people chatting.

She sipped her wine.

It was not bad wine.

But then right before their entrees came out of the kitchen, a sommelier arrived with three bottles and opened them, and when Taylor had finished her first glass and took a sip of the wine that had come from one of the bottles, she realized that the one she'd picked herself was neither all that good, either.

A flock of servers descended and began sliding plates onto the table.

Taylor swallowed a bite of her terrine. It tasted of herbs and butter.

She lifted her wine glass to taste that delicious dark spicy red and as she did she saw that Rocco was looking at her.

"HOW IS THE WINE, OKAY?" he shouted across the table.

She blushed slightly at having been singled out like that and smiled to cover the blush and nodded enthusiastically, yes yes, very very good! Very good, exquisite, thank you. This seemed to be all that he expected. He turned his attention back to his conversation with the guy sitting next to him, a fat and balding manager from U-Ful.


After the dinner plates had been taken away a tiny footed glass was placed in front of Taylor. It held a clear reddish brownish liquid. She sipped it. It was sweet and warming. Rocco caught her eye again and lifted an identical glass and smiled in a private toast that made her blush again and smile again to cover it again.

He must be satisfied that she had conducted herself well in the meeting yesterday morning. That she was going to hold things together for DipTych Digital. And why not? She was smart. She understood the stakes. She could handle any questions that might come up—answer the simple ones herself, deflect any that might be more complicated.

Hey. The interviews today had been a breeze. Kyle Shillelagh. How awful could he really be?

She took another sip of the reddish brownish liquid and picked out her dessert.


This time when they assembled to wait for their cab they were outside.

And Taylor found Rocco at her elbow, so that when the first cab pulled up to the curb he opened the door for her and gestured that she should get in.

"Ladies first," he said.

Ha. She'd pre-empted Basil's spot.

Rocco slid onto the seat next to her. "So how was your dinner? Okay?"

"It was delicious. Probably the best meal I've ever had."

"Good."

Darryl hit his head on the doorframe as he followed Rocco and muttered an approximation of a vulgarity.

And out of the corner of her eye—ha again. Randolph had out-maneuvered Basil for the fourth slot.

Take that, Basil.

She imagined the sour look spreading across his face as he hunted for a seat in the next cab.

Randolph shut his door and the cabbie said "where to?" and Taylor found herself pushed up against the cab door, and with Rocco's left thigh pressed full length against hers. She shifted her weight, pressed against the door a bit harder to open some space between her leg and her boss's boss's.

Rocco leaned over and locked her door. "Don't want you falling out." He smiled at her again. The sun had gone down so his face had an orange tint from the streetlights.

The cab pulled away from the curve.

*So this is it. This is me, now, Taylor Song, PR Manager, DipTych Digital Corporation.*

Basil and Darryl were discussing their meals. Taylor gathered that they had both chosen the Coastal Elegance tapas flight.

*And I'm doing pretty well, aren't I. I'm handling this pretty well. My new job. My new career . . .*

"My beefsteak petite fours were a little on the dry side," Basil was saying.

*And Rocco knows it, too—no question. He sees that I'm smart, and capable, and that I have a future.*

The cab wove and darted through the city streets, then up onto an expressway. Fewer streetlights, the cab interior darkened.

*Here I am, me, Taylor Song, PR Manager, DipTych Digital Corporation. Business trip, our biggest trade show of the year, and now I'm sitting next to my boss's boss. My boss's boss . . . my boss's boss's HAND IS ON MY LEG???*

It couldn't be it couldn't be—but it was. Most definitely. Dropped there, casual as if it belonged—as if it were invited.

She could—what? Pick it up and drop it back into Rocco's lap where it belonged? Slap him? But . . . to raise a fuss . . . and then—oh thank god the cab veered all of a sudden onto an exit ramp, and as it rocked around the serpentine curl of the ramp she used the movement to shift her leg and give it a slight shake and thank gawd the hand fell away.

He must be drunk, she thought.

He hadn't spoken or looked at her.

Perhaps he hadn't even realized he'd done it.

In any case it was over.

She'd just make sure to keep a little distance between them, that was all.

He didn't say a word to her or look at her when they climbed back out of the cab at the hotel.

They straggled into the lobby—Taylor assumed on their way to their rooms.

But no.

"C'mon," Rocco said. "A night cap. On DipTych."

She looked longingly at the elevator doors at the far end of the hotel lobby. But Rocco's pronouncement was more command than invitation—not that the others seemed to care, she suspected they would have agreed to a strychnine tab had it been offered to them as "on DipTych."

So they took a left and entered the hotel bar, and stopped to assess their options. There was an empty table at the far end of the room, encircled by assorted club chairs—and on one side, a couch.

Ew.

Taylor jumped a bit ahead of everyone and lurched into one of the unoccupied chairs.

She'd had enough of shared seating for the night.

Rocco waved commandingly at the bartender. Who returned a few minutes later, bottle of wine in one hand, fingers of the other hand wound around the stems of a half dozen wine glasses.

She needed to pee.

Stood up and made her way to the back of the room.

The hotel was an impressively mazy building. The rest rooms weren't even adjacent to the bar. You have to walk down a little hallway, take a right, another little hallway/alcove, and there is the door to the ladies room.

Taylor stepped inside. Pretty posh. The sink's glass bowls mounted on granite counters. A stack of cloth towels for drying your hands—no paper here, no noisy blower.

She looked at her face in the mirror. She was flushed from the wine. Tendrils of hair curled down around her temples.

She pushed the door open and stepped out into the alcove.

And found herself face to face with Rocco.

"Having a good time?" he asked.

"Yeah, sure." He was blocking the way. If she stepped forward, she'd be in his, uh, personal space. If she didn't step forward, she was basically trapped.

"You've got a piece of lint," he said then, and reached out to remove it from her shoulder, and then his other arm encircled her waist and he planted a kiss on her mouth—she felt tongue—she yanked her head back, pushing his arms off of her as she did.

"Got to get back to the others!" she said brightly and slipped around him and out of the alcove without turning around to see if he was following.

Wiped her mouth against the back of her sleeve as she walked.

He had not followed. He didn't return to the table, in fact. Which, as it turns out, was worse, because now she didn't know where he was. So she decided to bide her time, in case he was waiting out there somewhere between the bar and her room. Not that she expected him too—she sensed that he would not press things if it meant risking a direct rejection—but to be on the safe side, better to wait a bit, long enough so that if he was loitering about somewhere under some pretense he would lose interest and give up.

A half hour slid by.

The group's numbers dwindled, until only Darryl and Taylor were left.

The wine was gone.

Darryl had switched to cognac.

"Ever tried it?" he said when he noticed she had finished the last of her wine.

She shook her head. "I really shouldn't have any more."

"It's on DipTych," Darryl said glumly. He stood up, tottered slightly, and made his way over to the bar.

A moment later Taylor took the snifter from him and watched out of the corner of her eye as he swirled his cognac and took another sip.

She followed suit.

Realizing as she swallowed that she was now a more than a little drunk.

Three men seated at the bar were passing a Blackberry around and laughing at something on its screen.

Two women in pantsuits at the next table were finishing their meals—they must be there for Kich-N-World, they looked weary, they'd been talking earlier but now just chewed their food and sipped their wine.

The bartender washed some more glasses in the hidden sink under the bar. He'd done that so many times he didn't even need to look down, instead his eyes swept the length of the bar, checking to see if anybody needed anything from him.

Darryl didn't seem much like he wanted to talk. But she felt she ought to make conversation, and after casting about a moment came up with something suitable.

"The reporter from *Kitchen Retailer* asked for your contact information."

Darryl nodded.

"I gave him your email address. I thought it was a bit odd—wouldn't he normally just work with PR?"

"He wants us to buy ad space," Darryl said. "He knows you don't handle that budget."

"Ah." So that explained it.

Darryl swirled his brandy.

Taylor settled back in her chair and looked around the room. Yeah, she was definitely drunk. The thing with Rocco seemed silly now, inconsequential. The bottles lined up along the back of the bar were glistening now, bubbly bright as holiday lights, almost pretty.

She lifted her glass held it under her nose. It smelled citrusy and floral, and reminded her suddenly of Orwin's.

She sighed. "I'd say the show was going alright though, wouldn't you?"

"Yeah. They always do."

"Really? Things always work out?"

"Always. Spend months and months worrying yourself silly and the show finally hits and everything you thought would go wrong doesn't, and everything you thought you had covered turns out you didn't need to do anyway." He was on the couch. He shifted his weight slightly and the leather creaked. "You see, it's largely an illusion, like a reflection on water. It looks real. But it's nothing but the surface. Know what I mean?"

*Sort of.* "Yeah."

"Trouble is, I'll forget that within the next six weeks. By the time we're getting ready for next year's show, it'll be the same circus all over again."

"Wow. That's—" She stopped herself.

"Depressing?"

"No! No—it's . . . good to know. You know, for next time."

Darryl grimaced and lifted his snifter.

The women at the next table were done eating. They signaled the bartender for the check.

"Graham Woodsbury is stepping down from the DipTych board of directors."

"Sorry?" DipTych board of directors? She hadn't even begun to get her head around the DipTych board of directors.

"The name they're floating as a replacement is Brenda Song."

"Oh." Taylor avoided looking at him. "That's my mother."

She took another sip of cognac as an excuse to peak as him again. He didn't look at her or move a muscle. Such a homely man, yet there was something beyond homeliness about him too, the way he sat there so still, you could imagine him as an ancient stone god awaiting your prayers with inscrutable stillness . . .

"She got me the job. But I didn't ask her to. I didn't want it—I had a job. I was a florist."

The spell broke and Darryl swirled the Cognac in his snifter. "So how about now? Do you want it now?"

"Yeah."

But she got the feeling he wasn't thinking about her any more, or about Kich-N-World or DipTych. That—that was almost a smile on his lips. What was he thinking about? What in Darryl's life had the power to raise a sad sad smile . . .

She must not intrude on it, whatever it was.

Let him be.

She re-focused her attention instead on her cognac, on the hot biting smell of it, then took another taste . . . but her thoughts were being tugged away by something, something there . . . some nugget . . . it didn't have to be large, it didn't have to be a lot, some small little nugget of sanity was all she needed to fend off the great slouching craziness—not just of DipTych but of life, of everything, the cruelty and hurtfulness and bleakness and who knows, maybe even death itself. Just one little nugget to carry in her pocket like a talisman, it wouldn't turn the world sensible, she bore no illusions in that regard, but it would make it bearable—

"Oh, I just remembered." She stood up, knocking against the table as she did. "I have to make a call I'm sorry. Excuse me, Darryl."

He didn't answer or look up. He hadn't heard her. He was dreaming, lost in that sad dreamy half smile.

She peered warily around the lobby. No Rocco.

No anybody. Perfect.

Held her phone to her ear, heard the first ring.

And realized as she heard it that she had nothing to say to him.

She was scriptless.

Terror.

Too late.

"Hullo?"

"Hi . . . Miles. It's Taylor."

"I thought maybe. 'Sup?"

What had she been thinking? She had no idea what to say.

"Uh, I'm here. At Kich-N-World."

"Isn't it kind of late?"

"No. I mean—I didn't mean at the show. Right now. We had dinner and you know. Drinks and all that."

"How sweet."

"Yeah."

Pause. She licked her lips. That was her heart, thudding.

"So is the show going well? EasyCan setting the world on fire?"

"Yeah, I guess. Only . . . "

"Only you're a bit drunk."

"No, I mean yes, possibly, a bit."

"So what else is going on?"

"I'm not sure. I mean—there was something I needed to tell you but . . ."

"But?"

Her heart was beating so hard the room throbbed. "Uh, I'm not sure how to say it."

Was he smiling? "That might make it difficult."

"It's about DipTych. Sort of. But not really."

"Uh huh. Well, that clears things right up."

He was definitely smiling. That smile that rose on his face when he wanted to tease her but was holding himself back.

"It's about how DipTych is . . . a crazy place, Miles. Insane. And it drives people insane. Miles?"

"Yeah?"

"What's the difference between a pigeon and a rock dove?"

"Nothing."

"So. They're the same thing."

"Yeah."

"Okay. Just wondered."

"You know, Taylor, you do sound like you might be a bit drunk."

"Yeah. You know, I was thinking my job was okay for me, but now I'm not so sure. I think I might actually quit, Miles."

"Good idea. But perhaps you should take a little nap first."

"Yeah, I have an early day tomorrow. Can I call you back though?"

"Yep.

"When?"

"After your nap."

"You'll be there?"

"Yeah, Taylor, I'll be here."

"And it's okay—I mean, it's okay for me to call you back?"

"Silly girl, you know the answer to that question. Now go crash, okay? You have more press interviews tomorrow, right?"

"Yeah. Yeah. Okay. Miles?"

"Yeah?"

"You mean that, that I can call you back?"

"Yep."

Darryl's snifter had been topped off again.

"I think I'm gonna turn in," Taylor said.

"Right-o." He turned his head slightly in what passed for a friendly gesture. "We'll see you in the a.m. Chips and Clicks panel."

She noticed as she left that he was the last person sitting in the bar.

# STEADY, LASSY

*"Your source for inside information on the kitchen industry. Authoritative. Comprehensive. Influential. Honest."*

—masthead, *Kitchen Industry Insider* magazine

Headache headache headache.

Worse than a headache. The sort of headache where you also feel sickish, where the only way you feel anything like human is when you are in bed. Asleep.

But Taylor was not in bed asleep.

She was standing in the back of a conference room at the Kich-N-World trade show, watching the Chips and Clicks panel members take their seats.

Standing, because her first press interview was after the panel was over. She had to position herself for a quick escape.

Ow. Her head just hurt.

She looked around again for Darryl.

No sign of him.

No sign of anyone from DipTych in fact—except, of course, Rocco.

He was standing with the other panel members in the aisle between the two blocks of folding chairs.

He'd seen her when she'd first walked into the room. He'd ignored her.

Which was fine with her. A relief, in fact.

Back to her old spot—way down here, well below any VP's notice.

And in a few hours she'd be back on a plane, heading back to

Borschtchester . . .

Butterflies tumbled through her rather queasy stomach.

Miles butterflies.

The panel members had started talking.

She forced herself to focus. Rocco was speaking, now.

What was he saying?

"The biggest trend we see emerging is what we call Tangential Integration."

The other panel members nodded.

Tangential Integration?

Weird. Well. That wasn't anything like the EasyCan messaging. But he was a VP after all. Guess it was okay for him to go off-script if he wanted.

Another panel member was speaking now. "As digital technology becomes more ubiquitous, manufacturers need to ask themselves how to give it a place in the kitchen that doesn't displace the star. The cook."

Rocco nodded but interjected as soon the other panelist was done. "The cook is the star, sure, but digital technology is the producer, and the spotlight, and the supporting cast. That's why Tangential Integration is so important— if your stage hands don't speak the same language as your cast members, the cook is going to be lost in the broth."

Audience members nodded and Rocco raised his chin and smiled in the splendor of his self-satisfaction.


Taylor ducked out after the first few Qs of the panel Q&A.

Made her way back at the booth.

Everything looked eerily the same as it had the day before.

This caught her slightly by surprise. How strange that the convention center, ugly as it was, could somehow keep its contents pristine—it could keep this temporary city so shiny and clean despite the heavy load of commerce that it permitted to trample through.

She bent down to return her purse and briefcase to the hiding place beneath the cloth-covered table.

She stood back up—which made her head throb even more for a moment—and then she saw that there was another blue-border-badge person in the booth.

Looking at her.

Balefully.

She knew immediately who it had to be.

Kyle Shillelagh.

He turned his baleful eye from her and toward the computer screen, with its bright EasyCan brochure unfolding in a series of magnificent fades and wipes.

Taylor forced herself to breathe. Knelt again, pulled a press kit from her briefcase and thrust it at him while summoning her most brilliant and dazzling smile. "So nice to meet you, Mr. Shillelagh. I'm Taylor, we spoke on the phone."

He took the folder, opened it, flipped directly to the glossy insert that featured the EasyCan schematic, pulled it out, looked at it, looked at Taylor, and returned it to the folder. Her business card was mounted in the slot inside the front cover. He removed it and thrust it into his sport coat pocket.

She could smell him, cigarette smoke breath and something funky coming off his clothes, like the smell of a wet Labrador retriever. His eyes were red-rimmed and puffy.

She tried again. "So can I answer any questions?"

"Yeah. Why was my interview with Rocco cancelled?"

Uh oh.

"He had a schedule change and—"

Kyle had pulled a rolled-up copy of the Kich-N-World show guide from his back pocket. He had opened it while Taylor was speaking and now pointed at the page with the schedule of events. "I just saw him. At the Chips and Clicks panel."

"Yes—"

"So where is he now?"

"I—I'm not sure what his schedule is, exactly."

He could tell she was hiding something. She knew it. She felt it in his eyes. They had narrowed slightly.

He gestured now at the computer screen. It was displaying an image of the EasyCan schematic.

"About this," Kyle said. "I have some questions."

Taylor noticed that her lips were dry, resisted the impulse to lick them. "I'll do my best to help you and, uh, if there are any questions that I can't—"

"Good. Because I'm having trouble figuring out just what the hell it is."

Taylor was ready.

"It's a rendering of a schematic of EasyCan, of course."

"It doesn't look like any schematic I've ever seen."

Okay, so she wasn't ready. In fact, she was not cut out for this job. Despite what she had told herself last night in the cab—before her boss's boss had felt up her leg—and do you know why? Because she was a terrible fibber. Terrible.

"I was told you'd have a demo unit at the show."

"No. Well, at one point we'd hope to, but we—"

"How far behind schedule are you?"

Wow. They hadn't exaggerated when they'd warned her about Kyle Shillelagh.

"It's, uh, a very sophisticated product. It's not always possible to be exactly sure, in advance, to uh, anticipate everything that might be involved."

If Kyle's eyes narrowed any further his lower lids would meet his eyebrows. "When can I speak to Rocco?"

Phew. Rocco. Yes. Give this all to Rocco. Dump it right in Rocco's pervy little lap. "I'll check and let you know, okay? We can possibly do something after the show—by email or phone."

Kyle pulled a narrow spiral notebook from his hip pocket. "You know the last time DipTych brought out a digital product?"

He looked at her.

She knew that he knew that she hadn't been around the last time DipTych brought out a digital product.

"I wasn't with the company the time, but I'm aware—"

"It was a joke," Kyle said. "And we said so."

"I'm sure that this time—"

Kyle snorted. "Sorry, but I call bullshit. And you can tell Rocco I call bullshit. It's just another line of DipTych crap. Not only are you guys probably a year, two years away from a prototype—"

"Oh no, not at all—"

But Kyle cut her off with an even louder snort. "Even if you weren't, the world does not need a digital can opener. Much less a digital can opener—" he flipped the notebook open and began quoting Rocco "'that will transfigure as it evolves into an uber-sophisticated management console for tomorrow's high end digital kitchen.'"

Rocco. If force-planting a kiss on her face hadn't made him look as stupid, in Taylor's eyes, as he possibly could, that quote sure did.

And now she was supposed to . . . defend him.

Protect him.

She looked at Kyle.

He'd missed a spot when he'd shaved that morning. There was a faint strip of stubble streaked along on the edge of his chin.

"Well, Kyle," she said. "If Rocco were here. Which he is not . . ."

Nope.

She couldn't keep it up.

"Okay, start over. This is off the record, okay?"

Kyle's expression changed. His eyes were still narrowed, hostile, but she detected as well the barest hint of curiosity in his eyes.

Taylor leaned forward.

"You see. Nobody really knows what nonsense to take seriously. Know what I mean? And that's not really anybody's fault."

Kyle stared at her.

"Know what I mean?"

He shook his head. "No. No, I don't really understand your point, Miss

Song." He shut his notebook. "DipTych Digital Can is a joke, and I'm going to be saying so in print. So let Rocco know, okay? And if he wants to talk, I'll be back in my office on Monday."

"That was off the record, remember," she said to him as he walked away.

Where was Darryl?

Headache.

Headache.

She dialed Darryl's cell.

Pick up. Pick up.

He picked up.

"Darryl. I just got finished talking to our friend Kyle Shillelagh. He seems to have some kind of problem—he isn't really buying anything about EasyCan at all, really. He says—he thinks we're b.s.ing. He said he thinks this whole thing is a joke and that's what he's going to print."

No answer for a minute.

"He wants to talk to Rocco. On Monday."

"Right. Okay. We'll, uh, we'll deal with it somehow. Don't you worry about it for now."

He sounded like he felt pretty much like Taylor did.

The computer presentation had looped around to the screen with the schematic again.

How could you not tell, looking at it, that something was terribly wrong? It was obvious.

And now Kyle was going to expose it and make DipTych Digital Can the laughing stock of the entire kitchen utensil industry.

And Taylor didn't really give a damn if he did.

# AND A WOMAN'S TOUCH

*"You're asking me what happened? Well let me give you a clue. The advertisers make a nice big soft fluffy bed and throw the covers back and invite everybody in sight to jump in and to join them. It's one big slut-fest. How's that?"*

—Kyle Shillelagh, senior reporter,
*Kitchen Industry Insider*

Darryl had booked a suite.

He always did, when he traveled.

Because he wouldn't know how to sleep on an actual bed.

He needed a room with a couch.

The blinds were still drawn, heavy hotel blinds designed to block out all but the faintest blur of light.

Darryl was unclothed except his briefs. He sat now on the couch, sheets tangled up around his legs, narrow chest with its thin pelt of hair lit pinkish by the gleam of the smoke detector LED on the ceiling.

He had picked up his phone.

"Hedy."

He shifted his phone to his other ear.

Long silence.

Then: "Well. Darryl." Hedy's voice. "How are you."

He winced.

Cleared his throat.

"We've got an issue with Shillelagh. That reporter from *Kitchen Industry Insider.*"

"Mmm. So you're saying this isn't a personal call."

Darryl winced again and rubbed his face. "This Shillelagh, he's threatening to pan us. He also wants to talk to Rocco."

"Well, we'll just have to move some money around then, won't we. How much have we got with them for ads?"

"With this book, nothing. We'd decided to pass on them this year."

"Sounds like it's time to re-evaluate our ad buy priorities."

"Works for me."

"My office will be in touch with the publisher within the hour. And have your PR girl tell our reporter to phone my office about the Rocco interview."

"Thanks, Hedy."

"Any time."

"I have to run, now, on my way back to the show. Just about to walk out."

"Oh. Are you sure?"

Third wince. "Got to run."

He pressed End.

And slumped back onto the couch. The AC was on in the room and now he was chilled all the way through.

He pulled the covers back up around his shoulders.

Groaned.

But quietly.

And only once.

Only once, is all . . .

# BRAD'S LUCK

*"Yeah, I remember him. You can tell the type. He pretends he's loaded to the ladies, but when it's time to buy a round for the guys, he just realized he left his wallet home on the dresser."*

—Jon, bartender, Loopy's

It was 6:30 p.m., the time of day when Loopy's began to come into its own.

Loopy's was no Middlin's. It was further away from DipTych Corporate, by nearly three blocks. And it didn't rely on a corporate lunch clientele. Its core customers were the DipTych employees who stopped by for drinks on the way home from work.

Nothing else about the place was particularly special. The interior was narrow, flanked on one side by the bar and on the other by a row of cheap dinette style tables. The barrel back bar stools (helpful for keeping the serious drunks from tipping off backward), the chipped veneer of the bar itself, the draft keg handles, the glasses, the mirrored wall behind the bar and the bottles arrayed in front of it, the television screen where SportsCenter played on endlessly and soundlessly, all was dulled by the faintly grimy patina that is the unmistakable mark of a middle-aged neighborhood bar.

During the day, the bathrooms' odor—old urine and cheap disinfectant—tended to waft into the barroom itself, but now, as the door opened again and again to admit DipTych employees, that odor gave way to the smell of men, and beer, and bourbon.

Miles was there.

He'd come in an hour ago, seated himself at the far end of the bar and asked Jon, who tended weeknights from 4 until closing, for a Sam Adams.

He drank the beer from the bottle and read the day's edition of the *Deign & Pontificate.*

Then the bar began to fill up, and he was joined by a group from the U-Ful division. He was acquainted with them all. Some because they also patronized Loopy's. Others because he'd worked with them at one time or another.

Brad Tankard, on the other hand, knew only one or two of them.

But they knew him.

"That's the guy I was talking about."

Chuck, U-Ful Insides Sales Rep, was looking toward the door as he spoke. Miles followed his glance.

Brad was scanning the room. He recognized Chuck and lifted his hand, nodded his head, started towards them.

"Guy dresses like he's rich as a mobster," Chuck said into Miles' ear, "but always manages to disappear when it's his turn to buy."

Miles leaned back in his stool. "Maybe he can afford the suit because he doesn't blow his money on beer like us poor slobs."

"There's a thought." Chuck signaled to the bartender and pointed at his and Miles' beer bottles. "You watch." He raised his voice. We're ready, Jon."

"Bring me a Heineken too while you're at it, would you?" Brad, standing behind them. "Hey, Chuck, what's going on?" He tapped Miles' shoulder. "I don't think we've met," he said. "Brad Tankard."

Miles twisted around slightly to shake Brad's hand. "Miles."

Jon set three beers on the bar and lifted an eyebrow at Chuck.

"Yeah, put it on my tab," Chuck sighed. "You got the next one, right, Brad?"

"Sure thing," Brad said.


But when it was time for the next round Brad was no longer standing near Chuck and Miles.

He was working the room.

Networking.

He wasn't sure exactly why—although he had his suspicions—but Andrew Spittleton had hinted that he wouldn't have budget to keep Brad on past the end of the month.

So he made his way down the bar, introducing himself to people, and telling them he was a contract writer and on the DipTych Corporation approved contractor list.

Being on the approved contractor list was a big deal for DipTychians in search of vendors. It meant they could hire him without having to fill out as much paperwork for Procurement.

He didn't get back to Chuck and Miles until Chuck had settled his tab and was standing up to leave.

Chuck wasn't the only one calling it quits. The bar was thinning out quickly. People were ready for the final few hours of the day—home, dinner, television, sleep.

Waves of fresh air blew through the room as they left.

"See ya, man," Chuck said to Miles.

Miles nodded.

"See ya," Brad said.

He took Chuck's seat. He was feeling pretty good, but he wouldn't mind one more before he headed home himself. "So where do you work? Miles, right?"

Miles nodded. "DipTych."

"Oh yeah? I'm just finishing up a contract with DipTych. What division you in?"

"Digital."

"Huh. Me too." Brad eyed Miles a moment. He'd never seen the guy before, so he couldn't be attached to the R&D group at all.

That left marketing.

Marketing might need writers.

"What do you do for Digital?"

"Draw pretty pictures."

Brad eyed Miles again, but this time his expression was different. More alert. "So, you're graphics."

Miles didn't answer.

Brad sipped his beer, set it down on the bar. Picked it up again. Set it back down, this time without drinking.

"I don't suppose you worked on the Kich-N-World stuff," he said finally.

"Yep. Sure did."

"Show's going on now, isn't it?"

"Yep. Last day, today."

Brad took another drink, giving himself another minute to collect his thoughts. "My boss, for that contract work I mentioned, is Andy Spittleton in R&D. Know him?"

"I've met him."

"He heads up the EasyCan development team."

Miles' head didn't move but his eyes flicked slightly in Brad's direction.

Okay, time to get to the point. "The schematic Marketing used for the EasyCan drawings, what did you think of it?"

Miles laughed. "Jon, ring me out when you get a chance," he said as the bartender walked by, behind them, with a basket of chicken wings.

"What's so funny?" The sheen on Brad's face was picking up bluish highlights from the light of the television screen.

"What do you mean?"

"Why'd you laugh?"

"Didn't realize I did."

Brad leaned over. "I could tell you something about those schematics."

Miles took another pull from his beer.

"Don't breathe a word about this."

"Scout's honor."

Brad leaned closer. "There was a screw-up. There are no EasyCan schematics. The original you had—it was a drawing by my son."

"You don't say."

Brad studied him for a moment. "You know about it."

Miles shrugged. "There's always rumors going around about things."

Jon was back at the register, ringing up Miles' tab.

"What gets me about the whole thing?" Brad said. "My boy doesn't get any credit."

"Credit?" Miles counted out some bills and handed them to Jon. "Fuck credit. What about cash?"

Brad stared at him. "You've got a point."

"Hell right I've got a point. That drawing of your son's, you know it's the star of the DipTych booth."

"Jesus."

Miles glanced at Brad. "Oh, yeah." He lowered his voice a bit. "We designed our whole campaign around it."

Brad's face had reddened noticeably.

"Our whole campaign," Miles repeated.

"I'm such an ass." Brad's lips were tight as he spoke. "I never even thought about that. Never even occurred to me. Jesus."

Miles stood up. "You know what I'd do."

Brad waited.

"I'd push them. Hard. That drawing of your son's, it was exceptional. He's got a real gift. He deserves to be fairly compensated, in my opinion."

He kept an eye on Brad's face as he spoke. Then he picked up the bills Jon had dropped in front of him, extracted a five, and pushed it to the back of the bar. "See ya, Jon," he said.

He let himself smile, finally, as he stepped out onto the sidewalk.

Fools can always be counted on to act like fools.

Wait til he told Chuck that his buddy Brad the moocher was now trying to get DipTych to pick up the next round.

Brad didn't watch Miles leave.

He was staring at the mirrored wall behind the bar. Bits of his face staring back between the bottles.

"Is this seat taken?"

A blond.

She'd startled Brad from his reverie.

Then he got a look at her, and she startled him again. Because wow. She was pretty hot for being what, in her late 30s maybe? No, older . . . but it hardly mattered, did it, this one was smoking hot.

Brad straightened up and shook his head. "No, nobody's sitting here. Uh, can I buy you a drink?"

"How are the martinis?"

"Couldn't tell you, I'm a wine and beer man myself. And uh—" He looked around. "I'm not sure this is the place for—can I take that?"

The woman shrugged her shoulders out of her coat and sat down. She was wearing net stockings. Brad caught a glimpse of her calf muscles through the nettings and her black stilettos as she tucked her legs under the stool.

He hung her coat on a rack along the back wall of the bar.

"I know a place that makes a first rate martini," he said as he sat back down. "But it's south of town."

The woman glanced over at the door. "I'm meeting someone here in a few minutes, so I guess I'll have to pass on that," she said.

"Then by all means try one from Loopy's." Brad waved and snapped his fingers at Jon. "Anything special?"

Jon strolled over, stopping on the way to gather some empty glasses and slosh them in the sink under the bar.

"Grey Goose, painfully dry, three olives," the woman said.

"Ah. So you're a serious martini-ite." Brad shot a look at Jon intended to hurry him up.

"I prefer to think of myself as a classicist." She'd drawn a compact from her purse and now fixed her lipstick.

Jon had made his way to their end of the bar, finally. Brad repeated the order and turned to look at her again. She was wearing a silk top and a freshwater pearl necklace that fell just above the dark arrow of cleavage at her shirt's neckline.

"A classicist."

So. Intelligent, too. And her scent. She smelled like—what? Vanilla. Something spicy . . . he shook himself, forcing himself to focus. He didn't have much time. She'd said she was meeting someone. Husband. No, no ring. Boyfriend. Had to be.

Big guy, probably.

Brad rubbed his jaw protectively.

But . . . but he couldn't just sit there . . .

He was a man, after all.

He cleared his throat. "Uh, so, do you come here often?"

"No, first time. I'm not from here—I'm in town on business."

Jon shook her martini a last time, dropped a toothpick skewer of olives into a martini glass, strained the drink into the glass and pushed it toward her.

He looked at Brad. "You got this one?"

Brad nodded and lifted his hip so he could pull out his wallet.

The woman's name was Kitty.

"How's the martini?"

"Not bad." Was she leaning toward him? She was. That scent. "So what do you do, Brad?"

"I'm a writer."

"Wow, no kidding. I've always wanted to write a book."

"What about?"

She told him. She was tilting her head, smiling as she spoke, looking sideways at him from under her lashes.

She'd started glancing a lot at her watch.

"Your friend late?" Brad asked.

"Will you excuse me a minute?" she said. She stepped off the barstool, pulled a cell phone from her purse, and left the purse on her stool. "I need to make a quick call. Watch my purse, would you please?"

Brad watched her walk over into the back corner of the bar.

She was smoking hot, that one.

And interested.

In him.

No question about it.

He covered his left hand with his right on his lap, worked his wedding ring loose, and dropped it into his pants pocket.

"Cancelled," she sighed a moment later as she slid back into her seat.

"Well then," Brad said. "I'm ready for a change of scene anyway, aren't you? How about we sample the martinis at that other place I was telling you about? I'll drive. Where'd you say you're staying?"

"The Strathheimlich. Do you know where that is?"

"Sure do. Tell you what, we'll have a martini, maybe some dinner, then I'll drive you to your hotel. Good deal?"

"I've got a rental car . . ." She sighed slightly.

"No problem, I have to come back this way in the morning, I can pick you back up then."

"That would be lovely. I thought I might be left high and dry tonight—"

"No reason a woman as beautiful as you should ever be left high and dry, Kitty."

He held her coat for her, and handed her purse, and touched her back as she preceded him out of the door.

Jon watched them leave as he wiped down the bar.

The crowd wouldn't pick up again, now, until after 9.

He picked up the three coins Brad had tipped him and promised himself he wouldn't spend it all in one place.

# TIME FOR PLAN C

*"I'm sorry, I can't comment on matters pertaining to our agency clients. May I take a message for Ms. Fusee or Mr. Madelaine?"*

—Receptionist, Fusee & Madelaine

"The next step," said the architect, "would be to build a scale model."

Rocco nodded.

The two men stood.

Shook hands.

"I'll walk you out," Rocco said. "This is excellent. I'm very pleased."


Back in his office, Rocco unrolled the architectural drawing again and drank it in with his eyes.

The cannery.

His cannery.

It was all going just as he'd planned. Exactly as he'd planned. Yes, the snafu with the EasyCan drawing had stirred things up for a bit, but nothing had come of it—whatshername, Darryl's PR girl had apparently handled the press interviews, and Fusee had handled that nasty little *Kitchen Industry Insider* fellow when he'd gotten a little too uppity.

Rocco laid the drawing on his desk, smoothed it flat, caressing it—

His phone rang.

Scally.

"Yes, sir?"

And then the color bled away from Rocco's face.

"I see, sir. No worries. We will handle it. Yes, at the division level. I'll get my team on it right away."

He hung up and spat expletives out into the air over that perfect architectural drawing, then picked his phone up again and dialed Darryl.


"Darryl. That goddamned EasyCan schematic—how the hell did you say you got your hands on that goddamned schematic again?"

The drawing of the cannery had been rolled back up. It leaned now against the wall, in the corner of Rocco's office, forgotten.

Darryl did not answer Rocco's question.

Rocco didn't particularly expect him to. "The problem is," he said, spitting as he spoke, "the problem is not that the kid's father can win a penny from DipTych, because he won't. The problem is, just when we thought we'd gotten through the trade show without any negative publicity, here we are, back at square one, again."

"We just have to keep him quiet," said Darryl.

"Do you know who this Tankard's lawyer is?"

Darryl's face tightened. Bracing himself.

"I'll give you a clue. He's also Bo Valgus' attorney."

"Oh, Christ." Darryl sighed. "Does Bo know?"

"I don't think so. Not yet. But it doesn't matter, because Scally knows. If we'd caught this before Scally found out—but we didn't."

They looked at each other.

"It's time to call Hedy," Rocco said.

"No." But Darryl's voice was weak and he slumped slightly as he spoke.

"This all comes back to you, you know," Rocco said. "You're the one who came up with this drawing in the first place."

Darryl's throat made a slight noise.

"So you call her, or I will."

Darryl pulled out his cell.

Rocco stood up. "Get her in here today if at all possible. 6:00. Here, in my office."


Darryl didn't have a clean shirt in his office.

If he only had a clean shirt. A shirt that wasn't damp—he must smell—if he only had a clean shirt, he might be able to survive this thing.

But his clean shirts were all at home.

And he couldn't make it there and back in time.

5:49.

He shut down his computer.

His staff had all left. Gone home.

The only sound on the entire floor was the despondent hum of the fluorescent lights overhead.

Darryl shuffled toward the elevator.

He stopped once.

To sniff at his armpits and wince when he felt the damp cloth brush against his nose.

This was no way to meet Hedy.

Rocco looked again at his watch.

"You told her six, right?"

Darryl nodded.

Unlike the lowly contractors like Brad, Hedy had full security clearance. So she did not need to be escorted. She would make her own way up to Rocco's office.

Darryl tried not to watch the door for her.

And then the wait was over.

She was there.

Glorious in her four inch heels and that immaculate skirt and sweater ensemble and the dangly gold earrings and her perfect blond bob.

"Oh, Darryl," she said when she saw him.

He cleared his throat quietly. "Good to see you, Hedy."

"Rocco." She took Rocco's hand.

She sat in the chair next to Darryl.

He focused on remaining immobile.

"So tell me, you boys have some trouble to clean up?"

"Well," said Rocco. "It's this EasyCan schematic issue."

Hedy nodded.

"We thought we were out of the woods, but his father has surfaced. He's threatening to go to the press with some story about us—that DipTych's entire digital venture is based on . . . well, a six-year-old's drawing."

"That is rather the truth of course," Hedy said.

Rocco scowled.

"You should know," Hedy leaned forward slightly, "not everyone is in full agreement with every aspect of your little venture, Rocco."

"What do you mean by that?"

Hedy smiled briefly and touched her hair. "The city has other suitors for the old FairARTS! space."

Rocco stood up, slamming his fist on his desk.

But he didn't speak. Because he saw the look on Hedy's face and realized he would be a fool to speak.

"Don't get overly excited, dear," the woman said. "Nothing's been decided."

Darryl had turned his head slightly so that he could watch her.

"We have an excellent plan," Rocco whispered. Then a bit louder. "An excellent plan. Scally—"

"Scally's not happy about this whole drawing business," Hedy interrupted.

"That's it!" Rocco's voice rose another notch. "That fellow—that Brad Tankard—the nerve, to go to Scally—"

"Oh, I told him to."

"Excuse me?" Rocco said.

"I told him to go to Scally."

Darryl's eyes had not moved from her face. She knows everything, he thought to himself. She knew it all before it even happened.

He wondered if Rocco knew, yet, just how much she knew.

Rocco's eyes were bugging slightly. "Hedy. Why would you—" And then something else hit him. "What about Bo—does Bo?"

"Yes, he's been briefed as well."

"Hedy." Rocco's face was white. "Don't—I—people have a lot riding on this, here."

"Oh, don't worry, Rocky. Things have a way of working out."

Rocco winced. "It's just that—"

"Switch will handle Bo. And I'll handle Brad."

"But the cannery—"

"Don't worry," Hedy said. "There's always a Plan C."

She stood up. "If you boys will excuse me now, I have a dinner date. Darryl, dear?"

Darryl had fumbled to his feet. "Yes, Hedy."

"Set up a meeting. You, me, Brad."

"When, Monday? Here?"

"Oh, no, not here. Monday's good, though. A dinner meeting."

"Dinner?"

Hedy stood up touched her hair, smoothing it. "You owe me a date, you know, Darryl."

"Shouldn't I be there?" Rocco was standing now, too.

"Next time, maybe, Rocco. Eight o'clock, Darryl. At Deft Palate."

Deft Palate being Borschtchester's highest high end restaurant.

And then she was gone.

Rocco was staring at Darryl.

None of it made sense. None of it—if it only made sense he'd be able to see what was going on but it didn't make sense, he couldn't see what was going on—

"Why you?" The only question that could form itself in his mind. "Darryl.

What the hell does she want with you?"

Darryl stood up unsteadily. "I don't—"

"If I didn't know better, I'd think she was into you."

Darryl didn't answer. He fell toward the door, then three giant steps out into the hall, just get himself and the stricken look on his face the hell out of Rocco's stricken office.

# DARRYL ON A DATE

*"Lies. All lies. My family comes first, they always have and they always will. People are vicious, people will say anything. But let them say it to my face. I dare them."*

—Brad Tankard

If you saw Deft Palate from the outside, you would think it was a marginal restaurant at best. After all, who opens a high end restaurant in a strip mall storefront. Except that Deft Palate's owner was clever enough to recognize that anti-pretention is the new pretention. Having to walk past a big box drug store and a dry cleaner with a cheery Alterations Done Here sign in the window and a narrow dank little liquor store, it turns out, can function as a purification ritual of sorts, a way to show your solidarity with the little guy before you sit down to your $40 plate of homemade pasta with braised tenderloin tips and shaved truffles.

Our Darryl, of course, needed no purification ritual. He'd just lived through 72 hours of personal and sleepless anguish. No pilgrim ever reached his shrine looking more wan or thin or pitiable.

He was a good hour early, so he sat at the bar and ordered a vodka and diet coke, which he drank too quickly, which gave him gas, which he tried furiously but silently to belch back out before Hedy got there—then switched to bourbon neat for his second drink in the hopes that the effect of the alcohol on his GI tract might work to his advantage.

If only he could stop his mind from babbling on so.

Brad got there next.

Hedy was never exactly late, but she was always the last one to show up.

Brad eyed Darryl defiantly as they shook hands.

"Maybe we should ask them to get us our table," he said. "You guys are buying, I hope."

Darryl nodded.

He was in no shape to do anything but let himself be led.

The hostess took them to their table.

They sat down to wait.

"I don't know what you guys expect to accomplish," Brad said finally.

Darryl tried to figure out what he was talking about. Oh. That was right. The drawing—Brad was talking about his kid's drawing.

"It's, uh, Hedy's meeting," Darryl said. "We'll have to wait for her."

Brad grunted.

The server brought Brad his first drink, and Darryl his third.

Darryl spilled a little bourbon on the table's white linen when he picked up his glass. He set his it back down over the spill to hide it.

Then he stood up.

Hedy, just inside the door, scanning the room coolly, saw him, she was walking up—

"Hedy," Darryl said.

Brad turned, then jumped to his feet. "Kitty!" he cried.

"In some respects," Hedy answered. She leaned over to Darryl and her lips brushed his cheek. "Bourbon?"

He nodded.

"Get me one, too."

Brad stared.

Darryl pulled out her chair and she sat.

"So, boys," she said. "I believe they've got their beef dumplings on special tonight. The porcini cream red wine reduction is to die for."

"You said your name was Kitty."

Hedy smiled, a gracious smile, but a smile that also made it clear to Brad that he had spoken out of turn and had better not do it again.

Darryl tore his eyes from her face and looked, then, at Brad. He was staring at Hedy, sucking hungrily at his bottle of beer as he did.

She has slept with him, Darryl thought.

He stood up.

"Darryl? Are you okay, dear?" Hedy looked at him, concerned.

"Yeah. Yes, I'm okay." The waiter had seen him stand up. Darryl raised his hand. "Just getting your drink."

He sat down.

He'd never met anyone she'd slept with before.

He looked at Brad. Brad's hand holding the beer bottle. It was an ugly hand, the fingers were puffy, the nails were broad and flat.

Sweat standing out now on Brad's forehead.

Darryl looked again at Hedy.

She'd slept with this guy.

And this guy was . . . married.

So Brad didn't matter anymore.


The server came over with Hedy's drink and recited the specials.

Hedy ordered the famous beef dumplings.

Brad ordered something else, not the dumplings, and Darryl—stretching now to his full height in his seat—changed his mind. He'd been thinking pasta but he decided on the Porterhouse.

The food came, and some more drinks, and then Hedy and Darryl pointed out desserts to each other on the dessert menu.

Hedy excused herself to go, she said, to the powder room.

Darryl watched her maneuver around the white linen-covered tables. She knew how to wear a dress, that woman.

She disappeared around the corner.

Darryl leaned over the table.

He seized Brad's eyes with his own.

And then he snarled—yes, Darryl snarled.

"Don't you ever—EVER—lay a hand on my Hedy again. Do you understand?"

"I don't know what you're talking about."

But Brad's eyes were glassy with panic.

Darryl leaned back again but his eyes didn't let Brad's go until he felt Hedy back at the table.

She smiled at them both and sat down.

The servers brought their desserts.

Brad ate his quickly. Excused himself. He had an early day tomorrow, he said. New job, not with DipTych, starting tomorrow.

"There, dear," Hedy said when he'd gone. "Didn't I say things have a way of working out?"

"Hedy," Darryl said.

"Yes, Darryl?"

And Darryl went home as well, about a half hour later.

Only not alone.

And not to his couch.

# HOW UTTERLY GAULING

*"We're very proud of our new plans for Candy & Nut. I've always said it's the division where we're most likely to find surprises. DipTych Candy and Nut, I tell people, we're doing a lot right, a few tweaks here and there and you'd have a real gem on your hands, a sugar-coated gem."*

—Paul Scally, CEO, DipTych Corporation,
analyst conference call

"You wanted to see me, sir?"

"Rocco. Come in."

Scally was standing by his window. The scaffolding had come down a week ago. Spikes now protruded from the stone of the exterior sill.

There wasn't a pigeon in sight.

Rocco stood in front of Scally's desk while the CEO settled into his chair.

"I've got a job for you, Rocco."

Rocco let the air ease soundlessly from his lungs. To think that—he'd been worried. As if Scally would have reason to fire him! Why would he ever want to do that?

"What do you need done, Paul?"

"It's Candy and Nut."

Candy and Nut? What was he—

"As you know, we've made a strategic decision to consolidate our Candy and Nut production facilities."

"Yes, I saw the report. It should drive some significant cost savings."

"I'd like you to head up the new organization."

Whoa.

Whoa.

Rocco. You snake. You did it—you sly snake you.

"Van has just come back from touring the new facility."

Hang on—now that didn't sound quite so nice. "New facility, Paul?"

"We've signed a ten year lease on a plant in Asia-Pacific."

Beijing? Bangkok? Hong Kong? Okay. This might work. Rocco in the global economy, Rocco as international executive—

"In Ulaanbaatar, Rocco."

Ulaanbaatar?

"I'm sorry, Paul, what did you . . .?"

"Ulaanbaatar, Rocco! The capital of Mongolia. Van did an extensive feasibility study. Weren't you copied?" Scally looked disturbed that Rocco hadn't been copied. "Highly favorable tax and regulatory structure in Mongolia today, Pinnoccho! Locating DipTych Candy and Nut production will be the catalyst, it will stimulate the emergence of a brand new regional confectionary superpower. Mongolia will soon be known as the Belgium of Asia!"

"The Belgium of Asia."

"And you're the perfect man for the job, Pinnoccho. A perfect fit. Anybody who can do what you did with Digital—the projected revenues you've achieved in only a few short months—accomplishments like that, Pinnoccho, that's what make this company great."

Rocco opened his mouth, then closed it again. What could he do? Point out that it was all paper numbers, that DipTych Digital had yet to sell a single product, how could you call a business successful that had never made a sale?

He could not. He dared not. Because if he did Scally would perhaps wonder how Rocco had managed to convey the impression that Digital had so outperformed the other DipTych Divisions . . .

"We need a Genghis Khan." Scally was saying, and he chuckled, pleased with the allusion.

"Sir—"

"Question, Pinnoccho?"

He needed to try something. Change Scally's thinking about this whole thing. "The only thing I'm thinking, sir, is that Digital—well, you know, there's still quite a bit that needs to be done right here in Borschtchester, and—"

"The mark of a good executive, Pinnoccho, is that he grooms his lieutenants so they'll be ready at a moment's notice to step into his shoes. Should he ever fall in battle. The way I've groomed you. Not that this is a fall, Pinnoccho. Don't get me wrong. Now you've got that one fellow, Darryl something—"

"Darryl. Yes, Darryl Fiegit, right, but as far as Darryl goes—"

"I understand he's been heavily involved in overseeing our EasyCan project to date."

"Well, yes sir, of course—"

"Funny thing too. Have you heard? That admin, Amber something—she used to work for me. Took a leave of absence some time ago to get married. I understand she's back from her honeymoon and this Darryl just hired her. Smart move on his part. She was a good admin."

"Yes, sir, about Darryl—"

"He's a good man. Then it's all settled, Pinnoccho. Ulaanbaatar. Van tells me the climate is not half bad, there, during the summer."


The elevator doors closed behind Rocco.

The floor sank down, down, down under his feet.

They thought they'd won.

They'd thought they'd won.

But they'd see.

He'd be back.

Ulaanbaatar would be his Gaul.

They'd see.

# IN WHICH THE HERO
# KISSES THE HEROINE

*"I'm speechless, to tell you the truth. This has been my lifelong dream—to own a retail business."*

—Trevor Mancely, at the
grand opening of Trevor Mancely Kitchen and Bath Supply

"So there isn't going to be a cannery?"

They were in the parking lot again.

Taylor was leaning up against her car.

Miles leaning against the car next to hers.

It was a few minutes before 8:00. The lot was already nearly full. And DipTychers were still arriving, threading their way to the door, their security badges swaying like oversize dog tags from their necks or clipped onto their breast pockets.

The air was damp—it smelled like spring, at long last. And that was a robin's voice in the tree between the lot and the sidewalk.

"Nope," Miles said. "The cannery's been canned. It's going to be the Bo Valgus  Kitchen and Bath Emporium and Design Center."

Taylor shook her head in disbelief.

"And guess who's going to own fifty one percent of it."

"Hedy?"

"Nope."

"Rocco."

"Gawd no."

"Not Bo."

Miles laughed. "No, not Bo."

"Who? Who?"

"Jelly."

"Jelly?"

"Yep. I told you he was loaded. It's a consortium of private investors, Jelly and some contracting outfit, of D'Signario I think. But Jelly's majority owner."

"Does that mean he's quitting his job?"

"Oh yeah. He's moving on. He's a business bigwig now." Miles chuckled.

"No more Jelly in the ceiling," Taylor said. "It won't be the same."

"It's going around," Miles said.

Taylor had been rummaging through her purse looking for a lip balm. Now she looked up. "What do you mean."

"I'm giving notice tomorrow."

"Oh no!"

Miles leaned forward, reached out, and brushed the bridge of her nose with his finger. "That's no way to congratulate your boyfriend."

"What are you going to do?"

"My novel."

She jumped up. "Miles Chacuderie. You never told me you were writing a novel."

"I'm not. I'm drawing it. A graphic novel."

"A graphic novel?"

"Yeah. I'm still looking for a writer, though. Want to be my writer?"

"That depends. What's it about?"

"A dysfunctional multi-national company and all the odd but loveable people who work there."

"You can't make it about DipTych. They'll sue you."

"Oh, it won't be about DipTych. I'll change everything."

"All the people."

"Yep. And the industry."

"Not kitchen stuff."

"No. Something else. In the consumer space, though. Car accessories maybe. Or how about a camera film manufacturer."

"Camera film."

"The hero will be an intelligent and talented graphics artist, and the heroine will be an intelligent and beautiful PR professional."

"In other words, you're changing all the people."

"Right. And you know how it will end."

"No idea."

Miles stepped toward her. "They fall in love, and the hero asks the heroine to marry him."

"I thought the hero doesn't believe in marriage."

"He only doesn't believe in it for other people," Miles said.

"I see," Taylor said.

"I'm going to kiss you now," Miles said.

And he did.

"And so then, that's the end," Taylor whispered. "That's the end."

# ABOUT THE AUTHOR

Novelist Kirsten Mortensen loves to hear from her readers. You can find her on her website, www.kirstenmortensen.com, or on Twitter @Kirstenwriter.

And please look for Mortensen's other fiction and non-fiction titles, including:

# *Loose Dogs*

Animal Control Officer Paige Newberry doesn't know what's worse.

Her man problems, or her dog problems.

First she opens a package from her boyfriend and finds The Ring.

That can only mean one thing: the guy she can't get over is about to walk back into her life.

Then she stumbles on evidence of a dog fighting ring—and realizes that without her help, a pit bull she tried to help is doomed to die.

She thinks she can seal the deal with her boyfriend with a little help from sexy lawyer Larry Crawford.

But she'll soon need another scheme—this time, to save her life.

Loose Dogs.

An unconventional romance.

A thrilling twist..

# *When Libby Met the Fairies*

Libby Samson has figured out the perfect way to rebuild her life after her divorce: invest her settlement in a 10-acre piece of property and start an organic vegetable farm.

But then, as she's walking across one of her fields one evening, a two-foot tall man stands up out of the shadows and greets her by name.

It's hard enough for Libby to come to terms with the fact that "little folk" exist, that she's able to communicate with them, and that they're giving the advice she needs to make her farm a success.

Then word of Libby's experience leaks onto the Internet, and things get crazy. Her property soon swarms with strangers hoping for a glimpse of fairies. Her sister thinks she should turn the farm into a New Age retreat ("It'll be bigger than Deepak!") The media show up. And hiding all this from her boyfriend backfires, as well—he never liked the farm idea anyway, and he's under a lot of stress since the biomedical research firm where he works was acquired by Dormet Vous Luster, late night television's purveyor of "Tight by Tomorrow" anti-aging cream.

Libby finds one person she can confide in: her next-door neighbor. Granted, Dean Milbrant's a bit odd: withdrawn and taciturn. But her attraction to him is powerful—and he seems to feel it too.

Until Libby discovers that trusting Dean was a huge mistake . . .

# A NOTE ON BOOK REVIEWS

Authors live and die on reader feedback. Literally!

DID YOU KNOW: If a book averages less than 3-3.5 stars, retailers will not display the book as highly in search results?

DID YOU KNOW: If a book averages 4 stars or higher, retailers make sure more people will find and read the book—helping to ensure the author gets paid?

Your rating makes a HUGE difference.

*If a book is "not for you," please consider explaining that in your review, instead of giving the book fewer stars.*

Thank you so much for your readership and support.